WHAT IF YOU DIDN'T MAKE THE GOOD CHOICE,
BUT MADE THE RIGHT CHOICE INSTEAD?

THE

COMPASSION

GIFT

KATY HOLLWAY

SozoPrint
SozoPrint.com

ISBN 978-0-9929404-4-7

Other titles in this series:
The Compassion Prize

Other titles from this author:
The Times of Kerim
The Days of Eliora

For Michelle,
You are one who loves fiercely and bravely.
I am honoured that you are my sister.

For Andy,
Your encouragement, kindness, words and humour are just a
sprinkling of your generous traits that draw out the best.

... And for those that have given the gift
that cannot be measured

Chapter 1

The cloud of black smoke billowed from the yacht and rose high above them until it became a dark streak against the red morning sky. They watched from the smaller craft.

Suddenly, the boom of the second detonation reverberated through the air, producing a huge ball of flames and blasting the starboard side to splinters. Luca gasped at the sound. The first explosion may have been an imminent accident that they had escaped from, but the finality of this blast that followed unnerved him.

He heard Kelsee gasp so he reached out and sheltered her in his arms. When he looked out to sea again, there was little left of Harland Barret's majestic toy, save a few shattered and smoking pieces of debris floating on the waves.

Luca hoped that the authorities in Tropolis would be fooled into believing they were killed in the explosion, but he did not rest in those hopes expressed by the man at the rudder of their smaller craft.

Eban turned his back to the wreckage. His normally cheerful manner had turned to sarcasm. 'Well, I guess we are going with you now,' he said to the woman at the radio. 'But, where exactly is that?'

Luca shifted uneasily in his seat and ran his hand through his russet hair.

The slight woman, dressed in a faded blue jacket, turned, only now distracted from her task by Eban's voice. She looked intently into Eban's dark face. She had not been shaken by the explosions which Luca now understood to be of her doing. 'I cannot divulge such information, Eban. I am sure that you understand.'

Kelsee's sobbing had quietened, but Luca could feel her trembling. 'We understand,' he began, 'but since we have just left one prison we would like to know we are not heading for another.'

'Campion Headquarters,' she announced without hesitation, keeping strong eye contact with Luca. If they were to be taken to such an official sounding destination, perhaps the blue, that both this woman and the man at the rudder were wearing, could have been some sort of uniform. 'But as for not heading to another prison,' she continued glancing at Kelsee, 'that would depend on your little friend.'

Luca drew Kelsee closer to himself. Kelsee had led them out of the danger of Tropolis but now that she was outside her home, she had become the one that was vulnerable. None of his friends had planned for this before they agreed to let her join them.

The woman stepped towards them and reached for Mercy's wrist who twisted in her seat and tried to pull her arm from the woman's firm grip. Eban leaned forward to protect Mercy who was still a little weak from the transfusion. Her porcelain like complexion was dull and only looked paler framed by her thick dark hair and Eban's skin. His resistance was physically blocked by the woman as she shoved him aside. Mercy's strength was not enough. A thin curved cuff had been clipped over her arm and ran from her wrist, nearly to her elbow.

'Hold still!' the woman commanded.

A sequence of small coloured lights flashed within the surface of the cuff, blinked three times then faded.

'What was that?' Mercy asked.

The woman slipped the device from Mercy's wrist and beckoned for Eban to move closer. He smiled crookedly, shook his head and didn't move.

'You're disabling the chip, aren't you,' Luca understood. He twisted his own wrist to see the slight bump under the skin. Only now did he realise that the chip he'd had implanted in childhood was not just the entry code to the rubbish pile gates on Outside. When it had enabled him to hear the sound from the tablets in Tropolis and he had suspected it had more sinister abilities.

'Smart lad,' the woman said looking at Luca intently. 'We don't want Tropolis to be receiving any signals from your chips anymore.'

Luca glanced at Kelsee before he offered his wrist. There was no doubt in his mind that he wanted to be invisible to Tropolis. He checked to see if he could sense any sign that perhaps Kelsee would think him a traitor in accepting help, after all, this Campion woman had plenty of animosity. But Kelsee's response surprised him. She almost appeared relieved when her hazel eyes peered heavenward and she sighed. Even her posture relaxed a little.

Eban, now understanding the necessity, gently gave permission. The lights flashed and then went out.

The woman glared at Kelsee and grabbed her wrist when she didn't offer it. She roughly fitted the cuff but there were no lit indicators. Kelsee, tense once again, tried to pull away.

'It didn't happen then,' the woman said narrowing her eyes.

Luca turned to Kelsee and frowned.

'Tropolites aren't chipped,' Kelsee quietly admitted. 'My grandfather wanted everyone to have them eventually. He tried to enforce it a couple of years ago but the people felt it was an invasion of privacy. He almost lost his job over it.'

'What about the Outsiders' privacy? Eh?' the woman spat before ripping the cuff away.

'Kelsee has risked everything for us, for that I am grateful,' Mercy declared to the woman and the man at the rudder. 'We,'

Mercy said circling her fingers to indicate the group of friends, 'would not be here had it not been for her.'

The woman shook her head and frowned, but did not say another word. She returned to the radio, nodded to the man at the rudder, who turned the small craft away from the shoreline and out to sea.

The small boat, with its undulating roof that imitated the water, accelerated over the waves, away from the vast wall that bordered the place where the Outsiders lived. Luca looked back at the greying wall that had held him for almost the entirety of his life. A few weeks before, he had detested living in poverty, gleaning an existence from the waste and rubbish heaps of Tropolis, but now he longed to walk between the crudely made houses and not know what was really beyond the wall. He could never undo what he had seen.

His relationship with Tropolis had always been one of love and hate. He loved the idea of living free and wealthy, the extravagant lifestyle of wasting whatever you pleased just because you could, but hating it for all the same reasons. He had suffered at the hands of Tropolis for fourteen years. The disappearance of his mother, later recounted as just a number in the death toll at the docks, had meant he had to glean to ensure that he and his father survived. She had been just another moment of waste for Tropolis; unimportant and insignificant.

The opportunity of the Compassion Prize had invited him into Tropolis. He was grateful that Eban and Mercy had also been selected; without them he would never have understood what friendship was. They had completely changed him. Mercy was steadfast in putting others first, so much so that she had taken Luca's place in the Death Room. Eban was unmovable in his solidarity and he could be trusted with everything. Luca smiled a little at how fortunate he had been to be included and welcomed by them. They all had survived in Outside and wore its badge as a common factor. They each knew and had lived with hunger and loss.

Luca glanced at Kelsee. Her trembling had subsided but she still clung to him. The woman at the radio paid no further attention to them, but her words had stung. Luca smoothed Kelsee's wild hair away from his face. She was different from them, and should, of course, not even be there. He understood the suspicion, but in the short time he had known Kelsee, he had found she could be trusted. Her family may have been the instigators of the hierarchy of Tropolis, but reflecting it back onto her was unfair and unfounded. She had been the reason the friends had managed to escape and still be together. Without her, Mercy would have been trapped inside Tropolis, treating the Tropolites and being experimented on to find a cure. But the woman's comments had already scattered his thoughts with a seed of doubt. Luca tried to push it to one side, but could Kelsee really turn her back on all the wealth she had been accustomed to so easily? Could she run from her family and all that she had known? Luca stared at the woman and shook his head. She knew nothing of this girl, so she could not pass judgement.

Luca had thought that the Compassion Prize and Tropolis would be the solution to everything, but both had failed to provide. The memories of his behaviour; his desperation for votes; the danger and hatred he had received from Thickset and some of the other contestants; all of which left him feeling chilled. Tropolis had created a competition for entertainment, and for the most popular, a prize consisting of a twisted version of compassion. Luca was still unsure if the prize existed at all.

Crisp, a crude nickname given to the Tropolite worker who had overseen their training as contestants, had at one time been a contestant himself. Crisp had never seen the fulfilment of the prize as his family were never summoned to the apparent luxury of Tropolis. If they had been, Luca would never have known Outside. Crisp was his mother's brother, a man Luca was unaware of until he had helped them escape. This clean shaven and smartly suited man was his uncle Alec. He had been the secret mediator with Campion.

The wall of Outside was distant and the shoreline was fading. Luca watched the woman at the radio. She had headphones on and was intently listening. 'Message received,' she answered. 'We have collected the consignment of goods and have gained some contraband. Maintain radio silence from this point on. Explosion cover has dissipated. Over and out.' She switched everything off and peered over at Luca and scowled. He turned away, angry that Kelsee would be referred to as an illegal import. 'Radio silence from now on, and that goes for you lot too.' She shuffled over to the rudder man. 'Headquarters want us at Tower 2, approach on the eastern side.'

The man at the rudder raised his eyebrows. 'Understood.'

They sat in silence. Eban smiled reassuringly at Luca, obviously sensing the nervous atmosphere. Luca had so many questions and not one of them would be answered in this little craft. He fidgeted uneasily on the hard bench. All sense of rejoicing at being free was ebbing away. He clenched his teeth, holding back all his new uncertainties.

From underneath the shimmering, camouflage canopy that would make them so difficult to spot, the silence was full of tension. The woman sat stiffly, occasionally peering at her watch, but no longer looking at any of the friends. Kelsee had pulled away and fiddled with the hem of her top, her head bowed. Luca could feel his face heating, but Mercy leaned over and gently patted both his and Kelsee's hands. He looked up and saw the familiar and confident smile. He could not understand her calm, but chose to trust her once again, since she had a way of not letting worry crowd out all sense of hope.

The waves no longer crested like they did closer to the shore, rather the water rose and fell in smooth undulations lifting the small craft as it continued to speed out to sea leaving the land far behind. Luca had coped with the motion in the larger yacht, but now that the excitement of escape had dissolved away and with it all the distractions, he was suffering.

Eban patted Luca's back as he leaned over the side. 'Not much longer mate,' he whispered. The Campion boat was so susceptible to the vast sea. 'I think I see where we are heading.'

Luca spat into the water, pushed himself away from the side and looked up. On the horizon where several dark shapes that, at first appeared to be vessels. They weren't streamlined and elegant in any sense, but as the boat drew closer, Luca saw that they perched above the water's surface. The quiet hum of the engine propelled the tiny boat ever closer to the foreign forms that towered over them. The bulky and angular structures were raised high over the waves on tripods of concrete.

Seaweed and barnacles clung tightly to their manufactured homes, miles from their relatives at the seashore. The underwater grass swayed in the tidal flow and ebb as the boat passed closely by the two outer structures and approached the third. Not a single bird called. The waves broke against the concrete legs, splashing Luca and his friends as they floated past. Rust stains ran down the dull concrete from the metal structure above, although Luca could not see any rough rust holes. The metal structure was well coated in layer upon layer of thick, dark paint; the huge bolts and folded metal no longer had definition.

The man guided the boat from the right hand side to the centre of the tripod, pulled back the camouflaged hood and turned off the engine. The sound of the waves bounced off the structures creating eerie bangs and echoes.

Suddenly the water below them began to ripple. Chains rattled in the grooves of the concrete pillars and a thick net cradled the hull, lifting the boat steadily into the air.

Kelsee let out a small yelp and Eban laughed as he peered over the side. Both of the Campion crew began to pack away their things.

The boat rocked in the wind, Luca leaned over the side and retched.

The underside of the structure was almost within reach when the crane stopped. The boat hung enveloped in the dripping coils of rope, and was itself encased in the lower metal rim of the structure. They were sheltered from the wind and hidden from the horizon and the sea below. It was dark and cold.

All of a sudden, a square of stark white light appeared on the deck. Luca looked up as the hatch doors slid apart silently, the aperture widening. The bright flood light made him squint and step back just as a slender rope ladder was lowered from above.

Chapter 2

'Luca,' the woman instructed, 'You first.'

'We'll be right behind you,' Eban said.

He stepped forward and grasped the lightweight metal rungs. Taking a deep breath to calm his nerves, he began to climb. There were only ten rungs, but the ladder swung as he ascended and Luca was aware of the height above the sea they had already been raised.

The bright light was dazzling. As he lifted himself through the hole two sets of hands grabbed him.

'Hey!'

'This way!' A man pulled Luca to the side and into the low ceilinged square room.

'Luca?' Eban called. 'Are you alright?'

Luca pulled away and he was quickly let go. The flood light was aimed through the hatch, but enough light spread into the room for Luca to see that two men were smiling and seemingly friendly.

'Just helping you in mate, that's all,' one of the men said lifting his empty hands.

'I'm fine,' Luca called down to the others.

The rope ladder went taut again and the men crouched, ready to guide the next one in. Luca's attention was drawn away from the hatch. Hammered into the metal wall opposite was the Campion emblem. The flower, with its five heart shaped petals was not as delicate as the image on the notebook or Mercy's tattoo. Here, it appeared bold and stylised, huge and strong. Luca touched his pocket, reassuring himself that the notebook, his final glean from Outside, was still there.

Luca turned as Mercy peered into the room, her eyes scrunched against the light. He bent to help her up but the Campion workers got there before him. She stepped towards Luca.

'What is this place?' she asked Luca.

Luca pointed to the artwork. 'Campion headquarters.'

Mercy instinctively touched her neck and frowned.

There were two means of escape other than the hatch; two sturdy doors that were firmly shut either side of the Campion flower. The walls were painted in the same dark paint as the exterior adding to the gloom of the space. Then Luca noticed the red blinking light of a camera in the corner of the room taking in every move.

Luca leaned close to Mercy. 'It doesn't feel right does it?'

'Maybe,' she whispered back.

Soon they were joined by Eban and Kelsee and the boat's crew.

The men saluted to the woman who had brought the friends to Headquarters. 'Take her to the hold,' she commanded pushing Kelsee towards them.

'Leave her alone!' Luca protested as he rushed forward with Eban and Mercy. The woman and other crew man held them back.

The woman shook her head. 'She will be kept securely until we are certain she can be trusted,' she said as a statement of fact.

'I'll be fine,' Kelsee said quietly and confidently as one man opened the door to the left and the other guided her through, holding her arm behind her. 'Please, just tell them I'm not like my grandfather.'

The door shut and the friends were released. Luca could feel his heart beating hard. He had not expected to be made so unwelcome.

'Follow me,' the woman said as she turned the wheel to open the door on the right. It clicked and banged as the metal mechanism worked. Luca looked back to the other door that Kelsee had been taken through and felt his stomach churn. He had already let her down.

Small round lights that were fixed to the metal walls interrupted the gloom with a warm glow to the windowless space. The short corridor was wide enough for two people to pass one another, but left little room for anything else. At the far end were a flight of stairs to the left and a door with the small portal window to the right.

The woman pushed the door open and walked inside.

Luca squinted into the glare. Daylight filled the room as it pushed through the salt smeared windows and obscured the view. There were at least a half dozen men and women sitting at desks, focussing on screens and tapping out text. The floor was carpeted in mismatched, tough, square tiles. A large image was flickering on the table at the centre of the room where a tall woman stood. Her severely cropped hairstyle may have, at first glance, grouped her with the men in the room. She looked up as they approached.

Luca's guide saluted.

'Excellent work, Captain Scout,' the taller woman said acknowledging the guide. She then turned to the friends. 'Welcome to Campion Headquarters, contestants.' Luca heard Eban grunt beside him at the use of the title. Luca found this woman difficult to gauge. Every aspect of her appearance from the buzzed hair to the deep lines etched into her brow from frowning, described a stern woman. Yet her voice was weirdly gentle despite the abrupt way in which she spoke. 'I am Major Thomas. During your stay here, you will address me as Major, is that clear?'

Luca nodded slowly. Captain? Major? He peered around the room once again. The people at the desks all wore similar shades of blue; they were in uniform. Some of the screens showed different images, and each of them had the Network symbol in the corner. Other screens were full of scrolling, apparently random letters and numbers. This group of people were organised and efficient making Luca think of a military unit. A clear but disjointed message sounded from the desk nearest to them.

'Roger that. Search party to the explosion site due to be dispatched.'

'Due to be?' a familiar cross male voice shouted. 'Get them out there now!' Luca recognised Harland Barret's anger.

The Major leaned over and plugged a lead into the radio. The message quietened to a small buzzing in the earpiece at end of the cable.

'It appears that you have bought an unexpected guest with you,' Major Thomas stated.

'What are you going to do with her?' Luca asked aggressively.

'I don't think that has anything to do with you!'

Mercy gripped Luca at the elbow. 'She was kind to us and helped us,' she interjected quickly.

'Be that as it may,' the Major replied, 'she will be held securely. She will come in use again, no doubt.' The Major smiled. 'But as for you three, you will be useful now. Since we had no choice but to get you out of there, I want to know what is happening in the city at ground level. Tell me, what are the actual people feeling about the leadership? There is only so much you can *glean* from the propaganda that is broadcast.'

Luca's senses prickled at the use of the word glean. It was not a word that he had ever heard anyone in Tropolis use. His mind raced. She wanted what they had; information, and it was valuable. He quickly stepped forward. 'You won't be hearing anything from us until we are back with Kelsee.' He peered at Eban and Mercy and was grateful for their nods of agreement.

Major Thomas frowned then smiled sweetly as if nothing had been said. 'It seems that we have started in a somewhat poor manner,' she began. 'You must be hungry.' She pulled up her sleeve slightly and tapped her shoulder then spoke into the communicator at her wrist. 'Have a full English breakfast sent for three to B6.'

'Yes Major,' came the muffled reply.

'Captain Scout, take these children up to room B6. Make sure that they are made comfortable.' The Major looked fiercely at Luca. He hated her use of the term *children* as if it were an insult to their intelligence and ability to survive without her. His mouth became dry. 'You must see that we need to work together, after all, we have rescued you from Tropolis and the massacre they label the Compassion Prize.' Luca frowned. 'There, we can't have you getting upset. I am sure everything will be much clearer after you have full stomachs.'

Mercy stepped closer to Luca. 'Not now!' she whispered.

Eban laughed a little. 'Breakfast would be great. I don't suppose there would be scrambled egg would there? Thanks.'

The tension in the Major's shoulders eased a little as she turned her attention to the image on the table.

'This way,' Captain Scout instructed, and left through the same door.

Luca followed in silence. The man at the desk nearest the door was reading a message from his screen. Luca scanned the screen hastily. The words were emblazoned in red at the top of the page, *URGENT INTERVENTION REQUIRED*. It was short note, but certain words were highlighted near the end. *Power must be restored, able bodies to be deployed to Outside within 48 hours.* Just as Luca passed the man called out, 'Major, I think you should see this.' Luca watched as the Major casually looked at the screen. She then leaned over the man's shoulder, to read more intently.

Chapter 3

47h 53m

Captain Scout led the friends up a steep flight of metal stairs, their feet clattering on the open treads. Scout walked ahead, unconcerned. When she came to a door halfway along the corridor she opened it and stepped aside.

Eban peered in then comfortably entered. Luca and Mercy followed.

Three pairs of metal bunks lined the walls. The mattresses were thin and lumpy and a pile of blue folded bed linen was stacked at the foot of each bed. There seemed there was little colour to the room despite the warm sunlight that tried to enter through the two small windows encrusted with dried salt water. A square table sat just below one of the windows.

'Your food will be with you shortly.'

Before Luca could turn, Captain Scout was gone, the door shut and a lock clicked.

The room was extremely quiet.

Luca scanned the room for cameras but there appeared to be none. He looked anxiously at his friends. Mercy had moved over to one of the bunks by the door and Eban smiled back. Despite Eban's peace, Luca only felt on edge. He rubbed his neck trying to ease the tension but it didn't help.

'It's good they've put us together,' Eban said nodding.

'We're locked in,' Luca replied shaking his head.

'Just for now, until they work out what to do.'

'Eban, how can you be so calm?' Luca twisted the door handle but the door would not open.

'You said yourself it was locked,' Mercy said resting her hand on his arm. 'So why are you trying to open it?'

Luca shrugged and then stomped over to the window. He rubbed his sleeve on the dirty glass but it failed to improve the view. He could just make out that the waves were starting to build and the sky was filling with cloud, but that was as clear as it got. Perhaps the saying was right and a stormy day was ahead since the dawn had been beautiful.

Luca knew that he had created an atmosphere. Eban's smile was gone and the springs creaked as Mercy lay on her unmade bed gazing at the metal bars holding the mattress above. Luca sighed as he pulled out the stool, slumped to the table and watched as the wind bought the storm ever closer. He wanted to ease the mood he had created but he could think of nothing to say.

They were not free.

The minutes passed slowly but eventually the lock clicked, the door opened and a man walked in carrying a tray with four plates of steaming food. Four plates. Luca peered around the Campion worker and saw Kelsee enter.

'Kelsee!' Mercy called while Eban laughed out loud.

Luca rushed to her side and hugged her tightly. When he pulled away he held her out at arm's length scrutinising her. She looked pale and her eyes were puffy.

The food was left on the table and the Campion man retreated.

'When are we getting out of here?' Eban called. But the man didn't reply and locked the door as he left.

'Are you alright?' Luca asked now that they were alone.

'I'm fine,' Kelsee said quietly. Her eyes filled with tears and her smile quivered as she rubbed her hands together then gripped her wrist and winced.

Luca turned her hands over and saw the red puncture mark and unnaturally raised lump beside it.

'Fine?' Luca replied, gently rubbing his thumb around the site. 'They chipped you?'

Kelsee nodded and her gaze dropped to the floor.

'They put a chip in,' Luca announced lifting Kelsee's wrist to show the others. 'Why would they do that?'

Mercy glared at Luca. 'I think we should eat.' Then taking Kelsee's hand she continued. 'Are you hungry? Come and sit here with us.'

Luca sat down but pushed his plate away watching Kelsee wipe the tear away with her cuff.

'It is unlikely that they are trying to poison us since they have just rescued us,' Eban said gently pushing the plate back to Luca. 'You should have something to eat, it will help you to think clearer. The scrambled eggs are fabulous.'

Luca smiled. Eban was right, but the chip and questions didn't sit comfortably with him. Luca took a mouthful of crispy bacon before he realised just how hungry he was.

'We were taken to meet Major Thomas,' Mercy said chatting with Kelsee, 'The leader of Campion. She wants to know what is happening in Tropolis. We didn't have anything to tell her.'

Luca chewed and swallowed fast before trying to speak calmly. 'They seem to be gathering as much information as possible on Tropolis. Their comms room was receiving signals from the Network.' He was grateful that the edge of fury in his voice had been dulled. 'What do you think they want?' he asked all his friends.

'They questioned me too,' Kelsee stuttered. 'He may be my grandfather, but I'm not in any official meetings and I haven't been in the same room as him for a long time. I don't know what is happening, not really,' she said pleading with them to believe her. 'I think this lot thought I could be more useful.'

Mercy rubbed Kelsee's arm. 'It means you get to be with us.'

'I did tell them about the Compassion Fatigue illness and the search for a cure but they said they already knew about that. They have known about it for years. They got quite cross when I mentioned it and then put in the chip.'

'I can't believe I only found out about the illness this morning,' Luca said looking at Kelsee. He bit down on his lip, concerned for her wellbeing. Her confidence seemed gone and she looked lost. When Eban and himself had gone to rescue Mercy with the help of Luca's newly found Uncle Alec, they had not thought that they would be meeting Kelsee. She had been mid treatment, connected to an unconscious Mercy, by a series of tubes and a machine at the time of discovery. Luca had no idea how long the treatment Kelsee had been receiving would last. She was Tropolite born and was therefore susceptible to the incapacitating illness that seemed to plague her people. Tropolites were restricted to their homes and close relations because of the deadly allergic reactions if they strayed elsewhere. Kelsee was fortunate enough to have family that would pay for expensive one to one treatment with an Outsider.

Mercy shook her head. 'We found information about *The National State of Compassion Fatigue* on the tablets when we were meant to be studying for the Intelligence test. Don't you remember?' she asked.

Luca recalled that the articles and videos were not on the study list but Eban had hacked into the Tropolis archives. They had been able to watch as the electricity supply to the cameras had been turned off and "lights out" had hit the city. The video of Kelsee's grandfather dismissing the poor had systematically outlawed charity and help for those in need. They had witnessed the birth of Outside.

Eban nodded and glanced at Luca. 'With all that equipment I'm not surprised they knew,' he said.

'I get the impression,' Kelsee said turning to Mercy, 'that they don't trust Tropolis and Tropolites like me very much.'

'Maybe,' Luca said nodding, trying to shift his worry. 'They could have found out using the equipment. But do you remember what Crisp ... I mean my Uncle Alec mentioned to us Eban?' Luca frowned. It was no good, his uncle's name just didn't seem to fit. Eban looked blank. 'He said that Campion were a people who had escaped. They'd come out of Tropolis, escaped the same way we did and that the Tropolites were too sick to stop them. If they had fled from Tropolis, they must have done so before they got Compassion Fatigue or they would not survive out here.'

'Perhaps,' Eban added, 'they can only survive out here.'

Luca stared at Eban. 'Do you think they're ill? Do you think they want to use us to heal them too?'

Mercy raised her hands a little. 'It's best not to get carried away,' she said calmly. 'Let's not forget, they rescued us.'

'Or captured us!' Luca stated forcefully.

Kelsee looked up, her brow furrowed. 'These people are Tropolites?'

'I guess that would explain the technology,' Eban stated. 'And I suppose why they haven't done anything about Outside.'

The wind battered the windows but the Campion sea fort stood firm as it had no doubt done for countless years. It would not be bothered by such things. To Luca, the permanence of this place dwindled his hope. How could these people know the urgency with which they needed to act?

Luca broke the silence of the room. 'My father is alone on Outside,' he said quietly as he put down his fork and pushed his nearly finished breakfast to one side. 'I think they are sending people to Outside to restore the power. Major Thomas seemed very interested in a message that had come through. What if Tropolis uses that excuse to hurt my father? I'm no longer in the Prize. What happens if he isn't safe? The message gives him under 48 hours.' Luca picked at the toast. 'And we are stuck here, for who knows how long. I need to help him. I don't know how much longer he will survive now that I'm not coming back for him.'

Mercy straightened up. 'Who said you weren't going back for him?' She quickly placed a finger to her lips.

Suddenly the lock clicked and the door swung open. Captain Scout walked in and held the door open for Major Thomas.

'I hope you enjoyed your meal,' she began but did not wait for a response. Major Thomas pulled out an empty chair and sat herself at the head of the table. She turned to Kelsee. 'Captain Scout tells me that you are related to Harland Barrett, is this correct?'

'Yes Ma'am. He is my grandfather.'

'I see. And you stole his boat, is that correct? He had no idea you were bringing your friends here on a little trip?'

'He didn't know, so I suppose I did steal it. But it wasn't me that blew it up.'

'No. That was unfortunate, but necessary for our safety. They are no longer looking for you.'

Kelsee slumped a little in her chair. 'I had no idea that here was even a place. She brought us, not me.'

Luca shook his head and puffed. 'What about our safety? The man that got us out of Tropolis said that you would be able to help us.'

'Really?' Major Thomas seemed mildly amused.

Luca tried to remember what his uncle had actually said. The truth was, Luca could only recall Alec saying that Campion would find them, both his uncle and himself had assumed it would be to give them assistance. Maybe their assumptions were wrong, or maybe Luca's belief in his uncle was mislaid in Crisp. Luca refused to let the doubt show on his face and kept eye contact with the major. 'So what are you going to do to help us?'

'First we need to run a few standard tests but we hope to have you moved to a more comfortable environment by the morning.'

The major nodded to Captain Scout who quickly produced a number of small glass slides. She took hold of Mercy's finger, wiped it with a swab and pricked it with the needle. Mercy gasped a little at the shock. Scout encouraged a large drop of red blood to form before dripping it onto the slide.

Luca folded his arms close to his body. Campion were performing blood screening. His distrust grew. They were considering him and his friends as being the cure to Campion instead of free.

'You see. A very simple test,' Major Thomas said. 'Mercy dear, I understand that you carry the Campion flower.'

Mercy nodded but did not reply. She sucked on her pierced finger.

'Is there a reason that such a symbol be tattooed so permanently to one at your age?'

Mercy removed her finger from her mouth and touched her neck.

Major Thomas pushed Mercy's hair aside and peered at the delicate image. 'Of course it is not as strong as our current brand.'

Mercy pulled away from Major Thomas and flicked her hair back to hide the flower. She shook her head and sighed. 'It was done when I was little. My parents did it,' she said looking away from Thomas and at her friends instead. 'They never told me why, but I guess that if you needed reminding of something that you never wanted to forget, you'd find a way of making it constantly seen.' Mercy shrugged. 'Maybe I carry the message that they wanted to survive.'

The major coughed slightly and moved on. 'Now, I understand that you may have questions but ...'

'Actually, yes we do,' Mercy replied turning once again to face the major. 'What are you planning to do about the people of Tropolis and Outside?'

'There is nothing that we can do at present.'

'Nothing?' Eban said in disbelief.

Major Thomas stood to her feet. 'I can see that today has been a very stressful time for you all and I suspect you could all do with some rest.'

Luca snatched his hand away from Scout. 'Is that your answer for everything? To lay down and forget about it, because I don't think much about that!'

Mercy patted Luca on the hand. 'You are right, we are a little tired,' Mercy began, 'But we have family and friends that need your help too. We are grateful for what you have done. You searched for us and bought us to this safe place, but there are so many more that need your help.'

'I wish we could help them,' Major Thomas said pulling at the chair as if she were to sit down once again. 'But there really is so little that we can do. My prime concern is for my own people.'

'I understand,' Mercy sighed, 'But our people are still suffering. Even Kelsee's people are suffering in Tropolis.' Luca shook his head. 'They are Luca. They are sick and need help too.'

'They've never done anything for us,' Luca replied.

Major Thomas laughed a little. 'You are correct there boy!' she replied bitterly. 'They have only used you for their own gain. They have manipulated you and discarded you much like the place where you come from. The only reason they ensure you to live is for their advance.'

'But my people need your help,' Luca appealed to the major. 'They have done nothing to you. I've seen the technology that you have here. You can't just leave them to die on the heaps.'

'What good would it be to go into Outside? Think about it!'

Kelsee drooped in her chair. 'If the Outsiders were free, Tropolis would die.' Luca frowned. Was Kelsee really saying her people were better than his?

'Exactly! We'd all die!' Major Thomas banged the chair on the floor. 'I'm glad you have some sense. Electrical power would be removed, the source of their experimental cure would be gone and then what? The factories and farms would stop producing food, there would be violence and devastation everywhere to all people groups. It is a fine line that we tread, if one thing steps out of that balance everything collapses.'

'This is a balance of destruction,' Mercy said letting the tears roll down her cheek. 'It will never change if we ignore it.'

Thomas raised her chin. 'We do not ignore it. We manage it.'

'You manage it by ignoring it,' Mercy retorted bravely. 'Please consider the choices that you are making. Campion are the only ones who have a choice.'

'I have no more time for this discussion,' Major Thomas replied, turned and left the room to a shocked silence.

Captain Scout was the only one making any noise as she began to pack away the glass slides. Her head was bowed and she cleared her throat. 'I have to agree with the Major, but I can't help but be disappointed that Campion just sit back.'

'What?' Eban asked. 'Do you want to do something about this?'

Scout looked up briefly. 'If there was a way to turn this around, I would willingly do it.'

Chapter 4
45h 32m

The light fittings buzzed a little as they shed the dull light into the room. The impending storm had darkened the sky so heavily that the sea fort was lit artificially despite it being only late morning.

Luca had felt the weight of despair as hope had left the room with Captain Scout. He sat, silenced by his inability to do anything to make things better. When he had experienced waves like this before he had grabbed his bag and sought out a glean on the heaps. He could always find something to prove to himself that life was not as bleak as it appeared. Even in Tropolis there was the goal of the prize to ease the tension, but here he felt completely trapped. The spark that the arrival and rescue of the tiny Campion vessel had ignited in his heart had been snuffed out by the immovable forces of their leadership.

Luca had not listened as Eban and Mercy chatted sitting with one another on the bunk. He had barely noticed Kelsee curled up on another bed, facing the wall, until her quivering shoulders caught his attention. He inhaled deeply and dragged himself out of his own spiralling thoughts.

He approached Kelsee, knelt beside her bunk and placed a hand on her back. He searched for words to somehow make it better but they were hidden too well.

'I'm so sorry,' she sobbed.

'There is nothing for you to be sorry about. You got us out of Tropolis alive.'

Kelsee turned over until she was face to face with Luca. Her skin was pale and she almost looked to be in pain. 'I should have let you leave without me,' she whispered, 'I've only made it worse.' Luca heard Kelsee speaking out what was deep inside her. He shook his head. 'I am no use to anyone.'

Her eyes filled with tears and quickly spilled over, splashing the pillow.

Luca bit down on his lip. Kelsee was hurting yet he could not help her since he believed the same of himself. How could he lift her out without then listening to his own words?

Luca stared at the tears as they clung to Kelsee's lashes. He had to choose.

'You are much more important to me than you realise,' he began quietly. He paused, then smiling a little he continued, 'Without you we would probably be in those medical rooms under some experiment to find the cure. You got us out of Tropolis ...' Luca took a deep breath. 'You got us out so that we could do something about what is happening.'

'How can I be worth anything when they aren't even looking for me anymore?'

'You don't know that,' Luca said. 'Campion don't know everything that is going on no matter how much they think they do.' He wiped the moisture gently from Kelsee's cheek with the soft part of his thumb. 'You are more important than you think. After all, we all know who your family are. I can't see them giving up that quickly. They have the fatigue and the storm to fight and I'm not sure how that works with a search party, but there must be some technology that they would be using to scan the sea for you. You have enormous value, that's that. Do you hear me?'

A faint smile flickered over Kelsee's face. 'Thank you!' she whispered and held his hand close to her face.

Luca could feel the steady drip of the words he had given to his friend affect him. He had spoken truth to Kelsee yet knew that he battled with applying it to himself. Luca purposefully straightened his back and raised his gaze. 'I won't give up. I can't!'

'Glad to hear it!' Eban called from across the room, laughing a little.

'We don't exactly have a plan,' Mercy said confidently, 'but I think we need to be certain of what we want to do.' She walked over to Kelsee's bunk followed by Eban. 'We want to free Outside and get those in Tropolis well and we think that Campion are the ones to help in this.'

'Small task then!' Luca scoffed.

'That is the aim,' Mercy said placing her hands on her hips. 'It doesn't have to all be done in one move and I'm not expecting that to be the case. But are we agreed that is what we want?'

'Of course that is what I want, but ...'

'Luca, that is all I asked. We don't need to worry about details yet.' Mercy stared at Luca almost daring him to answer back.

Everything in him wanted to trust her. It was all well and good to say those things, but how they could be accomplished seemed impossible. Luca nodded and briefly smiled back at Mercy. She had not let him down yet.

'I reckon that Major Thomas is just scared,' Eban announced.

Kelsee sat up. 'She is looking after her people and everyone else,' she said quietly. 'Perhaps my grandfather is just doing the same.'

Luca snorted. 'I doubt that!'

Mercy frowned at Luca. 'We don't know what these leaders are having to face or what decisions they are having to make under the banner of taking care of their own.' She opened her hands in appeal to Luca. 'We ought not to make rash judgements.'

'Rash!' Luca replied angrily. 'We have lived behind that wall for our entire lives and have never got anything from Tropolis.' He balled his fists. 'If taking care of their own means they are blinded to others we need to get them to take a long hard look at what they have created.'

'There you have it!' Eban said slapping Luca on the back.

'What?' Luca said shaking his head as he held his forehead.

'The plan, Luca!' Eban replied. 'We just need them to take a look.'

The afternoon passed slowly. A second meal had arrived but Luca paced, impatient for something to happen. Captain Scout had promised that they would be moved at some point and Luca regularly checked the salt misted window to keep track of the time of day.

The waves still crested beyond the fort, but the rain had stopped and the wind had died down before Scout appeared with several thick jackets folded over her arm.

'You'll be needing these,' she said passing one to each of the friends. 'It's time to go.'

Luca slipped on the coat even though he felt hot and uncomfortable. He tugged at the neck of his shirt willing for a little air to cool him down. He scraped his hand through his hair and puffed out. Mercy gently placed her hand on his arm and smiled reassuringly. Luca snorted a little, wondering where Mercy contained her calm demeanour and secretly wished he could tap into it. She smiled at him as she quickly braided her long, dark hair and tied it with the Tropolite ribbon she had pulled from her pocket.

Scout led them down the echoing hallways back to the hatch over the sea.

Luca glared at the bold embossed Campion flower emblazoned on the wall and his hand naturally reached for the notebook. The crumpled pages were still there, untouched and insignificant. The tension spread across his back before he released the notebook and began to ball up his fists. He felt foolish trusting in an idea as delicate as the illustration on the cover of the book. Campion had not lived up to what he had hoped for; they were not willing to rescue his people. Luca sighed and let the anger pass as he realised nothing had ever fulfilled his dreamy ideals. Perhaps now was the time to change his way of thinking. He sadly turned away from the emblem and caught Mercy looking kindly at him. There was someone that seemed to fulfil his ideals. Mercy had never let him down and had gone beyond what he had ever asked or expected when she had offered her own life in place of his, in the Death Room. In this moment, she was peaceful and yet knew that Campion had a part to play. She did not hold their passivity against them, but instead seemed to trust in their ability to change at some point in time. Luca felt great admiration for her but wasn't sure he was strong enough to stand in the same place.

The door to the left of the emblem opened. Luca reached back for Kelsee and grabbed her hand. This had been the place that had separated them before and Luca was certain he would get in their way if they chose to do that again.

Major Thomas strode into the dull room. A young Campion worker followed her.

'If you could confirm here, ma'am,' she said handing the Major the electronic tablet.

Thomas pushed the worker and his demands one side.

'So, it is time to leave,' she said approaching the friends, 'You are not required or permitted to speak of the events that have happened prior to coming to Campion. You are to start again here, with your new lives. Understood?'

'Where are we going?' Luca asked taking a step forward.

Thomas smiled a little but it faded almost as quickly as it appeared. 'You do not need to be here with us any longer. Captain Scout will escort you to a safe house.'

Eban leaned past Luca. 'Safe house? Who do we need to be safe from?' he joked; when he smiled it always seemed genuine. 'Have you really thought this through Major? I mean, nowhere is that safe, and it seems that the ones we need saving from are the ones who are refusing to do anything about anything important.'

'Young man,' Major Thomas said through pursed lips, 'You are forgetting that leadership decisions may not always be popular with everyone, but you can believe me when I say that I have my peoples' best interest at heart.'

Eban nodded. 'Yes, I can understand why you say that. You are frightened of what might happen if you stepped up and out for other people.' Major Thomas opened her mouth but Eban continued, unhindered. 'But you are failing to see that your decisions affect everyone, not just those in Campion.' Eban opened his hands. 'Please Major, be courageous.'

'Enough!' Major Thomas said reaching for the raised button by the door. 'Take them ashore,' she commanded as she walked to the opposite door. She snatched the tablet from her assistant and left the group alone.

An electronic voice rang through the space. 'Doors opening. Stand clear!'

The large hatch began to slide away into the floor revealing the suspended boat. A Campion worker tossed down the rope ladder and Captain Scout descended. She was closely followed by the familiar man who had navigated the boat. He looked even more weathered as he held the ladder steady, in this light than he had before.

'Let's get going,' Scout called up to them.

Luca stepped in front of the group.

'You're all coming Luca,' Scout said puffing. 'Pick up some speed, we don't have much light left.'

Eban clambered down first followed by Kelsee and Mercy. Luca took several deep breaths before he let his feet dangle over the edge. Reaching for the rungs below, he climbed down slowly. The sun had dipped below the clouds and the stark light startled him as he hung halfway between the fort and the craft. The contrast of the warm uninterrupted sunshine flowing over the rough water only led to further uneasiness in Luca's spirit. He grit his teeth as nothing felt settled.

Grateful for a seat near his friends once more, Luca's stomach churned a little as the boat was lowered to the water. The wind tossed the craft and it swayed slightly in the net cradle. The chains rattled as they let down the boat.

Scout and the navigator positioned themselves at the bow and stern of the vessel respectively. As soon as the hull touched the water they rushed to untangle the net from the gunwale and set the boat free. The waves rocked the craft violently but the two Campion's worked quickly and efficiently. The navigator started the engine and caused the sturdy boat to ride the waves as if it were second nature.

Luca turned and squinted. Tower two sea fort stood tall and silhouetted along with its neighbours against the sun brightened clouds. He was glad to be heading away but there was a knotted sensation in his stomach. They were heading to some other Campion location and further away from his father. The guilt that Luca knew he should feel at being far from Outside and the responsibility of care was not as evident as he thought it should have been. Perhaps the dark bitterness and anger towards his father was deeper and more hidden than even he realised. The clock was ticking; Tropolis may have decided to punish what they considered to be his only family. Here he sat, free from the fort but he felt very little urgency to do anything about it. He stared out to sea and avoided looking at the faces of his friends. Luca was ashamed.

Captain Scout lifted the camouflaged roof into place. The engine revved and the craft sped and jumped over the waves. Luca knew that the boat would be taking them to shore but the navigator seemed to be setting them on a different course from the one that had bought them to the forts.

No one spoke for a long while. Luca watched as Captain Scout fulfilled her orders yet she did not seem as alienated as the last time they sat in this boat together. She had said very little to them and engaged minimally as she gazed out to sea.

The sun kissed the horizon before the coast come into view. The rocky cliffs shone red in the fading light. Luca gasped as he picked out the line of a path slashing and clinging to the surface. He had been here before. This was the Endurance Test site, the place he had nearly died.

Chapter 5
38h 17m

Luca's mouth went dry as the boat failed to turn away from the deadly assault course. He could see the beach in the distance and hoped that they would change their path at any moment to head for the shore.

The cliff loomed ever taller in the fading light as the small craft and its travellers were dwarfed by the rocky face.

'I know this place,' Kelsee said almost gleefully.

Luca turned to her and frowned. This test had claimed some of the lives of those who had entered the Compassion Prize and had also almost taken his.

'You were amazing!' Kelsee continued. 'I loved the bit where you got to the beach and Eban and Mercy saw you. I almost cried.'

Luca shook his head. 'I almost died.' He leaned away from Kelsee. 'People were killed here. I'm sorry, I don't ...'

Mercy sighed and spoke softly. 'Kelsee, this is not a good place. Tropolis have turned the Prize into entertainment.' She took Kelsee's hand and gave it a gentle squeeze. 'Real people suffered here.'

Kelsee looked away from the rock face and towards Mercy. She glanced at Luca who shifted away from her. Her eyes widened. 'I don't know what to say. I ...' Tears began fill her eyes. 'I am a Tropolite ... and have never had to think that way. I've never known any contestants and I guess, well, it is real then, isn't it?'

'Yes,' Luca replied. 'Very real.'

'I'm so sorry,' Kelsee sobbed ignoring the moisture on her cheeks and reaching out to him. 'Please, Luca!'

Luca twisted away from her and rubbed his hands on his legs. He bowed his head as he focused anywhere but at Kelsee. He could feel the heat rising in his face even though he did not want to succumb to the anger he felt. How could she consider it all a harmless and pleasurable game?

'Luca, I'm sorry!' Kelsee pleaded.

Eban leaned towards him. 'She doesn't need your punishment. How would she know about it all?'

Luca glanced towards her. She was distraught and shocked by what had been revealed. She had lived as the enemy in the privileged Tropolis, yet had never been given the facts. He couldn't hold this against her especially, as now faced with the truth, her ignorance made her suffer. His bitterness washed away. Eban was right, how could he hold her way of life against her? He sighed. She just displayed the imprint of Tropolis. Raising his head and looking at her properly he finally spoke. 'Don't worry about it,' he said with a shake of his head. 'You weren't to know.'

'I don't know, I didn't know,' she said quietly wiping the tears. 'But I do now. All of it is real, isn't it?' She reached for Luca once more and he was relieved that he wanted to be near her.

Luca watched as Kelsee took in the cliff face with unblinkered vision, and his heart broke for her. He had known all along that life was not fair and that Tropolis ruled without care for anyone but themselves, but he believed that Kelsee was only just sensing the truth in this moment.

'Real lives,' Kelsee whispered to herself.

Luca didn't want to consider all the real lives that had been wiped out by the Compassion Prize, but he nodded in acknowledgment. He turned towards Captain Scout and watched her as she helped guide the boat ever closer. The waves smashed against the rock face in violent frothy swells. There seemed to be no reason to put their lives at such a risk, yet ever closer they crept. The man at the helm threw the engine into reverse to fight the pull of the water to the craggy wall.

The thundering sound of the waterfall could be heard above the thrashing waves. It must have been in the next carved out cove. Luca leaned over the edge and looked up past the canopy. He saw the small wooden platform high on the cliff face.

In the next moment a shrill whistle sounded and a dark object came hurtling towards them. Luca pulled Kelsee and Mercy to the floor of the boat and shouted to Eban to get down.

Captain Scout chuckled a little as she shifted past them to the back of the boat and began to fold the canopy away.

Luca released the girls and peered up. A long rope ladder with stiff rungs swayed from the platform. He shook his head. For a moment Luca recalled how Clarisse had helped them from this exact platform before she had been killed. The remnants of the storm did not help ease the memories. This, indeed, was a real place with real consequences.

'Up you go,' Scout instructed as she shifted her weight to one of the lowest rungs to tighten the dangling ascent.

The light was fading fast and the platform seemed so high to Luca.

Eban patted him on the shoulder. 'It's okay, I'll go first.'

Luca smiled at Eban, appreciating the kindness of his friend.

Eban climbed confidently and quickly while the others watched him. Luca could feel his heart beginning to race. Coming back to this place was making him revisit the fear he had faced before. He looked along the cliff face, searching for another way to get to the platform but there was none. Luca had thought that he had changed, so why was he trying to escape the fear that was building inside him. He looked up again as Eban disappeared over the edge.

'Are you alright?' Mercy asked trying to catch Luca's attention. 'Do you want me to go next?'

Luca nodded. He watched Mercy clamber up the ladder that gently twitched as she moved. Her jacket flapped and her braid would occasionally flick in the wind. Luca rubbed his hand over his face and looked away.

Scout beckoned for the next person to climb as she easily kept the rope taut.

'You go,' Kelsee said. 'I'll follow behind.'

Luca reached for the ladder and noticed the small smile on the navigator's face.

'No,' Luca said reacting to a deep instinct. 'You first, I'll follow.' Kelsee frowned and the navigator huffed. 'I'll be alright,' Luca reassured her, confidently knowing that she should not be left alone on the boat.

Kelsee climbed very slowly. Luca caught snatches of Mercy's and Eban's voices calling encouragement from above. Luca stood close to Scout and held the ladder. His feet left the deck a couple of times as the rock of the boat on the waves made it dip low and his grip on the ladder lifted him.

Eventually it was his turn.

'I wish you well, Luca,' Scout said quietly, 'And I am sorry that we couldn't do more.' Luca paused hearing the truth in her tone and turned to her. In the twilight, he caught a hint of real regret in her face. 'I won't be coming any further. Campion's land crew will take care of you.' Luca extended his hand and she took it.

'Thank you, Captain,' he said shaking her hand, 'I know that it isn't easy to step out and I hope that one day you will find the courage to do so.' He released his grip on her hand and forced himself to climb, quickly regretting that he had said anything. She had, after all, rescued them.

The rope was dry and his shoes gripped the stiffened rungs well. Luca heard a sniff and grunt come from the direction of the captain. Luca dared to peer at   Captain Scout just a few steps below but the darkness was too quick to hide her. He was grateful that she still held the ladder so that the tension did not change. Perhaps her passion to fulfil her Campion duties was so steadfast that she couldn't do to him what he felt he deserved for his outburst.

The guilt was a helpful distraction for a while. However, soon his cold fingers ached and the buffeting wind bought him to his senses.

He could no longer see the rough cliff face but he knew it was out of reach. The only thing he needed to concentrate on was the rung above him as it would carry him to the platform and his waiting friends. Determined to keep moving upward, Luca grit his teeth and continued to ascend. His breath was laboured and even though he knew he should be accompanied by the sounds around him, he heard nothing as he climbed. Luca desperately wanted to take a lungful of air so that he could blow away the memories that this cliff face represented but the further he went the more constricted his chest felt.

Luca shuddered when he felt the grip and pull on his coat. Startled, Luca realised that Eban was leaning over the edge of the platform and pulling him towards what little safety the platform afforded.

He clambered over the edge and quickly scrambled as far from the danger as he could.

Eban squatted next him and gripped Luca's shoulder.

'Thanks!' Luca puffed.

'You take your time,' Eban said laughing a little. 'Tough climb huh?'

Luca nodded as he quickly checked for both the girls. They were huddled up against the rock face talking quietly with each other. Then he caught sight of a shadowy figure approaching. Luca quickly stood to shield his friends.

'Steady Luca,' the man said sternly, 'You could fall.' He was dressed head to toe in grey, was clean shaven and had an assured, calming voice. 'Take these,' he said pushing a rough rope and woven belt into Luca's hand. 'You know how to use them.'

Luca had never seen someone this old before. The man was evidently older than any Outsider. His wrinkled face fascinated Luca. A thick woollen hat sat snugly over the man's head but strands of curly greying hair poked out at his neckline. His voice was gentle but his stature spoke of strength and fitness.

Luca glared at the items in his hands. He could make out the buckle and the clamp. Almost mechanically, he fitted the belt around him as thoughts on what was coming next assaulted him. Kelsee moved cautiously towards him.

'This place is far more real than I could have ever imagined,' she said soberly.

'Tropolis created this place, and it is far worse than their imagination,' Luca replied coldly. 'You haven't seen anything yet.'

'This way,' the Campion man said glancing at the group. His gaze lingered a little longer on Kelsee.

'What about Captain Scout?' Mercy asked.

'Just me. Brigadier Alard, this way.'

There was no time to question the man. He had turned and seemed to blend into the cliff face as he took to the wooden walkway. He was confident and appeared fearless at the prospect of the pathway. Luca swallowed hard and followed after him.

The ropes and belts were far more secure than the ones that Tropolis had provided during the Endurance test, but the pathway that clung precariously to the rock face had not changed. It was still terrifying and the near darkness only made it more perilous. The slippery boards felt familiar under Luca's careful tread. The circumstances were different now, he was no longer a contestant fighting for his life and the life of his father. His every move wasn't being scrutinised by the Tropolis public who appeared to see the Compassion Prize as some far off and harmless entertainment. But he was still fighting for his life on this walkway pitted with holes and deadly gaps.

Mercy followed after Brigadier Alard with Kelsee staying very close to her. Luca could hear Mercy's encouraging words, and although they were directed at Kelsee, he listened intently. Eban took the rear and several times Luca heard Eban's cheerful hum carried in his direction.

'You alright?' Eban asked with his reassuring crooked smile when Luca had stopped and glanced behind.

Luca whispered half to himself. 'Are you afraid of anything?'

'Yes,' Eban replied. 'But I choose not to let that fear define me.' Eban laughed a little at his own remark. 'Luca, you have already endured this place and passed the test. Who and what are you listening to?'

'I am listening to the waves below and that crazy waterfall coming up. You remember that don't you? This place hasn't changed at all,' Luca said gripping tightly to the rope. 'Even the weather makes it too familiar.'

'You're right,' Eban said, 'But *you* have changed.'

Luca turned away and bit down on his lip. He shifted uneasily along the path desperately trying to pull away from Eban and his bluntness but now it was difficult to concentrate and he was distracted. He ran his fingers through his hair and blew out a noisy breath. It was the fact that Eban was right that annoyed him. He had changed; he had been changed. Standing on this narrow wooden track fixed to the side of a cliff was a strange place to have such a revelation. The Luca that had left Outside was not the same one that stood here. He took another step forward. Would he have found friendship such a stabilising factor before? Would he have let others help? No! Friendship had kept him sane and safe. Friendship had taken his place in the Death Room, something he had never really thanked Mercy for. Would he have protected anyone other than himself or perhaps his father? Not at all. Yet here he was, keeping Kelsee, a Tropolite, alive despite her lack of grasp on reality. He was transformed. He could see the change, he could even feel the change so why did he constantly go back to this place of insecurity and fear?

Luca looked back to Eban who seemed so relaxed and confident. There was something that Eban possessed that Luca wanted and he knew his friend well enough to know that Eban would give it away willingly, or maybe he already had. Maybe Eban's remark that Luca had changed was not a rebuff but inspiration to live in the truth of it.

Luca eased the grip on the rope handle, the belt and safety clips would hold him. A shiver ran up his spine but he just turned to his friend and laughed.

Eban leaned forward and patted Luca on the shoulder. 'That's it!'

The cliff rose higher and it loomed dark even against the windswept, cloudy evening sky but it did not disturb Luca.

The roar of the falls indicated the presence of the river that poured over the side of the land, although the darkness hid most of the spectacle. Luca remembered the phenomenon; the white water racing to the edge and then tumbling excitedly to join the sea below. The walkway would stop suddenly and a balance beam would be the only obvious way to cross. Soberly, Luca thought that it would be suicide to attempt that in this light.

He watched as Mercy clambered over the barrier, just as they had done in Endurance. She was still following the grey clad brigadier. Luca began to laugh. Mercy had convinced him to take this route last time by suggesting it was not what Tropolis had wanted and he had felt rebellious, and here he was rebelling again.

Luca untied the rope, and climbed over too. His pulse raced as he stepped out onto the ledge then quickly pushed his back up against the rock face. Kelsee had squeezed herself as close to the cliff as possible and gripped the wall. She was moving very slowly and muttering to herself. Luca reached out and touched her fingertips. She turned to him and even in the poor light he could see she was wide eyed.

'Take your time,' he said calmly. 'We aren't in any hurry.' The path was shallow and plants made the surface slimy. 'Mercy will help you.'

The fine spray from the falls made everything slick and the droplets quickly ran from the end of Luca's nose but he was not brave enough to wipe them away.

Soon the ledge began to widen and the darkness deepened. The thundering water sent vibrations through the rock and air, saturating the space with sound. Luca knew that they were about to pass behind the falls and out the other side.

Suddenly a blue tinged light came on and lit the last few steps on the rock path.

Brigadier Alard held the small torch in his hand. A massive overhang of rock produced a thick ceiling to the cavern that was hidden behind the falls. Luca had stood in this place in the test but was unable to investigate.

With the way lit, Kelsee easily made her way to the hollow at the back of the falls and it only took a few moments for Luca to join her. He looked around, half expecting a camera carrying drone to force them back onto the path along the cliff as it had done before, but there was nothing there except them. The cavern was sheltered from the pounding water and echoed with the rushing torrent.

Alard pulled his hand from his pocket and handed a tiny torch to each of the girls. 'This way!' Alard commanded after passing two more lights to the boys.

Alard directed his beam away from the waterfall and into the cavern. Luca quickly found the power button and shone the light over the rock.

The Campion leader did not follow the path that would take them out from the falls but instead took the short path that branched off towards the rock face. A deep split in the stone stood taller than a person. Luca shone the torch light into the void. It appeared to be more than just a fissure since the light was swallowed and did not shine back from the rock. Alard's silhouetted form soon blocked all the light as he walked right into the gap. Mercy took hold of Kelsee's hand and raised her eyebrows in question.

'Where else are we going to go?' Luca stated. 'Stay close!'
Luca stepped into the broken rock and the friends followed.

Chapter 6

36h 27m

The overwhelming sound of the falls died in the cliff face tunnel. The roar seemed far behind them and the noise of their shuffling feet on the damp pathway filled the space.

Luca explored the passage with the narrow beam of his torch. The walls either side were roughly hewn and dripped with water. If he stretched out his arms just a fraction he would have been able to touch both sides of the irregular corridor. The pathway was mostly flat; a few pools of water lingered in slight divots. The ceiling above was uneven. In some places, the Brigadier could only just stand upright under the flat rock, but in others the rock split in jagged heights that the torch beam could only just skim. The further that they travelled on the twisting pathway, the more Luca felt that this tunnel had been created by connecting several naturally occurring voids.

There was a chill to the air that stayed constant. As the friends travelled deeper, they noticed less surface water and the damp walls eventually stopped running with water. Luca thought that perhaps they were moving away from the river, but wherever they were going, it was far from the cliff face and the walled Outside.

Luca followed Alard through a particularly low section of tunnel with rough and prickly walls. He had to clamber over uneven ground made from large rocks fixed within the bedrock, but the echoing sound that was coming from ahead drew him onwards.

As Luca straightened up he saw a vast cavern. A cool beam of moonlight filtered down through a hole high in the roof where vegetation was growing, and reflected off the flat lake at the base.

The path came to an abrupt end and became a rocky beach on the shoreline. The lake was all that was before them.

Mercy and Kelsee spoke in whispers and Luca could understand why. There was a charmed silence and stillness to the place that should not be broken.

Whilst the others shone their torches all over the cavern, Alard purposely pointed ahead, flashing the beam on and off. Luca watched as out of the darkness a second light mimicked his signal identically.

The lake's surface rippled and the water bobbed at the beach line. A small raft moved from the shadows and across the moonlit pool. The swells caused the reflected light to jump and dance over the cavern's walls breaking the enchanted stillness. The unmanned craft drifted towards them and stopped at Alard's feet on the shore.

He stepped over the slight ridge and placed himself at the far side of the raft. Alard beckoned that they follow.

Luca felt the raft give a little under his foot as he stepped forward. He offered his hand to each of his friends as they stepped aboard. Surprisingly the plastic craft hardly shifted even with their movement.

Alard had perched on the slightly raised edge and instructed the others to do the same with the beam of his torch. Mercy sat down to his right. As he raised the torch from the raft the shaft of light caught Mercy's profile. Alard paused and stared at the tattoo.

His eyes widened and his lips parted. The sudden sound of the tiny gasp amplified over the water.

Alard covered his brief and unguarded actions by continuing with his role as if nothing had happened. He took a small silver remote from his pocket and a few moments after the screen had lit, the craft began to move away from the shoreline. The base scraped the rocky shallows and the echoes of the hollow plastic raft dominated the cavern. After the juddering start, the raft moved away smoothly and with only a very soft humming noise.

No one spoke. Luca unzipped his jacket a little and bit down on his lip. Had the others not noticed Alard's reaction? Luca wondered if the tension and uncertainty of where they were being taken was playing with his mind.

Luca peered over the side and shone his torch, but there was no engine to be seen even though their progress away from the shore was steady.

The others were focussing their lights on the far rocky face. Luca thought he saw a flash of light shine back at them. He fidgeted in his space. Luca was grateful for the respite; his legs ached after the exertion on the cliff face and then the long journey through the rock tunnels, but he was eager to find out where Campion were taking them.

Eventually the raft came to a halt at what could have been a dead end at the far side of the lake. The raft bumped into the uneven hewn jetty wall. A rusty metal ladder clung to the side leaving orange stains on the rock.

'Up you go!' Alard commanded breaking the silence with what felt like a shout.

The rungs were cold and rough. As Luca climbed over the edge nervously, waiting for another Campion worker, he could feel a warm breeze. As he clambered to the top he quickly shone his light at the landing. There was no-one there.

'Luca!' Alard called. 'Take this.' He passed Luca a dripping rope.

The glint of light off a shiny surface caught Luca's attention. Next to the mirror was a hook connected to a set of cogs and a small motor. Luca shone his torch beam more intentionally onto the mirror a few times, the motor whirred gently, the cogs turned and the hook lowered and pulled back. Luca looked at the rope in his hand and noticed the loop on the end. He realised that there was no other Campion worker here because the raft had been held back by this weird contraption and had been released by Alard from across the lake.

Kelsee had followed Luca and was breathing in the fresh air deeply. Eban had helped Mercy onto the jetty and had moved over to assist Luca. Alard climbed up last. He leaned over to Luca and held another rope. 'After three, pull,' he said as he turned away. '1,2,3 ...'

Luca and Eban pulled at one rope while Alard the other. The raft clung to the lake, it slurped in the water below then lifted suddenly taking Luca and Eban off guard.

'Alright lads?' Alard asked. 'Keep pulling.'

The raft was light after the lake had released it. The plastic banged and grated against the rock sending echoes throughout the cavern.

Alard grabbed the ridge of the plastic craft as it came to the top of the jetty. He pulled it onto the rock pathway forcing Mercy and Kelsee to stand aside.

'Give me a hand,' he said to Luca and Eban strapping the torch to his arm.

The boys took hold of the other end just as Alard flipped it onto its side and almost knocking it out of Luca's hands. Luca grunted his irritation. Eban laughed a little and shook his head but his manner wasn't directed towards Luca. The hollow underside revealed four small propellers and an encased battery pack in the centre.

Alard marched at the head of the band, dragging the boys behind him. The raft wasn't heavy, just cumbersome.

Luca was concentrating so hard on not tripping up that he didn't realise that they had reached the opening of the tunnel until the ground beneath his feet became soft.

He glanced behind him. The opening of the tunnel was tall and obvious in the rock formation, but dark and intimidating. Luca was grateful for the moonlight that filtered through the trees. It seemed that the storm had passed.

The sound of the breeze against the branches was full of depth and space. The confines of the cave had restricted everything, but Luca felt revived in the open night air.

With his free hand Luca shone the narrow beam of his torch over the wooded area they were now in. They were following a dirt track and Luca's light caught a reflector ahead of him. Alard stopped at the back of the large truck. He lifted his end of the raft onto the flatbed and began to drag the rest of it into place.

'There is space for two more in the cab. The others will have to travel on the back.' Alard opened the truck door and called out, 'Torches off from here.'

'Mercy should go in the cab,' Luca said to Eban. 'She has had very little time to recover from the ordeal in Tropolis and then had to get here.' They both looked at Mercy. Luca saw that she was exhausted. 'We need to look after her.'

Eban nodded. 'One of us should go with her,' he replied in a whisper. 'I'm still not sure about leaving her with the Brigadier.'

'You go,' Luca urged and patted Eban on the back. Perhaps he hadn't been the only one to notice Alard's reaction to Mercy's tattoo. 'I need to talk with Kelsee. I need to take back some stuff I said.'

Eban smiled as he placed his hand on Luca's shoulder. 'Well done mate!' He turned to Mercy. 'Let's get you a good seat. In you go!' Mercy didn't object and wearily slid into the cab.

Luca boosted himself onto the back of the truck and then offered his hand to Kelsee. She allowed herself to be pulled up and then they both shifted away from the edge. Luca threw a thick blanket over the upturned raft and they sat down on it with their backs propped up against cab. Luca knocked on the window and gave a thumbs up to Eban inside.

There was a slight judder as the motor started but the hum of the engine was no louder than the rustling of the leaves on the trees; the truck made more noise as it rattled along the track. The moonlight played a game of hide and seek in the canopy and the clouds that scuttled past.

Luca had no idea what time it was as they had been travelling for a long time. Being underground had been disorientating but the moon had risen high so he felt certain that it was nearing midnight.

'I er, I'm sorry about earlier,' Luca finally said quietly.

Kelsee looked at him. They were sat quite close together but Luca was unsure of her expression. 'I don't think you really have anything to be sorry for.'

'Of course I do!' Luca replied.

'Luca!' Kelsee said raising her hands. 'I'm just saying, I think you were right.'

Luca furrowed his brow. 'Really?'

'Yes,' Kelsee replied calmly, 'I never knew that it was all real. It's like I'm seeing for the first time.'

'But I got angry with you,' he said lowering his gaze. 'I shouldn't have done that. You weren't to know that life outside Tropolis isn't a game.'

'You're wrong, Luca,' she said and he looked up at her. 'If I had really cared about anything but myself, I would have investigated it.'

'I don't think that it would have been that easy,' Luca said sighing. 'Eban got through to some stuff on the Network that has been filed away and isn't accessible by others.' He smiled at Kelsee. 'It isn't that easy to find evidence when you are in Tropolis.'

'But now I am outside, I see it everywhere.'

Luca sat silent for a while. 'First impressions aren't that good are they?' He laughed a little. 'Kidnapped from your grandfather's boat, locked away in isolation, chip implanted, Endurance test cliff climbing ... not sure that the outside world has started off all that well!'

Kelsee giggled. Luca was relieved to hear that again.

'Tropolis cannot keep this hidden,' she finally said, 'Life just can't be sustainable the way it is.'

'It seems to be doing quite nicely right now.' Luca could hear his own voice tarnished with criticism.

Kelsee rested her head on his shoulder and said nothing further.

For a while the truck left the path and joined a tarmacked road. The surface was breaking up and long grass grew down the middle. Either side tall and unwieldy hedges blocked the view. But soon, however, Alard had driven back onto another track where younger trees flanked the pathway.

The truck came to a halt and Luca turned to look through the fogged cab window. He gasped when he saw the shadowy rows of double storey buildings that were silver in the moonlight.

'This way!' Alard called to them as he stepped out of the cab. He pulled off his hat and wiped his brow with the back of his hand. Luca saw that Alard's thinning, curly hair was kept long. Alard replaced the hat to keep his bald patch warm.

All the windows in the buildings were dark. Luca's stomach churned at the familiar smell of rotting wood that reminded him of Outside.

Alard marched along the road that seemed clear of grass. He was unaffected by the unfamiliar place, to Luca, Alard appeared completely at home. Luca shivered but he was not cold. He picked up his pace so that he could walk nearer to Eban, he pulled Kelsee closer to the group. Alard's confidence grew as he wove through the quiet streets, while Luca sunk further into fearfulness. A haunting screech made Luca jump before he saw the dark creature run from the corner they had just turned. They had scared the scavenger just as much as it had frightened him.

Suddenly Alard turned and strolled through the small gap in the low wall. He approached the front door of the run down house. He put his hand through the slit in the door and pulled out an oddly shaped piece of metal, no longer than a finger, tied on a string. He pushed it into a slot in the door and the door opened easily.

'You'll be staying here at the safe house,' Alard said as he opened the door wide and beckoned them in. 'Your rooms have been made ready and are up the stairs.' Alard flicked a switch and warm orange light flooded the space. Luca blinked into the brightness, his eyes stinging at the sudden onslaught. 'Make yourselves comfortable,' Alard continued. 'I'll be back for you in the morning.' He walked out the door and pulled it shut. The four of them stood in the empty hallway.

Mercy slumped against the wall.

'You're exhausted,' Kelsee said as she caught her. 'Up to bed for you.'

Mercy didn't argue and allowed Kelsee to guide her up the stairs with the wooden balustrade to support her on her other side.

Luca and Eban followed close behind. The treads creaked a little as they ascended.

The landing led to two bedrooms and a bathroom.

Each bedroom had a double set of bunks identical to the ones in the sea forts. Luca ran his hand through his hair and sighed. It was an unpleasant reminder that they were still prisoners.

'I think we should stick together,' Mercy said quietly as she clambered into the nearest bed.

'She's right,' Eban agreed. 'Until we know what this place is, we should stay together.'

Kelsee bent down next to Mercy and untied her friend's shoes. 'I'll feel safer that way,' she said touching her wrist. She pulled the blanket over Mercy and sat on the adjacent bed.

When everyone else had got into their beds, Luca turned off the lights. The cool glow of the torch beam reminded him of the nights that they had sat up exploring the articles on the tablet during the lights out times over Tropolis when power had been cut. He shook his head, unable to compartmentalise the things that had happened over past few weeks.

He climbed up to the top bunk above Mercy and stretched out. The sheets were crisp and the blankets soft. It felt odd that he should find comfort in a soft mattress and other Tropolite luxuries when he had been so used to the conditions of Outside. Luca was weary from the day that had failed to deliver its promise of freedom. The frustration was not helping him to relax. He concentrated on the slow and steady breaths of his sleeping friends.

He tried not to think about Major Thomas' dismissal of his people, however, he did not succeed. He wanted to hate her for her choosing to ignore them, but if he did that he would have to hate himself too. He was no better than she was. He knew that the clock may be ticking for his father, and yet here he was warm, hidden and idle.

Chapter 7

23h 56m

Luca was aware of a sudden burst of light. He looked up groggily only to be faced with near darkness.

'Sorry, did I wake you?' Eban whispered. 'It is morning but with these blackout curtains it is hard to tell.' Eban pulled the corner away briefly and light flooded the room.

It looked to be warm and bright despite the grime coated glass.

'Do you think there is any food?' Eban asked.

Luca laughed a little and shrugged. He sat up and stretched.

Eban had already slipped on his shoes and had left the room.

Luca quietly followed taking care not to disturb the girls.

The little house had a distinct feeling of being unloved. The walls had been covered with patterned, coloured paper, although this seemed faded. In several places the patterns and colours of other layers peeked through where it was torn. It was physically clean but there was not the extravagance of Tropolis here in any sense, but neither was it similar to Outside.

Luca crept down the stairs and peered through the first door to a room which had a few soft chairs pushed to the sides and a large rug in the centre of the floor. The light from the hallway didn't reveal much detail.

The room, directly opposite the front door was a tiny but well equipped kitchen.

A narrow work surface stretched out wherever the wall would allow, broken only with a ceramic sink on one side of the room and a sturdy stove on the other. If you stood in the middle of the room you could probably reach everything within a few steps. The walls were yellowing where they had once been painted. Eban had already found the switch and turned on the light. He was searching through the cupboards and drawers.

Within moments Eban had found a large frying pan and was heating oil on the stove.

'Luca! Look real eggs!' Eban said his eyes bright with excitement.

Luca looked in the fridge. 'Milk and cheese too.'

Eban cracked a couple of eggs into cup, beat them then added them to the pan. The translucent mixture quickly turned opaque and golden. He crumbled some cheese on top which quickly melted. Eban flipped the omelette onto a plate and handed it to Luca with a fork.

It was so hot but Luca could not wait to taste it. He took a bite and fanned his mouth.

'Smells amazing!' Kelsee said peering around the door jamb.

'Hope there is enough for everyone,' teased Mercy from behind.

Eban laughed. 'A whole load of them.'

Luca had never enjoyed such simple food so much. They sat together on the soft seats in the other downstairs room. It seemed that with just their company, all the other pressures and worries faded.

His respite was short lived. They had barely finished eating when there was a knock at the door.

Eban jumped up and rushed to the door.

Luca heard Alard's voice, it seemed as stern as it had the night before.

Within moments, Alard had joined them and Luca had got to his feet stepping in front of Kelsee a little.

Alard strolled across the room and tied the curtains back. The low sunlight was welcomed in and took the chill from the air. Luca noticed the flecks of dust floating and glimmering in the autumn brightness.

'It is my duty to welcome you to our community,' Alard began. 'You may enjoy the liberty of this place as long as you play your part. All necessities are rationed and distributed fairly in exchange for what you bring to the community. You will be required to assist where necessary, but since today is our rest day, you will not be introduced to the jobs that have been set aside for you. There are some farm labouring, nursing and childcare work spaces. You will be assigned tomorrow morning.'

Luca tried to pay attention to what Alard was saying but the movement on the street outside was distracting. He turned towards the window and watched as a few people were walking past. The apparent discarded and abandoned street was a façade. People lived here. Free people lived here.

Luca pointed. 'Who are they?' he asked.

Alard glanced out the window. 'You want their names?'

'Are they Campion?'

'I see,' Alard said. 'Yes, they are. But they are a mixture of refugees from Tropolis and Outside. Many of them were even born here.'

Luca stared more intently. He wondered which was which.

Alard told them to stay within the boundaries of the village but that they were welcome to leave the house if they wished. 'You are fortunate that you have the day free. You will not be required to work until tomorrow.'

Luca felt his spirit rise. A day when they weren't required to be or do anything. A glancing thought for Outside pinched at his joy but he pushed it aside. Perhaps this wasn't a prison after all.

Luca looked to his friends, they all seemed brightened by this news and as soon as Alard had gone, they were putting on their shoes excitedly.

The morning was bright and the air chilled. A slight breeze played along the potholed road, blowing a few brown and curled leaves that were freshly whipped from the trees that seemed to grow everywhere. There were old and established oaks that towered high above them, filtering the sunlight, but also spindly and sickly specimens that grew out of walls and pavements. There could have once been a design and order to the place, but nature seemed to be fighting back. Luca wrapped his coat tighter around himself as he shivered. He was thrilled that there was a natural revolution going on, it felt comforting to see that what was once cut away and held back was now taking over. Luca smiled to himself.

The village street led up a low hill with houses that got increasingly closer together. Each window was dark as if the buildings were unoccupied but Luca suspected that they were existing homes. Then, as if to confirm it, a door to a house that stood directly on the pavement opened. A short, elderly gentleman hobbled out. 'Good morning to ya!' he said pleasantly before speeding up the hill at an alarming rate.

A second stepped into the road overtaking them. 'Fine morning!' he commented to them nodding his head.

Luca glanced at Mercy who was smiling. She seemed to be enjoying the friendly atmosphere. He was not feeling anywhere near as comfortable as she looked. She had seemed to be like these people when he had met her in Outside. Eban was humming to himself and appeared not to be bothered at all. Luca had learned to trust his friends and had been able to find his voice with them. He felt the tension mounting in his shoulders and pulled them lower so that he stood straighter. Talking to complete strangers was not what he was used to and this place was weirdly uncomfortable.

After three more people had passed by them and had greeted them, Kelsee looked behind her and called to an old lady who carried a wicker basket following close behind.

'Good morning!' Kelsee began. 'Excuse me, but where is everyone going?'

The old lady frowned. 'Newcomers?' she asked. Kelsee nodded and smiled. 'Ah! It be time to hear the stories up at library. You wanna come. I show you!' The lady beckoned them to follow.

The friends had to pick up their pace to keep up with the old lady who swung the basket jovially and glanced back to check that they were indeed following her.

There were plenty of buildings in this more densely populated part of the community, but there were also increased broken down walls and collapsed properties. Nothing had been done to stop the erosion as buildings either side showed signs of large cracks and bulging façades. The rubble and debris piled high and spread wide into the road. Plants had begun to grow and spread on these mounds and the fallen leaves caught in the crevices.

Luca shook his head at the lack of care these people showed to the place that they lived. He had witnessed and experienced the pride that people had in their homes and necessity to care for them in both Tropolis and Outside. Any Outsider would fight hard to live in the luxury of any of these buildings rather than makeshift shacks and hideaways, and a Tropolite would not stand for the mess and disruption.

The old lady pulled on a dirty glass door and ushered the group into the lobby. A second, wood and glazed door was to the right. Luca peered through the clean glass. A dark curtain had been pulled back on the other side and obscured the view a little, but he could see a large room with many people milling around.

'Go through dear!' the old lady instructed. 'No use being stuck out here!'

The noise of chatter flowed out through the open door. Luca frowned, he had never heard so many people's voices all at the same time before. A laugh over on the far left rose above the din but didn't stop anyone's conversation. The people stood and sat in groups of four or five talking and listening. The room smelt clean and flowery

'Hope you enjoy it,' the lady said before she wandered off to a group of other elderly women sitting all together.

A mixture of plastic, metal and wooden chairs were set out in a large semi-circle with several rows facing and extending from a single soft chair in the centre to the floor to ceiling windows. Light poured in, the blinds had been lifted as high as they would go and black gathered curtains were pulled right back to the walls either side.

After a few moments, the conversations around the room were taken to the chairs as the groups sat down.

Luca, Eban, Mercy and Kelsee sat at the far back. There were a few empty seats nearby, but the people here seemed to fill the room from the front row in excitement. Luca licked his lips, he felt he was going to be in for a treat.

This room was loved. Luca could see the carefully repaired shelves stacked with lines of books; large and small. The walls were free from dirt and marks, instead pictures and posters were neatly stuck in place. There were some framed paintings as well as a few children's drawings placed side by side, not distinguishing between which had more value.

The room hushed suddenly. The swish of the wood and glass panelled door behind them distracted Luca and he turned to see Alard stepping into the room. Alard shut the door carefully, removed his hat and slunk quietly to the chair closest to the exit.

The sound of a woman's voice rose in the room and Luca strained to see who it was. The woman had obviously sat in the chair while his head was turned and now she was too low for him to see. He settled back and listened.

She was reading. Luca closed his eyes and let the words paint a picture for him. Her voice was soft but rose and fell with dramatic tones. She had beautiful pronunciation, articulating the words and adding something more to the reading, she was bringing herself.

Luca suddenly stopped listening to her voice and heard the words clearly. The woman was reading from one of the very few books he had been able to glean when he was living in Outside. He recognised the character and section of the tale, remembered the scene and immediately fell into the story.

"The screaming preceded them," she read in a hushed voice then with a slight menacing tone continued. *"Bruja was drenched in sweat; his long hair clung to his forehead. His normally pale skin was blotchy and red from the exertion of his exercise, but he had not allowed the beast to travel too far ahead. Many others behind him complained of tiredness but continued to keep up their pace. Each and every one of them felt an indescribable excitement rising inside them."*

The chapter was coming to an end all too soon. *"I see the others quickly move to their posts their swords unsheathed, bows at the ready and their faces full of vigilance. 'And by the way,' I add with confidence, 'we will be victorious.'"* Luca blinked into the brightness, he stood his feet and began to applaud. He realised he was the only one standing but in that moment he didn't care. The reader had taken him to another place and another time and he was grateful for the escape.

He saw the reader for the first time, gasped and stopped clapping. The woman's eyes were wide but she quickly put a finger to her lips. The people gathered were watching him and laughing. No one saw her response but Luca. He looked at the faces turned to him and then back to the reader. She shook her head. Luca could feel the colour draining from his cheeks instead of flooding them. He huffed a tiny laugh and sat down.

What was his *dead* mother doing in this place?

Chapter 8
22h 32m

Luca listened intently to his mother's voice as she reminded the people present that the books were available to borrow before dismissing the meeting. No one appeared to take any books from the shelves but left the room for the street outside and hurried past the large window on their other errands.

'Alard left quickly.' Luca heard Eban say to Kelsee.

'He didn't look that comfortable being here,' she responded.

Luca hadn't even noticed. As the crowds moved away, the reader was the centre of his attention.

She stayed seated as a few went to her obviously saying kind words by the way she smiled in return.

She had changed. Her once beautiful russet hair that had matched his was now golden white. But when Luca looked at her he could see his own face hidden in hers; the shape of her eyes and her cheek bones, but her nose was angular and not rounded like his own. Her frame still appeared as slight even in the long skirt and thick cardigan that she wore.

'The last ones to leave have the duty of stacking the chairs,' Luca's mother said turning towards Luca and his friends. 'Would you mind?'

Eban laughed and began to stack the matched chairs.

'They need to go over by the far wall,' she said pointing behind her.

Luca moved straight to the front row so that he might be near her.

'Mum?' he asked quietly.

'Luca?' she replied. 'What are you doing here?'

He turned to face her. 'I could ask you the same question.' Luca clenched his fists.

'I couldn't come back to you, they wouldn't let me,' she said her voice quivered, betraying the pain. 'I wanted to come back for you and your father. You have to believe me.'

Luca stood over her, he could see the pleading in her expression. He knew what Campion was like, and was experiencing the subtle prison as she spoke. He bit down on his lip.

Luca's mother dropped her gaze. She stroked the cover of the book she had read from. She traced the sweep of the blue wing with her finger.

'I used to love that story,' he finally said, 'But you never read it like that to me.'

'It isn't really for small children,' she looked up at him again. 'I didn't want to frighten you.'

'I still have a copy. I would read it to myself when you were gone. It helped me feel closer to you again.'

'Luca, I'm so sorry.'

Luca pulled the wooden chair closer to his mother and sat down. She shook her head and glanced at Eban, Mercy and Kelsee who were now paying attention to Luca.

'They're my friends. You can trust them.'

'Friends? You never had them before,' she said laughing sadly.

Luca nodded and leaned in closer to her. 'I've missed you Mum. I am so glad you are alive.' He took her hand and she squeezed his tightly as her eyes filled with tears.

'I had no choice. You do believe me, don't you?'

'I know.'

Mercy had moved closer to Luca. 'Luca?'

Luca laughed and without looking away he said, 'Mercy, I'd like you to meet my mother.'

Mercy shrieked and began to laugh.

'Willow,' Luca's mother extended a hand to Mercy. 'It is very good to meet you.'

Eban and Kelsee came over to see what the noise was about.

'This is Luca's mum!' Mercy said joyfully. 'Eban,' Mercy said pointing, 'and Kelsee.'

Luca could almost feel strength entering his back as he sat taller.

'Please, grab a chair, they can be stacked and sorted later,' Willow said. 'There is so much to talk about.'

'We don't want to intrude,' Kelsee said a little confused. She turned to Luca and said in a hushed voice, 'I thought your mother had died.'

Luca released his mother's hand and pulled a chair up close to him. 'So did I!'

Willow nodded. 'I had gone to the docks as part of a demonstration. It was rumoured that Barrett, the leader of Tropolis would be visiting the recycling works.' Luca reached over to Kelsee and took her hand. She looked at him wide eyed. Willow stopped and watched for a moment. 'He never showed up, he never would. But the crowd got angry. I was near the front with some of the others that had planned the protest.' Willow lowered her gaze. 'Your father told me it would no use going and we spent too long arguing over doing anything to rise up against Tropolis at all. He wouldn't be part of it. He was right, of course. Tropolis is too powerful. Why would Tropolis change just because a few Outsiders demanded it?'

'You weren't to know,' Mercy said kindly. 'You were speaking for your people, you were standing up and letting Tropolis hear your voice.'

''My voice!' Willow huffed. 'My voice was not heard, there was no time for that. It was my own people that forced me over the edge of the dock and trapped me against the barge. I only remember being inside a boat for a while then recovering in a room at the infirmary. I did very little that day except abandon my family.'

'The fences went up quickly after you died, or at least we thought you had died,' Luca said. 'They told us it was for our safety.'

Eban disagreed. 'But it was probably for theirs. I think that what you did was threaten their power. Outsiders were given courage by what you did. It just wasn't the right time.'

'No time will be the right time. It is time that I have had stolen away from me,' Willow said angrily. She gazed at Luca and her posture relaxed. 'You've grown so big and I've missed it all,' she said as she ran her hand over his cheek. 'But what are you doing here?'

'I was in the Compassion Prize along with Mercy and Eban. I never understood what the prize was really about. I thought, that if I won, I would be able to get Dad to Tropolis.' Willow shook her head as she listened. 'But I wasn't doing very well and wouldn't have got anywhere without Mercy and Eban.' Luca looked up to his friends who had listened intently. 'Then your brother, Alec, he thought I looked like you, did some investigating and discovered that I was your son, well, he helped get us out. Kelsee is a Tropolite, she kind of came with us by accident.'

'Alec is alive?'

'Yes,' Luca said nodding. 'He told me that Tropolis had informed him that his family were dead. He wanted to make it up to you by helping me.' Luca's mother frowned and ran her hand over her face.

'We had no idea. I hated Tropolis for taking him.'

'He's safe and he is working with Campion. He may be in Tropolis but I don't think he is a Tropolite.' Luca tried to ease her pain. 'He's doing all he can, but it isn't enough.'

'What about your father? Is he ...?'

'When I left he was okay,' Luca said giving a half smile.

'But?' Willow pressed.

Luca snorted a little and shook his head at his mother's intuition that he was holding back. 'He isn't well. He hasn't been well since the accident.' Luca corrected himself, 'Since it was reported that you died.'

'Is he strong enough to glean?'

'No, but I had a stash of credits to help pay for food and there were still a few vegetables in the garden.'

'Credits won't help him, he can't use them,' Willow said.

Luca frowned. 'They're valid.'

'Yes, but your father isn't. He isn't an Outsider, he is from Tropolis. He has no chip so he can't redeem them.'

Luca sat back in his chair and stared at the wall of books to his right. How had he not known this? 'He can't glean either as you need a chip to get to the heaps now too. We can't leave him there. He's ill.'

'How ill is he?' Willow asked.

'I don't know,' Luca said starting to get agitated. 'It isn't like the Compassion Fatigue, it is something else. He hardly says anything and sometimes when he does, it doesn't make sense. He wants to sleep all day and never goes out to glean ... but then, I understand why he doesn't now.'

'Does he have friends?' Willow asked looking to Mercy and Eban.

'This is Outside we are talking about, Mum,' Luca said running his fingers through his hair. 'No one has friends.'

'I was being hopeful.'

'I've been worried about him,' Luca added wincing a little. 'But it seems that I can't do anything to help.'

'I wish we could help. I have tried to think of a way to get you and him out of there for years but there isn't anyone to help me. I have been trapped here wondering if you have survived.'

Luca could feel his stomach tightening and tension ran across his shoulders. He was relieved that he had been missed but his mother hadn't come to rescue them. 'Is there a Campion guard then? I didn't see anyone holding you here.'

Willow shook her head. 'There is no possible way that I could leave this place.'

Luca bit down on his tongue and looked away from her.

'Luca,' Mercy began, 'Did you not see your mother come in?'

'What does that matter!' Luca blurted to Mercy. 'She has chosen this life over her own family.' He stood up and pushed his chair away violently. 'I don't ... It doesn't matter! I'll see you back at the house.'

Luca didn't look back and would not turn even at their calls.

He pulled hard on the wooden door. It swung open quickly and banged satisfyingly against the wall. He rushed across the small lobby and pushed on the glass doors, then stomped out into the chilled air. The streets were no longer busy. The people had come out to hear Willow read and now seemed to be with each other along the streets or hidden away again.

Luca ran down the road, rushing away from the stuffy library. He sped around the corner and into a deserted alley, not taking care to head back to the safe house. He took gulps of the cool air as he slowed his pace. He stiffened his arms and tightly balled his fists. The spell was broken. His mother's appearance had sparked a flame of hope. Hope that he was no longer alone, hope that he belonged somewhere, hope that he was loved. Now that was completely extinguished. Willow had not cared enough to come back and rescue him and his father. The familiar grief of abandonment made him stoop under the weight.

He let out a grunt and then covered his ears.

His own father! How did he not know the truth?

Luca searched through his memories, looking desperately for any sign that he might have missed that would have told him that he was half Tropolite. Now, in hindsight, there were nothing but clues. His father had stopped gleaning soon after the accident when their chips were scanned at the rubbish heap gates and he hid away from others not wanting to be found. Luca considered his father's age, he was over the average Outsider life expectancy perhaps as a result of growing up in the affluent Tropolis. Luca sucked on his lower lip as he had never really thought about that before. Luca had never once wondered why his father had never spoken of his family, wherever they were, when his mother had kept hers alive with her memories. The final clue came like a blow the chest. Luca's father had never offered to purchase food with the credits because that was monitored even before Willow had gone. Luca growled at his own stupidity and his stomach churned as he considered the suffering his father would be going through that very moment.

He had hated his father for sitting back all those years and for forcing him to provide for them both. Bitterness towards his father and Tropolis had grown side by side and intertwined. His father's health demanded that he glean for a meagre existence and Tropolis provided only one way to do it. At least that was how he had seen it, but now, in the light of this revelation the world seemed to tip on its axis. The truth was it was the fault of Tropolis that they both suffered. His father could not provide for them both. How must that have felt without all the snide comments and cruel actions Luca had heaped onto him?

Strong shadows of the towering trees that protected Campion village patterned the broken tarmac. The narrow road, bordered with low stone walls covered with creeping plants smelt damp. The gutters were full of brown and discarded leaves. He kicked at the crisp layer and they flew high into the air and fluttered down whilst the wet mulch below fell around him. He wanted there to be a way to put this jumbled mess back into order. If he could just prove that he was worth it, or at least that his father was worth it, maybe Willow would be want to help rescue his father. Getting him from Outside and bringing him here might be what was needed to set him free from his dark illness. There was life in this place and life that seemed sustained and worth keeping. Luca angrily wiped his cheek and stamped his feet as he realised it was worth more than him.

The alley had twisted back and opened onto a familiar road. Luca peered up the hill. He had moved far enough down the hill to be out of sight from the library. He took a deep breath, straightened up and walked in the direction of the safe house.

How was he going to convince his mother that she should risk returning to Outside? The time was ticking away and he had already wasted so much. He should have left last night, should have escaped Campion at the first available moment and gone to his father. Luca hung his head and thought about how useless and selfish he had been.

Luca stopped. He swallowed hard. He had probably ruined it all by running off, but perhaps Willow would take them to Outside. Perhaps his family could be pieced together again. She could make his father well again, in every area that he had failed she could make it right. He looked up at the dark branches that fractured the sky and sighed. His father's life depended on him and not the bunch of worthless credits that he had left behind. He had to go back and face his mother. He needed to win her over despite his anger. And there was very little time to do it.

Everything in him wanted to return to the house and to wallow in self-pity. He clenched his jaw. Hiding and forgetting would be the easy thing to do, but he had wasted too much time thinking only about himself. He dragged himself up the hill on what seemed the longest and shortest walk of his life.

He approached the glass doors exhaled and entered. The small lobby was empty but he could hear the urgent voices of his friends and Willow in the library. He stepped forward to push the wooden door open but Mercy on the other side had got there first.

She opened it without looking into the space beyond and held the door wide open.

Eban pushed the wheeled chair, where Willow sat eagerly, over the threshold.

Chapter 9
22h 12m

'Luca!' Willow cried.

'I've come to apologize,' Luca said stiffly blurting out what he had practiced in his head. 'Why are you in that thing?'

'You don't have to apologize. I didn't have a chance to explain. In the accident at the docks my back got crushed and so now I can't walk.' Luca covered his mouth with his hands. 'I wanted to come back to you, but I just couldn't. Please, I need to say sorry to you.'

'You would have come back?'

Willow reached out to Luca. 'With all my heart.'

Mercy pulled Luca closer. 'Come back in.'

Eban backed up the wheelchair.

'Are you in pain?' asked Luca.

Willow smiled. 'Not anymore. Let's go in the back rooms.' She grabbed Luca's hand and spoke quietly to him. 'I'm glad you came back. Your friends wanted to follow you but they wouldn't go without me. Took that girlfriend of yours,' she gestured towards Kelsee, 'ages to find the chair.' She laughed a little.

Luca frowned at his mother and shook his head. She had not seen him in years yet how was she was able to read him? He could feel his cheeks burning. He bent down to her and whispered. 'She's just a friend.'

Willow nodded and directed them into a smaller room situated to the rear of the main library. There was only one armchair but next to it was a small table littered with books and magazines.

'We don't glean many of these anymore,' Eban said picking up a glossy title with what looked like the tablets they had used in Tropolis on the cover.

Mercy had gone through another door. 'Eban,' she called. 'Come and help me!'

Willow wheeled herself over to the armchair. She fixed the wheelchair in place and lifted herself into the comfy seat.

'You, Kelsee right?' Kelsee nodded at Willow. 'Can you grab some chairs from the other room? You know where that is right?'

Kelsee frowned, dropped her gaze and left.

Luca didn't like the tone his mother had used. He tried to ignore the bitter taste it left him with.

'We need to get dad out.'

Willow shook her head. 'I'm not sure that is possible.'

'He'll die there. We are his only hope.'

There was a clattering of cups coming from Mercy and Eban.

Willow looked towards them. 'There is some nettle tea on the stove. Just heat it up a little if you like.'

Luca followed after Kelsee if only to control the anger rising in him once again.

As soon as he was near enough to Kelsee he apologized for his mother's behaviour.

'It's alright,' Kelsee replied graciously. 'She didn't like it when I told her she should go after you.'

Luca frowned. 'What?'

'I don't think she wanted to go outside. She wasn't happy when I found her chair,' Kelsee straightened her jumper. 'I don't think she likes me very much.'

Luca could see the confidence in Kelsee ebbing away again. 'She's just jealous of you. You don't have to be useful to have value.'

'That's not true,' Kelsee said smiling sadly. 'I was only of value to you because I was useful; I got Mercy out. I'm here by accident.' She had grabbed two chairs, 'Like you said.' She turned to the back room and pushed the door open before Luca could formulate a reply.

Luca huffed in frustration.

Before long Luca had returned with the remaining two chairs. His mother had made the mistake of being cruel to Kelsee out of spite. Luca set out the chairs whilst Eban had bought in a tray with several steaming mugs and cups of nettle tea.

When they had settled Luca turned to his mother but she had already begun.

'Has Compassion Fatigue spread to Outside yet?' she asked, avoiding eye contact with Luca.

'Not at all,' Mercy replied. 'We didn't know it existed until, well, until Eban hacked into the Network and found the files.'

'It's here too,' Willow admitted.

'Really? How bad?' asked Eban.

'Not too bad, it seems we have a milder stream but Campion have been following the guidelines from Tropolis in terms of treatment. It appears to be working. Unfortunately, it was only those that had escaped from Outside that were able to create a cure or temporary cure in some. Campion have been working on the pointless task of searching for the gene that makes us immune.'

Eban raised his eyebrows. 'How is that going?'

Willow shrugged. 'All I know is that they keep coming back for more blood. I expect you and your friends will be on their testing list.' She nodded. 'Those that have only ever lived here don't suffer at all, they all seem very happy and are part of the community. The ones who have come here from Tropolis are a bit of both. Some recover really well and only require a few treatments and then their life is free from the fatigue, while others, mainly in the Campion ranks, seem to suffer more.'

'What about Alard?' asked Eban.

'He's an interesting one,' Willow replied. 'He used to suffer a great deal but since he has been coming into the community more, I don't know, it appears to have lifted.'

Luca frowned. 'Do you think there is a connection?'

'Yes, I have been thinking that for quite some time.'

Kelsee leaned in closer. 'Is the cure even in the blood?'

Willow raised her eyebrows as if surprised by the question. 'When the transfusion occurs there is some form of healing that takes place.'

'I've suffered from Compassion Fatigue for ages, lost count of the transfusions I have had.' Kelsee frowned and spoke quietly. 'The ones that always had the longest lasting effects were when I sat with the ones donating their blood. Although, donating may be a rather twisted view now that I know truth from the other side. If what you are saying is right, I could have been made better just by being with people who had a heart for me without taking their blood?'

The room went incredibly still. Luca turned to Kelsee and smiled widely.

'What did you just say?' Willow asked, her eyes narrowed.

'I was just saying that, what if, maybe, just sitting with the Compassion contestants made me better without having to take their blood too.'

'Could it really be that simple?' Willow shook her head. 'I read something, somewhere in this place, on one of these shelves, but I can't remember where! It went something like, "protect your heart because what is in there pours out into other parts of your life". I don't know! I guess what I'm saying is, this fatigue began in Tropolis and hasn't spread to Outside, yet Tropolite workers are there too so it isn't contagious. In Campion it is the escaped Tropolite workers that have suffered the most, but they are getting better and not needing treatment all the time. It could be genetic

I suppose, but what if it was a disease of the heart? What if the Tropolites are ill because their hearts, their attitude to others is sick.'

Kelsee squeezed Luca's hand. 'Tropolis only helps itself, it is selfish, I see that now. Campion are helping the ones that have either escaped from Outside or Tropolis and they are recovering.'

Luca sighed. 'I get what you are saying, but Outsiders tend to be self-sufficient and only look out for themselves.'

'Really?' Kelsee said almost laughing. 'Where would Tropolis be without Outsiders? I mean, your people clear our waste and make our energy. You send your children into the Compassion Prize and do so without fighting back.'

'We never did that because we wanted to,' Luca scoffed. He noticed his mother's approval at his tone. He cleared his throat and spoke, instead with kindness. 'The Compassion Prize was about escaping the heaps and finding a better life. We didn't know it was a means to a cure. You've no idea how much I wanted to stop doing things that would benefit Tropolis.'

'Okay, but you never did stop. You continued to serve my people despite what we do to you,' Kelsee said. 'What if your serving us has kept you healthy? What if the bit in your hearts that wanted to destroy us was overpowered by the part that did what was right instead?'

'Luca,' Mercy began gently, 'I'm not sure that you really knew the people of Outside that well.'

Luca shrugged. He remembered one of his first encounters with Mercy. She spoke with the people of Outside, she engaged with them like no one he had ever seen. They knew her and she knew them. So many Outsiders were genuinely sad to say goodbye to Mercy at the Compassion Gate at the beginning of the Compassion Prize contest.

'The Outsiders I knew thought similar things. They believed that they were just working to survive but they had hearts that would reach out to one another too.'

'I never did that,' Luca confessed. 'I only did what I needed to do to survive.'

'You cared for your father,' Eban said patting Luca's knee. 'Don't underestimate what is in you, mate.'

Luca looked up at his mother as she swiftly shifted the conversation away from his father again. 'I think the quote is more about what you hold onto dearly,' Willow interjected. 'What Tropolis has held tightly to is oppressing the weak and poor. They value wealth and power above people.' Kelsee sighed and hung her head. 'There is nothing we can do to change them. We can only help those that leave.' Willow shifted in her chair. 'And we haven't had many of those recently.'

'You can't expect to be able to help others if you are just waiting for them to turn up here,' Luca said irritated by his mother's inaction. 'You have to go to them.'

'Which I can't,' Willow said through tight lips and gesturing to her legs.

Luca sighed. She would not be moved, but the mother he had once known would not have let this stop her. He pushed his shoulders back, determined not to let her hopelessness seep into him. If there really were no guards as she had said, there would be nothing but her to hold him here.

Luca fidgeted and looked at the undrunk mug of nettle tea still sitting on the tray.

'I 'd like to go out,' he finally said. 'We've been stuck inside for so long.'

'You should take a look around,' Willow said in approval.

'Will you show us the sights?'

'It is a bit cold for me. You go. It will be very difficult get lost.'

'We can wrap you up nice and warm.'

'No, I have things to do here,' Willow said stacking the magazines neatly on the side table. 'I don't really have the time.'

It seemed that Kelsee was right. Willow was going nowhere.

'Alright.' Luca turned to his friends. 'Anyone else want to come?'

Every one of the friends got to their feet and grabbed their jackets. Luca was unsure if they felt as uncomfortable as he did.

Willow leaned over to Luca and grabbed his hand. 'Leave the chairs in here,' she said, 'But could you stack them to the side for when you visit next.'

Eban quickly did as she asked.

'I love you, Luca.'

'I'm glad I found you,' Luca said bending down and hugging her. She held him tightly.

'It was really good to meet you Willow,' Eban said cheerfully as she let her son go.

'Bye!' Mercy bent and kissed Willow's cheek.

Eban and Kelsee had already left and Mercy was close behind. Luca turned to his mother.

'Make good choices,' he said and her eyes glinted at the memory of what she used to say to him when he was small. Luca saw the delight in his mother and swallowed hard. He hadn't finished what he wanted to say, he had only paused. He took a deep breath then spoke loudly looking her straight in the face. 'I take that back. Don't make good choices, but make the right ones.'

He saw the sharpness of his words pierce her and he didn't regret them as he walked away.

Chapter 10
21h 41m

Mottled shadows danced on the pathway. The autumn sunlight filtered through the branches but did not take the chill from the air. Luca stood in a patch of light, closed his eyes and lifted his face to the rays. He knew Mercy had heard what he had said and was scrutinizing him, he was choosing to ignore her. Red and orange flooded his senses and he allowed the light to expose all the darkness and banish it.

'Which way?' Eban asked.

Luca shrugged. He opened his eyes and watched as Eban and Mercy chose the route away from the safe house. Perhaps they really did want to explore this place.

Nothing was as it appeared in this village that was inhabited by Campion. The old dilapidated buildings and abandoned homes were not as ill managed and deserted as they seemed. Nature may well have given the illusion of decay and neglect but that was all it was; camouflage. The façades may not have been decorated for years, but there were small signs of repair. Luca saw that a middle aged man was filling a large crack in the wall on the side of one double storey home. A woman worked on some recently rendered repairs, painting it not with a fresh colour but a dirty shade that matched the old walls. The closer Luca looked, the more he noticed. These properties were being excellently maintained to appear forsaken.

Many people were pausing in the street to chat to one another, busy with friendship and community that Luca had only ever witnessed when Mercy had displayed it on his final day in Outside.

In the busiest part of the settlement, the buildings sat close to the pavement and had large windows, but nothing could be seen of the inside from the street. The windows were boarded, blacked out or closed off with curtains.

'They want to disappear,' he exclaimed. 'Campion are hiding here.'

Kelsee looked at him and squeezed her lips tight before replying. 'You can't hide a whole village.'

'But you can,' Luca said speeding his pace to catch up with Mercy and Eban. 'They're hiding aren't they?'

'I think so,' Mercy answered, nodding.

Luca smiled but saw Kelsee's confusion. 'Just look. The houses look uninhabited, they even appear to be falling down, but they're not.' He pointed. 'The windows are all blacked out so that no one can see in. They want others to think that there is no one here.'

Kelsee raised her eyebrows. 'They want Tropolis to think that they are not here?' She reached over and touched Luca's arm. 'They're frightened, aren't they?'

'I think they are happy here,' Mercy replied. 'They don't want it to be taken away from them.'

Luca witnessed the cheerful and relaxed inhabitants and wondered if this way of life would work for him. Campion village was almost idyllic but its fake façade could not disguise it. He could smell their type of freedom, and it stank of damp and mould. Under the guise of abandonment, all Campion were really embracing was rejection of the world around them. They had secreted themselves under the trees and could no longer look up and see the expanse of sky. Luca wished he could forget all that he had seen and heard, he wanted to just stay here and be safe, but his father was probably dying in Outside. Even if the Tropolites being sent into Outside were solely ordered to restore the power and would therefore ignore his father, he couldn't do the same. But he feared that perhaps the Tropolite workers would have more than one task to complete. Three contestants had made a fool of Tropolis.

Luca understood that he was the only hope that his father had. Luca knew that he could not settle for hiding. He would always have his father's blood on his hands if he stayed away and he could not bring himself to be just like Willow.

The friends hardly spoke. Luca hoped that they were pondering staying here, where they would be protected, because he knew that his journey would lead back to Outside. His hands began to shake so he forced them into his jacket pockets. He could feel his breathing accelerate. He peered timidly at the strangely silent Eban whose mouth was turned down and eyes were not cheery. Mercy walked in tune with Eban. She smiled at the passers-by, but joy didn't linger on her face. Luca hesitated before glancing at Kelsee. He thought that if he had stood any closer to her he might have heard her growl. They weren't going to sit back and let him do this alone. Each of them had a mission.

They had reached the outskirts of the village, but none of them suggested returning. The road was potholed and had a healthy strip of grass growing down its centre. Oranges, reds and browns coloured the hedges that grew tall and attempted to stretch across their path. The buildings here were sparse but large.

'I can't stay here,' Luca finally said stopping in the middle of the roadway. 'I need to help my dad.' He bit down on his lip and blinked away the moisture in his eyes.

Mercy grabbed him and hugged him.

'Count me in.' Eban responded with the light returning to his face. 'Your mum will be fine.'

Luca shook his head. 'I'm not asking you to come.'

'Mate! We're coming anyway!' Eban laughed as he patted Luca's shoulder. 'Remember, you don't need to do things alone.'

'So where do we start?' Kelsee asked. 'Does anyone know how to get to Outside from here?'

Luca wrapped his arm over her shoulder. 'Are you sure you really want to do this? You won't be able to un-see what we will find there.'

'Luca, your dad needs help,' she said seriously. 'I'm sure.'

'Outside is on the coast. Anyone have any ideas?' Luca asked looking to the others.

Eban began to walk away then turned and spoke quietly. 'I say we get out of here first, find some high ground and hope for a sighting.'

Mercy laughed and began to follow.

Luca turned to Kelsee. 'You're really sure?' he said in a hushed voice.

'Please, stop asking!' Kelsee replied, irritated and marched off after the others.

Luca blinked hard and shook his head. She had no idea what Outside was like and he was only trying to protect her.

He jogged to catch up. 'Sorry,' he said as he pulled on her sleeve.

'Fine,' Kelsee answered abruptly. 'Just leave it alone now.' She spread her hands as if she were dropping something to the floor. Luca watched her intently and she eventually made eye contact.

'I am sorry,' he said sincerely.

'I know.' Her voice was softer again and Luca dared to give her a small smile. 'You need to understand,' she began, 'everything has changed for me. My whole world is not what I thought it was. I can't live in that place anymore.'

Luca bumped her with his elbow. 'I get that. I'll try not to do it again. But just for the record, I'm looking out for you so I might slip up sometimes.'

'And I get that too. Caring is what friends do right?'

Luca smiled and ran his fingers through his hair. Friends cared; that was a very true statement of the friends that he had. But Kelsee wasn't like his other friends. He felt fiercely protective of her.

They walked on in contented silence. The sounds of the countryside still thrilled Luca; loud bird song that had a shrill tune rather than the calling of gulls, the rustle of the wind through the leaves and even the odd squelch of a footstep in mud. Each time they were met with an alternative route, they took the path that led higher. There were hardly any houses alongside the roadway this far outside the village. There were however, lines of large brick barns with vast corrugated metal roofs. The buildings were not covered with plants as they were sat, exposed to the elements, on large concreted yards. There were no trees to offer any shelter or hiding places for Campion. The windows, if they had them were blacked out and boarded. It was evident that Campion maintained these barns too. Someone had done a good job of creating the illusion as the large metal doors showed signs of rust and age but this had been camouflaged much like the village.

They had walked past several barns before Eban wandered close to the towering wall of one of them and ventured towards the doors. Luca followed. Campion felt these buildings were important for some reason and he was inquisitive.

Eban tugged at the padlock and chain that held the doors shut. The lock was firmly shut but the doors pulled open ajar. He peered in and gasped.

'What?' Luca asked as Eban made space for him to look.

Luca held the door steady and squinted as the unexpected brightness took him by surprise. The windowless barn was flooded with clear light filtered through thousands of leaves that stretched high to the ceiling. Layer upon layer of large trays were suspended from tall mechanical frames. The differing trays contained varying degrees of maturing plants and fruit. The artificial light surged from the underside of each tray, concentrating on the plants a little below them, creating their own personal sun. Luca noticed the gentle clicking that accompanied the incredibly slow movement of the plant trays that appeared to be rotating much like a wheel towards the roof and then down the ground.

'You might want to see this,' Luca said stepping aside. 'There is enough food in there to feed all of Campion.'

'And there are so many barns on just this industrial site.'

'It's not all ready to eat now,' Mercy said. 'They are completely self-sufficient and can just keep on producing what they need.'

Eban sighed. 'They don't need to interact with anyone else.' Eban turned to Luca. 'I hate to say it, but Willow was right. Campion will wait for people to come to them but appear to have no intention of going out to help others.'

As Luca shrugged and turned away he noticed a smaller wooden building tucked into the trees at the far edge of the concrete. Wanting a distraction from thinking about his mother, even if it contained more evidence of Campion's lack of true compassion, Luca strolled over to investigate. He was only a few paces away when he read the sign stapled to the planks.

HIGH VOLTAGE – DANGER OF DEATH

Part of him wanted to run and hide back in the safety of the invisible Campion village, to escape the memory and fear of the death room, but his body had already responded instinctively. He surprised himself by defiantly stomping towards the hut, fists clenched and deaf to Eban's calls.

He pressed his hands up against the wood. This building had not been here for long, the plants had not yet claimed the boards and the edges were still crisp and un-weathered. He let his fingers trail along the wall as he walked its perimeter. At the rear of the building the earth had been disturbed in the form of a long raised mound. Luca assumed it was to bury something. He kicked at the loose soil where no one had trampled and only young weeds had grown and died back in the cold weather. With just a little bit of persuasion the earth gave up the secret. Just under the surface, a curved, plastic pipe lined the gully. Luca had seen this type of pipe carrying water but since this was feeding directly into the high voltage shed he thought otherwise.

The slightly raised earth gently snaked its way through the trees.

Luca could hear Eban calling out to him.

'You might want to see this,' he replied. 'I think I know how to get to Outside.'

Chapter 11

20h 09m

'Campion have to get power from somewhere.' Luca exclaimed excitedly pointing to the plastic piping. 'Where do you think electricity comes from?'

'Outside!' Kelsee laughed. 'So we just follow the cables, right?'

Mercy shook her head slowly. 'They have technology and ideas, why would they steal power?'

'Because they can ... and they don't care.'

Mercy frowned. 'That isn't fair, Luca.'

'And that would be a lot of cable,' Eban suggested raising his eyebrows, 'Where would they source that?'

'Do we want to get to Outside?' Luca asked. Mercy nodded. 'Well, it doesn't really matter what I think then. The cables will lead us there.'

'It's a great idea,' Kelsee said happily before turning to follow the soil trail.

The buried cable took a route that began to lead them on a slight decline through a densely forested area, but Luca continued to pursue the course with confidence. The conifers shut out much of the light but the near bare strip of earth in the carpet of needles made tracking easy. Luca hadn't noticed the lack of bird song until he stepped out of the shadows and into an area of open lattice branches. Here the trees were older and more haphazardly planted compared to the regimented rows of pines. He could feel the age in this place.

Twisted trunks seemed unevenly balanced with many fallen branches either littering the ground or clinging to the main trunk by a splinter. Rotten logs demanded that the friends weave through the labyrinth.

Luca's heart beat faster when he saw the red cabling through a poorly constructed joint in the exposed pipe. No one had bothered to bury it here, instead they had threaded the cable through the undergrowth in as straight a line as possible.

The temperature had dropped a little and as Luca came to the edge of a steep bank he understood why. A watercourse ran through the wood. The pipe hugged the top edge of the bank. Even when the mud clung stickily to Luca's trainers and his feet began to chill in the wet, his spirit would not be dampened.

'Luca wait!' Mercy called.

He turned to see Eban bent over the pipe a few strides back from where he was.

Eban looked up, 'You should see this, mate.' Then he carefully stepped down the bank towards the water.

'There's a second cable,' Mercy said pointing to the joint in the pipework.

'Come down and see this,' Eban called.

Luca peered down the bank at Eban whose gaze was fixated on the water. Luca squinted at the patch where Eban was focused. Luca tilted his head at the slightly out of sync and strange shimmering.

Eban beckoned to the group and one by one they gingerly made their way towards him.

It was only as Luca approached that he saw what was really there. A thin but wide canopy, similar to the one on the Campion boat had been stretched over the watercourse. Below its camouflage, the river had been artificially narrowed with rocks and logs forcing the water to run faster through the gap. Three, large barrels, spinning with the flow of the water were regimentally lined up. Each was connected to a metal frame that stopped the barrel twisting but allowed it to rise and fall with the water. At the edge of the bank three thick cables had been grouped together before they disappeared into the sealed end of the pipe that must have inevitably led up the bank.

Luca lowered his head and breathed a heavy sigh. 'They're making their own power aren't they?'

'They really are!' Eban replied excitedly. 'I wonder how much power these things generate.'

Kelsee looked on in wonder. 'Not enough for all that light in that warehouse, but the pipe up there was still going.'

Eban happily climbed the bank and followed the pipe further. Luca no longer wanted to lead. He stuffed his hands into his pockets.

Mercy pushed her hand through Luca's arm and tense posture. 'Is everything alright?' she asked quietly.

'The pipe won't take us to Outside,' he replied grumpily.

'No, but all rivers lead to the sea.' Mercy smiled as she spoke. 'And the coastline will take us home.'

The tension in Luca's shoulders seemed to melt a little with her words.

They walked in silence for a while until Eban dashed down the bank towards the river and announced that there were more barrels and further cables.

Luca clenched his teeth.

'Ok, Luca,' Mercy said drawing Luca to a halt. 'What else is bothering you?'

Luca tried to avoid Mercy. His fingers touched the notebook that had been his lifeline to freedom and home. He pulled it out. The corners were crumpled but the delicate Gibraltar Campion illustrated on the cover had not faded. The heart shaped petals were still as detailed and as fragile as they were before, nothing like the Campion he now knew.

'This contains the details of the ones that were freed,' he said jabbing his finger at the notebook. 'Ones that Campion played a part in freeing!' He tossed the notebook down the bank and walked on without a backwards glance. 'They don't care anymore!'

'Luca!' Mercy exclaimed, staring at him. 'Don't give up on them yet.'

Luca raised his eyebrows and snorted. 'They produce enough food here to feed many if not all the Outsiders, they have managed to survive without the intervention or authority of Tropolis, they have technology, and I guess many other forms of survival that we haven't seen. Yet they do nothing. They are not saviours, they are selfish.'

Mercy nodded. 'All that is probably true, but you fail to see the time it has taken to get them to this point. They have worked hard.'

'Yeah right!' Luca laughed. He watched Kelsee scurry down the bank.

'Don't Luca!' Mercy said crossly. 'They have worked hard. We met the community at Willow's reading earlier, there aren't that many of them,' she appealed softly as Eban joined them. 'It must have taken a great deal of hardship and diligence to get where they are now. Imagine digging these channels for the pipes. In fact, you don't even have to go that far, imagine gleaning the things that they have. There must have been planning and vision for them to have got this far. And the things already established in the village, well that probably needed repairing too, just like the homes there. They have had to adapt what they found to make work.'

'But they are done now.'

'True,' Mercy added, 'But hardship makes a community weary. They can't help others until they are well themselves.'

'But they are well now,' Luca said firmly. 'They have far more than the Outsiders.'

'And probably more than Tropolis too,' Kelsee said offering Luca his notebook. He shook his head but smiled at the support she was giving his argument.

'True again. They have everything that they need and more. They are also healthy and ready to help,' Mercy paused, 'But, they don't know it yet.'

'That's the same thing as just choosing not to help,' Kelsee said sarcastically, looking at the notebook before putting it in her pocket.

'Far from it!' Mercy replied. 'They have been preparing to take care of a multitude of people for years. They have everything in place from food to electricity to homes. They just don't know how to step out from their organised preparation and into action.'

Luca laughed sadly. 'They will never change.'

'Well then,' Mercy said calmly, 'We shall have to force them one way or another.'

'Nicely said!' Eban agreed.

Kelsee frowned at Eban. 'But how?'

Mercy shrugged. 'I guess we could start by sending them some refugees from Outside when we get there. It is good to know that Outsiders could find safety here.'

'The sooner we leave this place the better,' Luca said grateful that Mercy wouldn't vindicate Campion completely. He peered down at the river trying to make out the barrel generators under their camouflage canopy but there was nothing there but an unusual shimmer. 'You said all rivers lead to the sea. So, we need to head this way.' Luca tried to no longer pay attention to the pipe but it still mocked him. He chose not to join in with any conversation, instead, his thoughts turned to the reasons why he would assume the worst of Campion. They had not come to rescue them from the Compassion Prize, but his uncle Alec had felt the need to remove them, and even that seemed like a pointless act from this distance. Campion had collected them from the sea but had done nothing about meeting them where it was most dangerous. They had also treated Luca to imprisonment and then separated the friends, firstly from each other and then from the sea forts as the only place that appeared to have any action. Campion cared only for itself and remained unseen, had no influence and was insignificant to any need of the people of Outside. Luca wanted all this to be true and even as the anger began to build, his ears still rang with Mercy's reasoning.

Viewing the situation from his own standpoint, Campion looked like cowards but Mercy had a habit of bringing things into focus. Under her argument, Campion weren't sitting back but were actually taking action. Despite Luca's need to blame Campion, Mercy's positive slant could also be true and when he sought out what he deeply wanted, he hoped Mercy was right. The weight lifted from his chest a little.

They walked the shortest course with the waterway. Before long, a number of smaller streams fed into the creek making the journeying watercourse wider and lazier. As each new brook came into view Luca's frustration grew. In order to follow the main river, the friends would have to navigate the brook to a place where it was narrow enough to leap across. When the main flow of water branched into two the feeling of foreboding grew and Luca could only hope that they would be the correct side of the river when the time came. They had little choice but to continue on their side of the water way.

After a while the water led them down a steep incline where it rushed and foamed but the energy was short lived. The density of the wooded landscape gradually reduced as the ground flattened and opened up before them. Pipes and generators had been left far behind where the water ran faster. The river drifted around wide curves and the stubble of reeds, some distance from the water's edge, must have meant that the river often flowed even wider.

Luca's feet were cold and very wet as each step sank into the soft grass and sodden earth, but he was not discouraged. The flood plain had cleared away the woodland and instead, on the distant, flat horizon there glinted the sparkle of the sea. His mood lifted with the brightened hope.

Eban drew the group onto slightly higher and firmer ground but the closer Luca viewed the horizon the slower his approach felt. The grass and bog area continued to expand even as they drew nearer the sea and the land on their side of the river spread out flat before them. The land on the opposite bank rose rapidly to a sweeping grassy hill.

Luca peered only occasionally at their approach to the sea. The journey seemed to progress much faster when he wasn't focused on the distance. Before long, the earth became littered with shingle which then rapidly became pebbles. A wooden sign, weathered by the wind stood at the edge of a water-damaged concrete path, indicating that they were approaching a nesting ground. Luca had very little hope for any bird choosing such a place to lay its eggs. The deep and wide gully ran from the bank of the river, now some distance on their right, to the very edge of the path. Shingle and rocks piled up so high ahead of them that the sea view was almost lost behind it. Had it not been for the continuing sweep of the deep nesting ground that curved out to the ocean, they would not have noticed the waves at all. In the bowl of the gully a gentle trickle of water ran continuously from the upper edge of the river and then meandered its way against the path and out to sea.

Eban had hummed to himself as he had walked the path, but now something else had caught his interest. 'I'd say Campion have been here,' he said. 'Look, this path has been repaired.'

'What would they want that is out here?' Kelsee asked.

Luca shook his head. He had no idea what Campion might want anymore.

The almost sheer drop into the nesting ground meant that the friends were funnelled out onto the beach. The concrete path was buried somewhere deep in the shingle, but a narrow bridge straddled the gully. The tiny trickle of water faded into the stones, no doubt to meet with the sea secretly.

Luca paused to look at the vast body of water and beach.

To the left the stony beach eventually swept out of sight behind growing cliffs that could be hidden by the breadth of a finger they were so far away. Luca thought that the profile may be familiar and wondered if they were almost close to the site of the Endurance test. The Campion village was far inland and hidden. There must have been a reason that Major Thomas had sent them as the light faded and Alard had collected them at the falls. Perhaps the powers at Campion wanted Luca to believe that somehow Tropolis were holding Campion in hiding and that access or escape was difficult.

Luca squinted at the grey rocky face in the distance and sighed. He may just have picked out a single darker line that might have been the timber clinging to the sheer cliff but he was not certain. If it was the site, that route would lead them back towards Campion.

Turning away Luca viewed the tranquil hillside on the other side of the river that dipped gently onto the extensive beach. He ran back up the path and crossed the narrow bridge. Only a rickety and rusty handlebar protected him from the drop. He wished he had chosen to go down into the gully and struggled up the steep bank on the other side instead of the weathered boards.

When he reached the other side, the pebbles slipped from under his feet. He bounded down the beach to the edge of the tide and river to glimpse beyond the grassy bank and further around the bend. The foot of the hillside met the mouth of the river and the beach then swept into a cove. The knoll then inclined dramatically before the sea had created the first white knuckle of a stumped cliff.

That little bit of distance had allowed Luca to see past that first small cut in the hillside and onto a few of the taller white pillars that rose like steps, carved out of the by a ferocious sea. But the furthest of the white pillars rose above the others, wasn't as sloped or weathered and it caught the low sunlight as though it had a polished surface. Luca knew that it was undeniably human-built.

In the distance stood Outside and the domineering and confining structure that made it impenetrable. *The wall.*

Chapter 12

16h 15m

Suddenly, Luca felt the exertion of the day and the potential wasted time. He slumped to the ground.

The river hurried towards the open waters of the sea, its gushing mouth blocking the way toward Outside. The concrete pad stones and posts at the river's side could have once held a bridge, but that was long gone. He considered if he would be able to swim the distance, but the loud drag of the waves across the pebbles made him recoil. The currents would be confusing even for a boat to navigate let alone a fragile swimmer and taking a wide berth out to sea would not be wise. Luca had seen the inadequate swimming skills of Mercy and Eban and knew that would put them in danger. He had no idea if Kelsee was able to swim.

The clattering of pebbles behind him announced the approaching friends.

Luca retraced the river in his mind. He wandered over the flatter ground the steep drop and white water, the place where the river branched and right back to the barrel turbines. The only place where they may be able to cross would be where they had started, where the water was possibly shallow enough to wade through. He rubbed his hands across his face and sighed.

'It's cruel how close we are!' Luca whispered. He turned to Kelsee. 'Outside is just there,' he said pointing, 'You can see the wall in the distance, but we can't get there.'

'You give up too easily!' Kelsee said. She took a few steps closer to the river. 'Looks deep.'

'It won't be safe to cross here.'

Eban was about to sit down next to Luca, instead he offered his hand. 'Then I guess we cross over further back. I wouldn't sit there if I were you, the beach is still a bit wet.'

Mercy was watching the waves. 'I think the tide is nearly out. I don't think that we'll be able to cross here.'

Luca shrugged. 'Why couldn't they have looked after the bridge,' he said pointing at the concrete posts. He grabbed Eban's hand and pulled himself up. 'We should go back upstream. We need to get over there as soon as we can. I think we've wasted too much time as it is.'

The regular rumble of the pebbles on the beach was joined by another sound. Luca looked toward Kelsee. She was stood on the concrete block that protruded at the head of the shingle bank where it met the river. As she bent and stood up straight repeatedly the metallic clicking continued and a rod with teeth to one side began to lift out of the top of the concrete post.

Eban had already noticed the noise and was going over to investigate. 'What is it?'

'I wasn't sure to begin with, but I think it is a lock of some kind.' Kelsee pointed over to the gully and then kept turning the metal handle.

The gentle trickle had been transformed. A steady and growing head of water was now flowing into the nesting ground.

'You're diverting the river!' Eban announced. 'Keep going!'

At the point where Kelsee was turning the handle several smooth concrete posts began to protrude from the part of the river that was flowing out to sea.

Luca watched excitedly. As soon as the gully was a quarter full of rushing water, the dropping river level began to reveal a structure that was hidden under the normal flow.

He glanced up to cheer Kelsee on but other movement caught his attention. In plain view a figure dressed in grey was running toward them.

'You've got to go faster!' Luca shouted pointing, as he rushed past Kelsee. He could see she was exhausted. Eban was at her side and within seconds was turning the handle with her.

Luca grabbed Mercy's arm. 'Move! Campion have found us!'

Clambering up the loose shingle was challenging but they made it in time to see a pathway of stepping stones emerge from the flowing river.

Luca pushed Mercy forwards. 'Go!'

The water level flowing out to sea was still dropping as the nesting ground now roared with foaming life.

The Campion runner was nearing the edge of the gully and was dashing for the bridge. A snug woollen hat held his hair from his face.

'Kelsee, go!'

Eban stopped turning the handle and had grabbed a large stone. He bashed the base of the handle which rocked in the socket. He took hold of the bent metal rod with both hands, rested his foot against the concrete post and pulled so hard that he tumbled to the ground when the handle popped free.

Luca grasped Eban's forearm and got him to his feet.

'Campion will catch us,' Luca said with wide eyes.

'Just run!' Eban shouted.

Luca rushed and tumbled over the pebbles as he jumped from the concrete pad stone. He lowered himself onto the slippery hidden path that was brown with silt and slime. A plastic handgrip ran between each post but that too was covered in slimy weed.

The water began to flow over the path in various places. Luca dashed forward, as there was no time to think of the danger. Water splashed under his feet as he sped towards Kelsee and Mercy on the other side. Both of them looked pale from fear and anxiety.

'Keep going!' Luca heard Eban yell from much further behind him than expected. Luca turned, concerned for his friend.

Eban was still at the lock gate. He grit his teeth and swung the handle at the catch rammed in the teeth of the rod that held open the gate the edge of the post. Immediately the metal rod dropped back into the concrete with a crash and the flow into the gully ceased. 'Run!'

'Hurry, Eban!' Luca yelled.

Water now reached his ankles, and despite the need to reach the other side he had to slow his pace as each movement was amplified by the force of the water and its desire to drag him away.

Luca looked back. Eban had reached the stepping stones but they were concealed by the rising water level that was flowing fast as the river was taking back its normal course.

Luca had gained half the distance when his foot slipped. The water now knee deep. He turned.

Eban hadn't even ventured after him. Luca watched as Eban tossed the metal handle into the deep water.

'NO!' Luca shouted.

Ringing filled his ears and his heart felt like it would explode from his chest. The rush of the water tugged at his legs but his arm hold on the handlebar enabled him to gain his feet again.

Mercy reached out. He pushed himself up onto the ledge.

Luca propped himself on the edge.

On the other side of the river, as the last sight of the bridge disappeared below the water, an angry Alard stood, with his hands on Eban's shoulders.

Chapter 13

16h 07m

'Make sure your father is alright!' Eban shouted.

Alard pushed Eban to one side. 'Get back here!' he commanded.

Eban then said something to Alard who threw out his arms and gazed into the depths of the river.

Luca too realised that there was no way of crossing the river to fulfil Campion's command. The metal handle had been plunged into the river. Luca peered into the water but he could see nothing in the murky depths.

He clambered to his feet and caught Mercy nodding to Eban.

'What?' Luca asked. 'What can we do?'

'Eban wants us to go to Outside.'

'We can't leave him here,' Luca protested.

Kelsee pulled on Luca's arm. 'We can't get to him and we can't stay here, they will be after us in no time.'

'They won't harm him will they?' Luca asked frowning at Mercy.

She shook her head. 'Kelsee is right, we need to go. He'll be safe with them, but maybe they won't be safe with him!' she said smiling a little. 'He wants you to go to your father.'

Luca turned back to Eban, only to see Alard leading him back towards the bridge. 'Alright, let's go!'

The pebbles rattled under his sodden feet. Luca's stomach churned as he thought about his ability to walk away only because of Eban's sacrifice of freedom. Luca curled his shoulders in and let his gaze drop to the uneven beach as he considered how he would ever be able to repay his friend. Eban being trapped with Campion could not and would not sit comfortably with him. He balled his fists and resolved to be a better friend if Mercy, Kelsee and himself managed to come back with any Outsiders.

They rounded the sheltered curve of the beach and were immediately assaulted by the strong winds.

Luca peered up. The wall of Outside was so far off yet so vast. Any tiny seed of hope that Luca carried seemed to shrivel up and die, but there was no option to return. His father was likely to be in more danger if he didn't pursue this meaningless task.

Mercy and Kelsee followed on behind. They kept a fair distance from the cliff face after Mercy pointed out the piles of recently fallen rocks and chalk. The waves relentlessly battered the shoreline but the water was receding further away from the cliff as the tide continued to go out. There was very little talk. Luca wondered if they missed the ever positive influence of Eban as keenly as he did.

The hopelessness was exhausting. Even though Luca chose not to look at the wall he could still feel it looming over everything. His feet felt heavier, his breathing laboured and his mind seemed lost in negative thoughts. The approaching night and buffeting wind that twisted and spun off the white cliff fingers, deepened Luca's mental sense of cold by chilling him to his bones.

The sky had significantly darkened so Luca assumed that the sun must have already dipped below the horizon just beyond the wall, although he had seen no sign of it through the growing and threatening clouds.

The white cliff fingers had come to an end and the depleted company of friends stood at the edge of an expansive man-made beach. Large, irregular shaped concrete blocks were piled high and apparently haphazardly. The pebbles had seeped over the edges where they could, but Luca knew that further in there could be deep pools where sea water would collect.

Luca smoothed his jacket and took a deep breath. The sight, although daunting, had set his heart racing again and he could feel a little heat flowing though his body. These fake rocks were familiar. His Outsider home was on the far outskirts of the walled city and just beyond that was the place where Willow had taught him to swim, although he had no memories of swimming on days like this. He remembered the concrete rocks that formed the pathway down to the gap in the wall where the horizon was empty of anything but water. It almost felt like he was standing on Outside's foundation, he was nearly home.

Luca stepped onto the nearest block and clambered to a high point. The land seemed to double back on itself with access to Outside at the far reaches of the peninsular.

Outside was the dominating feature in view. The white walls, somehow not so pristine anymore, towered and were lost into the dimming sky. The city that held Luca's father and countless others rested out to sea and away from the mainland. At this distance Luca was able to make out a thread, a connection between Outside and the shore. He was certain it was a path.

Urgency gave Luca the energy to keep moving. He offered his hand to Mercy and then Kelsee.

'We need to get to that pathway, see?' he said pointing.

'It's getting dark, Luca,' Mercy stated. 'This place is dangerous.'

'I reckon we may have enough light left to get to the path, after that it will be easy.' Luca swallowed hard. 'Perhaps not easy, but ...'

Kelsee had jumped over a small gap to the next boulder. She then walked effortlessly on the flatter surface to the next.

Luca smiled. Kelsee's actions had spoken much louder than any words. She had rushed to agree with him and understood his desperation. He didn't wait for Mercy but knew that she would also follow.

After skidding on the seaweed for the third time, Luca's enthusiasm ebbed. He peered at the graze on his hand and brushed away the sandy grit.

'If we go further inland, the ground may not be so slippery,' Mercy called.

Luca peered at the sky. The light was so nearly gone, but there really was no other choice. 'Kelsee!' Luca called. When she turned he gestured to follow Mercy.

The further inland they went the flatter the blocks had been laid. Maybe they had settled that way so that other concrete could be imported and set up. Luca still had to leap the gaps but without slime and the haphazard gradients they travelled faster and further. Even with this new speed, the light disappeared fast.

Kelsee and Mercy shone the narrow beams of their torches over the ground. The soft white circles of light danced on the route just ahead of them.

Luca pulled the torch from his pocket and frowned as he twisted the handle to charge the light. There was something quite treacherous about using Campion's provisions. He flicked the switch and wondered once again, how Campion could hold back from helping Outside when they were essentially so close. Thoughts of Eban being held by the group were riddled with worries over his potential treatment. Alard had been so angry at their escape and Luca was concerned that Eban would bear the brunt of their actions.

Luca was concerned that the spots of light against darkness would draw attention. The only other option was to sit it out until morning but Tropolis would have sent in the extra workers by then. He was grateful that neither of the girls had suggested such a thing, they had to press through before the weather closed in and his father suffered further. The wall was still a long way off and out to sea, he had to trust that the light would not be noticed.

The wind beat at their faces and rain had started to fall but they were not faced with a steep and dangerous climb up to the path from the lower beach. The route inland had been a wise decision. Here, the concrete blocks flowed easily onto the thread of a path that Luca had seen in the distance. He shielded the torch light with his hand and directed the beam at what he had thought was the narrow walkway. The path turned out to be more of a fairly well maintained road wide enough for vehicles. Luca knew that this would lead them directly to the wall of Outside. He looked up at the distant wall to scan for any movement but the rain filled Luca's eyes and the darkness revealed nothing.

Luca switched off his torch and tucked it back into his pocket. His jacket was already dripping with the rain but he pulled it tighter around himself and set off at a renewed pace. Kelsee and Mercy followed after him.

Very soon, the sound and spray of the waves told Luca that they were out to sea. Even in the buffeting wind the waves did not overwhelm the elevated road. The slightly raised edge and gutter made the route easy to trace even in the darkness.

Tired, hungry and wet, Luca's mind went back to the warm beds found in Tropolis. He turned and called to Kelsee.

'You alright?'

'How much further?' she answered quietly.

Her tired voice was tossed by the wind. Luca slowed down and caught sight of her shadow. 'It can't be much further,' he reassured. Luca shook the water from his hood and then looked a little higher. There were no indications of the wall except perhaps a darker patch against the sky. 'Not long now,' he said encouraging himself.

'I think we are getting closer to that faint light directly ahead. Do you see it?' Mercy asked. 'It hasn't moved so I think it might be attached to the wall.'

Luca stared nervously at the glow. There was no other way to get to the wall, they had to stay on this road and that meant they had to get closer to the light. Mercy was right though as it did remain stationary. He hoped that she was right and if not, that there would be a place to hide.

The speck of light had carried much further than they had thought; they had perhaps only been halfway along the road when Mercy had spoken about it. Luca thought that he could feel the growing presence of his home as they trudged towards the gleam but he had no way of measuring the distance to the dominant wall. It towered above him, swallowed by the darkness which in turn masked any sense of scale or perspective.

The lamp was very close. Luca slowed his pace and watched for any other movement. They were alone. The lashing rain obscured his view and it was only as he drew very close that he could see it was a barred external light. It was fixed to the wall above a pair of wide and solid doors that almost spanned the road. Luca tentatively pushed against them but they would not move.

'How are we going to get in?' Kelsee asked.

'Not this way.'

Luca recalled the height of the wall and knew that it that loomed far above him but he was within touching distance of it once again.

Luca's feet and legs were saturated and chilled but his jacket had resisted the rain enough for him to know he could keep going in the atrocious conditions.

'The docks?' Mercy suggested.

'We'll never get past the fence even if we made it to the dockside.' Luca looked at Kelsee and then at Mercy. The glow from the security light caught the glistening droplets on their coats and faces. 'I know you are wet and tired, but I think there is only one way to get in.'

'Go on then!' Kelsee said gesturing with her hand to get him moving.

'No, you don't understand,' Luca began, 'We need to go around the wall to the gap where I used to swim but I'm not sure how far it is. It must be on the far side because I don't remember seeing any land. I used to believe that Outside was an island far out to sea and completely separate from anything.'

Kelsee smiled. 'I've come this far Luca, I'm not going to give up now.'

'Which way?' Mercy asked.

'Sun set that way,' Luca indicated with his right hand, 'so I think the other way would be our best option. We used to go first thing in the morning before gleaning. The sun would still be low in the sky.'

Kelsee again, reacted immediately. Luca shook his head, her courage astounding him.

Luca stepped over the ridge at the side of the road and onto the massive concrete blocks that had been butted tightly together close to the base of the wall. The width of the flat surface would have fitted at least ten people shoulder to shoulder. The white enclosure reflected what little light there was onto the wide ledge, before it seemed to sink heavily, into the ground.

The waves were pounding somewhere far below. The sound of the water's force being broken on the carefully positioned blocks was a strange comfort. Without the confusion of the dragging pebbles but with the amplifying effect of the echoes bouncing off the wall Luca felt oddly safe with the familiar splashes and crashes of the sea.

The solid wall dripped with water but Luca could not help but run his fingers over the surface. He was so near to home that the tension in his muscles began to soften. He pulled his hand away quickly as if his fingers had burned. He had missed this hideous prison. His stomach lurched as he was almost sick.

Luca picked up his pace once again, dashing away from the disgusting thoughts. He skirted around Kelsee. 'Keep up!'

The forced march was only interrupted by the substantial supports that jutted at regular intervals from the main structure.

They had to take more care when navigating the outer reaches as the flat surface nearer the base of the wall only stretched as far as the limits of the supports.

As they advanced further into the shelter of the wall, the wind died down and the rain was considerably lighter. Even though Luca was aware of this, he could not rest. He had to keep moving.

'It's so huge!' Kelsee dared to speak.

'Yes, bigger than I remember,' Mercy said sadly.

Luca turned. The clouds had broken and moonlight was breaking through. The cool night light made both Kelsee and Mercy appear pale and fragile. Night was deceptive. It played with how Luca perceived time, distance and scale, but most of all it lied to him about his companions. He would not believe what the moonlight told him, Kelsee and Mercy were far from fragile.

'Not long now,' he said breathing deeply, 'Then we can rest.'

The wall's relatively plain and smooth surface that had curved away from the road and the beach was now pitted with missing chunks of render. In places there were very clear vertical lines as if there were joins or sections of the thick concrete hidden under the masking top surface. The gentle moonbeams, that played hide and seek in the wind tossed clouds, caught sections of the wall.

Luca was bought to a halt as a dark stain was thrown into contrast on the pale wall. Paint had been smeared over the render and long skinny drips had trickled down the surface before the painting had dried. The image was old and weathered but it was unmistakably the five-petalled design of a Gibraltar Campion. It was not delicate like the artist's impression on the notebook Luca had once owned, nor was it the striking tattoo on Mercy's neck, neither did it have the force or militant feeling of the metal image at Campion's sea fort. This was a hurried and desperate message; a fearful rebellious cry to anyone who might see it.

He pulled out his torch and quickly flicked it on. The beam touched the wall.

'Turn it off!' Kelsee warned.

'If only Campion would come and see this!' Luca said loudly as he pocketed his torch once again and thumped the image, then he peered about in the darkness hoping that no one had heard him. But they had not seen any evidence of a guard since they had arrived. 'We need to keep moving,' he said brushing the image more gently.

The rain had completely stopped. Clouds scuttled across the face of the crescent moon, throwing the wall into silver light one moment then shadow the next. The friends had now circled far enough that the wind battered them a little again.

Kelsee could not help but remark at the size of Outside several times, each time her voice would lose a little more power until she just whispered in disbelief. Luca knew that she was shocked.

The wall was damaged and eroded. The sea winds and storms had obviously been attacking the surface for many years yet there had not been any repairs. Perhaps Tropolis knew that it wasn't just the wall that held the Outsiders here.

Luca had slowed his pace knowing that the gap that had become his breach in the strict imprisonment of Outside must be found nearby. The concrete blocks were still tightly packed at the base of the wall but there were also natural rocks that gleamed in the moonlight.

Memories flicked like photographs. Luca could see the gentle water, and feel the chill of stepping in. He could hear his mother's laughter and delight. He gasped as even the picture of his father resting against a rock with a high back that curved like one of the chairs in Tropolis came to mind and then into physical view.

'We're .. s s s so near!' he stammered in a hushed voice clutching his chest.

His father had been there whilst he learnt to swim. Luca had never recalled that before. He breathed heavily as he tried to push away the numb sensation. Had he locked away other memories too? He knew that there were so many things that he hadn't thought about for many years with regards to his mother, but now maybe with the knowledge that she was alive, his soul was seeking them out. Luca swallowed hard as he realised that in his grief he had also banished his father.

Luca's search for the doorway became urgent. Without thinking, he pulled out the torch and began to scan the base of the wall.

'Wait!' Mercy said excitedly, 'Up there!' She grabbed Luca's hand and directed the beam to the corner of a supporting buttress that jutted out from the main wall, perhaps his height off the ground.

The beam fell on a neat angular hole. Luca frowned then nodded.

'That's it,' he said. 'My dad used to lift me up to Willow who would pull me in.'

The render below the entrance had been chipped away to from hand holes and climbing up would be relatively easy.

Luca turned to Kelsee. 'Are you ready for this?'

'I think so,' she replied.

Chapter 14

12h 42m

Luca climbed up first.

The hole was smaller than he remembered and his torch light seemed intense in the tight space. He gasped. He had expected to see a thick and solid mass of concrete that had been excavated, but instead he found that the main depth of the wall was empty. The outer rims were just slabs of rendered concrete bolted to the steel cage structure. He marvelled at the patience and persistence of the person that had cut their way through and wondered if they knew the secret before they began.

He stood up and shone the beam into the void. The metal lattice work was geometric and had the markings of Tropolis in design. He could have easily walked through the organised maze but since the wall was sealed, there would be little point. The wall was not what he had thought it was at all. The monstrous thing that had held the Outsiders in their poverty was hollow.

The noise of scratching grit below his feet was amplified by the space.

Luca peered out of the crack to beckon Kelsee and Mercy inside. Mercy was already following close behind but Kelsee was taking advantage of the clearing sky and drinking in one last look out to sea.

He retreated back into the gloom. Outsiders didn't have the luxury of open spaces.

'Did you know?' Mercy asked in a near whisper from behind.

Luca shook his head. 'I don't remember any of this.' He turned the beam towards the small hole that led to Outside. 'Why don't I remember?' he said half to himself. He had been a small child and it was before his mother had gone. His father had retreated into the shack and they had not visited again. It was as if the wall was completely impenetrable. 'I don't know why I have no good memories.'

'They are in there somewhere, Luca,' Mercy said with quiet confidence, 'They've just been hidden for a while.' Luca took a deep breath and turned away. 'You do have them,' she continued, 'It's just that all this other stuff, all these piles of rubbish and responsibility have more prominence.'

'I don't know why I can't,' Luca lowered his voice seeing Kelsee approaching, 'recall any happiness as a child.' Kelsee frowned a little. 'We're nearly there,' Luca said louder.

Luca shone his torch at the far side of the wall extending the beam to the left and right. The steel supports were thick and coated in deep red paint, standing out against the grey concrete façade. A narrow and short crack caught Luca's attention. It was nestled next to a girder at the base of one of the slabs nearly opposite. Approaching the gap, he could see that the hole had been covered from the other side and wondered if this had been his father's doing many years before.

He crouched down and crawled in. A thick plastic board had been laid across the exit.

Luca pushed against it and it gave a little. He could hear the unmistakable tumble of rubble on the other side. Placing his hands at the highest point he pushed again. The board shifted forward then sprang back.

'What is it? Is everything alright?' Kelsee asked.

Luca directed the torch light back towards the girls. He peered around awkwardly. Kelsee was squinting in the beam. Luca returned to what he knew was the exit. Creating a sharp edge to the side of the crack was the steel frame and there was very little room to move. Luca backed out.

'It's fine,' Luca said as he returned to the gap but went in backwards.

The distance from the steel post to the plastic barrier was not deep. Luca rested his back up against the board and bent his knees to his chest. He shifted his feet until both were poised on the edge of the steel. Then he pushed. He gritted his teeth and let out a grunt. The vibrations of the moving rubble started as a trickle but after a few larger bangs he was slowly able to straighten his legs.

He looked up to the sky, the night was finally clear. The shear face of the wall loomed above him, but Luca was captivated by the familiar bright pinpoints of stars.

Luca twisted enough to squeeze through the partly-blocked space and quickly began to pull away the rocks and stone that had been piled up. He lifted the board out of the way.

Kelsee squealed a little as the debris tumbled into the exit.

'Everyone alright?' Luca asked quickly.

'We're good!' Kelsee said popping her head out of the hole. She pushed the rocks away and clambered into Outside; and then began to cough.

'Sorry about the smell,' Luca said with a hint of sarcasm as he reached down to help Mercy out. 'But it really isn't that bad just here.'

Luca slipped down the rubble bank. The slim exit to the free world was stationed between two shacks that leaned away from each other. He had no intention of concealing it again. As he made his way to the path at the front, he knew where he was almost immediately. This was where he used to live before he had decided to have a quieter and less hostile existence, like they had before his mother had died. There were container homes nearby for the more influential members and easier access to the heaps and docks along the straight roads, but enough distance to not be overwhelmed by the stench.

'This way.' Luca followed the purpose built, potholed road out into the settlement before taking a smaller path to his left. It had been fairly easy to avoid the large contained puddles of the road, but the muddy pathway squelched under his feet. The moonlight was not bright enough to reveal the shanty town for what it was. The buildings remained in the shadows.

'I would never have dreamed of such a place to live.' Kelsee said under her breath. 'Are we going to split up?' she asked in a whisper. 'Aren't you going to your family, Mercy?'

Luca's step faltered briefly and listened intently.

'I have no family,' Mercy said.

'You've been alone? How long?' Kelsee questioned.

'For as long as I can remember.' There was a pause but Luca didn't dare to turn around and show his ignorance and lack of care. 'I have plenty of friends so I was not alone here.' Mercy continued. Luca was certain that she had spoken in response to some non-vocalised reaction that Kelsee had given. All of a sudden, a new pang of guilt over Eban hit Luca hard. He swallowed and tried to believe that Eban would be safe with Campion, but knew that he should, in fact, be here with his friends.

As they moved further away from the main roadway, the shacks were forced closer together and the pathways snaked one way then the other.

A dim light suddenly appeared ahead of them followed by a rumble of chatter. A dark figure stepped out from the doorway. The person seemed to be in a hurry and was rushing past them when he stopped and let out a yelp. He leaned in closer to Mercy and grabbed her arm pulling her into a hug.

'It's you!' he breathed, 'You're back!' He began to drag her towards the door he had only just come from. 'They will want to see this,' he exclaimed to Luca and Kelsee.

'I can't come with you now,' Mercy tried to explain resisting his strength.

'But you must.'

'Gunter?' Mercy asked, and then smiled.

'Yes miss! Please, you must come,' the man named Gunter said and turned releasing Mercy's arm. 'Bring your friends too if you like.'

Mercy paused. She was looking at Gunter in a thoughtful manner. She then reached out to Luca. 'I think I should stay, just for a while and find out what is going on. You must go to your father. Where will you be?'

'Lower-end Quarter.'

'That's a spread out section.'

Kelsee pulled the notebook from her pocket. 'Draw a map,' she said handing it to Luca.

He bent down, opened the pad and rested it on his knee. He dabbed his finger in the sticky mud puddle and started to draw. He heard Kelsee huff and tried to overlook her ignorance. This was Outside and you used what you could.

'This is the wall,' he said smoothing the line, 'The Compassion Gate … You need to go way past the containers and into the Lower-end Quarter. My place is this side of the settlement, nestled into the rocks about three rows back.' Luca carefully tore out the page and smiled at Mercy. 'Thank you!'

Mercy nodded. 'I've got that. Go and find your father. I'll be there as soon as I can.'

As Gunter opened the door once again the vibrant cacophony of chatting voices seemed to give a collective gasp before exclamations of surprise and joy flowed out onto the street.

Luca frowned as the street went dark. He ran his hand through his hair, trying to work out what was so unsettling. A gathering of

Outsiders was not something he was familiar with, but even that didn't seem to be the answer.

'Mercy has so many friends,' Kelsee said. 'It is good to know that she wasn't alone when she was here.'

Luca swallowed and then bit down on his lip. He remembered the day when the contestants lined up at the Compassion Gate and Mercy had so many people wish her well. She appeared to know everyone. Now she was home again, he would have to share his friendship with others. Jealousy left a bitter taste in his mouth.

'Let's go!' he said handing the notebook back to Kelsee roughly.

The maze of paths and shacks were as familiar to Luca as his own hands. Nothing had changed on the material surface of Outside. The shacks still looked as precarious as ever, as if a strong wind would rip them up or tear them down. Of course, the sea wind swirled through Outside on a regular basis, but somehow, the fractured homes made from the discarded riches of Tropolis still held together despite the haphazard building style. Perhaps the plastic casings, bent fibre board, broken glass and other rubbish were strong when attached to others, perhaps there was hidden strength in this place.

The familiar silence that accompanied exhaustion, was not evident in the settlement. Luca could hear the buzz of voices from behind the doorways. His heart beat faster and his pace quickened as he led Kelsee from the centre of what could now, strangely, be described as a community, to the outskirts.

The wall seemed more overbearing in stature as they approached the Lower-end Quarter, but even that didn't feel real anymore since Luca now knew its secret. The slippery pathways juddered between low lying rocks, but Luca was grateful that they were now close.

Tall rocks naturally stacked up either side of the walkway. Homes were tightly fitted into the gaps and the shacks were determined by the rock formations.

He came to a halt and shone the beam of his torch over the large leaning rock. Fused plastic formed the undulating melted walls that could be crushed had the stone ever chosen to fall. He was home.

He slid the door to one side and rushed in, focussing his light on the bed. The tattered and stained blanket lay draped over the hunched form of his unmoving father.

Luca dashed forwards.

'Dad! Dad!' There was no response.

Chapter 15

11h 56m

He pulled the blanket to one side and bent low, resting his ear to his father's chest. A quiet but unmistakable rattle of breath echoed. Luca exposed his father's face to the torch light. His face was pale and incredibly thin and his lips were dry.

'Grab some water!' Luca commanded.

Kelsee span round scanning the small room.

Luca quickly got to his feet grabbed the mug from next to the rain water butt and sank it under the surface.

'Sorry ... I didn't know!' Kelsee stammered.

'Dad!' Luca propped up his father and offered the cool liquid to the frail man's lips. Luca's hands trembled as his father sipped from the mug.

'Luca!' the man said opening his eyes a little.

'I'm here. Just drink.'

After a few moments Luca's father drifted off to sleep once again. Luca laid him down gently then stood and reached for the lamp suspended from the low ceiling. He flicked the switch but nothing happened. Grabbing for the torch, Luca moved to the far corner and began to scrabble on the floor. He found the battery and reattached the loose wire. The stark, blue-tinged light began to glow.

Luca clambered over his bed, lifted the hatch in the wall and climbed out. The small garden was dry and the leaves on the plants were brown and shrivelled. Luca sighed. He grabbed at the pumpkin that was now only attached by a dead stem and broke it off.

Stepping back into the room Luca jumped in surprise as Kelsee leaned forward to help him. He had forgotten that she was there. She had taken off her sodden coat and hung it from some jutting wall material. She still looked cold and damp. Her hair was limp but her eyes bright.

'Do you know how to prepare this?' he asked. Kelsee shook her head. Luca put the pumpkin on his bed. 'Can you make soup?'

'No. Sorry.'

'Over on the side by the hob is a big metal pot; grab that, and the chair seat we use as a cutting board. It's underneath it.' Luca rummaged in the container that had a few utensils and pulled out a dull knife and a spoon. He took the plastic seat pad and placed it on the floor with the pumpkin in the middle. Carefully and slowly Luca began to cut away the tough outer skin. He had managed to peel one quarter before he aggressively began to saw into the hard flesh of the fruit. The muscles in his arm burned as he finally cut out the slice.

'I need you scoop out the seeds,' Luca said passing Kelsee the spoon. He half-filled the metal pot with water then put it on the hob. He puffed out the breath he had been holding when the central light dimmed a little but the hot plate began to glow. 'I'm not sure how long this will last, so we'll have to just cook a small bit.' He turned to Kelsee. 'What are you doing?' he almost shouted.

Kelsee had collected the seeds and was about to throw them into the water butt. 'I'm looking for the waste.'

'That's not waste! That is my next meal and my next harvest.' Luca could see the colour rising in Kelsee's cheeks and the tears welling in her eyes but he was not sorry for it. 'This isn't Tropolis! We use, we don't throw away,' he stated harshly and collected the seeds into a bowl.

He returned to the slice of pumpkin and began to cut it into small cubes, dropping them into the pot each time he had created a handful. Soon the room was full of steam and the sweet earthy smell of cooking. Luca opened two small pots; these were expensive, credit bought goods. He added a pinch of salt from one and a generous sprinkling of curry powder from the other to the pan. He pushed the pumpkin mixture up against the side of the pot with a fork, crushing the cubes until the contents became a thick soup. He bought a little to his mouth, blew on it and tasted it. He screwed up his nose and shrugged turning off the stove.

Grabbing two mugs and a bowl, Luca poured out the soup.

Kelsee was sitting quietly on Luca's bed. 'Here, it's not amazing but it is hot,' he said gently, slightly regretting his anger earlier and handing her a mug.

He took the bowl over to his father. 'Dad, I have some food.' His father's eyes opened a little. Luca lifted him into a sitting position. It did not require much strength.

Luca carefully spooned small amounts of the soup into his father's mouth whilst his father smiled kindly at him.

'When was the last time you ate?' Luca asked. His father shrugged a little and sighed. 'I left you credits.' Luca waited for an excuse but the frail man remained silent. 'Why didn't you tell me you couldn't use them?'

'Why do you say that?' his father said, his voice crackled from misuse.

'You can't use them, can you?' Luca could feel the warm prickle of tears. He blinked them away. 'All those years and you let me think you were a lazy parasite. Why did you let me hate you?'

'What I deserved.'

'How is that even logical?' Luca asked angrily.

'Willow.' The man looked away from Luca. 'I sent her there.'

Luca knew that he should reveal the truth. He dared not look at Kelsee and she was staying silent. 'You sent her to the docks? Why would you do that?'

'Freedom,' his father said weakly. 'I knew a place where we could have freedom.'

'Why didn't you go then?' Luca shook his head. 'You knew about the hole in the wall.'

'She would not go without all the Outsiders.'

Luca frowned and his breath caught in his chest. That sounded like the woman he remembered as his mother but not like the coward in Campion. 'She wanted everyone to be free!' he whispered.

'Luca?' Kelsee muttered.

His father peered over at the bed and caught sight of Kelsee.

Luca batted his hand but did not look at her. 'Why didn't you go get this freedom and take me with you after she was ... gone?' he accused.

'Sea took her. Didn't want it to take you.'

Luca was still. He had truly had his father wrong all this time. If Luca was able to put aside the fact that fear had controlled his father's life and therefore his life, he was able to see that his father had only wanted to protect and keep Luca safe. The method was all wrong, but the motivation softened Luca.

'I wish you had taken me through that hole and risked the sea, but I guess I get it now.'

'You, always my little boy. My Luca. Then, too late. You grew up. Had to stay.'

'We don't need to stay now.' Luca put bowl down and gently grasped his father's bony hand. 'We can have freedom.'

'But you need to build up some strength first,' Kelsee said kindly, 'It's a bit of a journey.'

Luca's father tilted his head and squinted at the stranger on his son's bed.

'Kelsee,' Luca introduced.

'Amil,' his father said smiling. 'Kelsee familiar.'

'Probably not dad. I think it is time to rest now.' Luca straightened the cushion and lowered his father down.

'Freedom exists Amil,' Kelsee said kindly.

'Can't be free in here!' Amil replied placing his hand over his heart.

Luca caught Kelsee's look and nod, but lowered his gaze to the floor.

'Fine!' she said quietly and took a deep breath. 'Amil, we have some amazing news for you.' Luca glared at her but she was undeterred. 'When we left Tropolis we were taken to a free village, away from Tropolite rule and hidden from the authorities. When we were there, we found your Willow. She's alive!'

His father began to shake. 'How?'

Luca was desperate to be angry at what she had done but in reality, he was grateful. 'Campion,' Luca explained. 'They rescued her. You can go and be with her.' Luca had seen this man grieve for years. His father had lived with the debilitating sorrow day and night and Luca, despite what he felt for Willow, knew that she could ease the pain.

'When?'

'As soon as you are well enough.' Luca was defeated.

'I can move. I can come.'

Luca looked with pity at his frail father who would have to move sooner than he would like. The time was ticking away and there was no possibility of running from it. Luca could only hope that his fears for his father's safety were not what Tropolis had in mind. 'Rest now. We'll have you ready to leave.'

His own portion of soup was cold but he did not waste power to heat it up. He sat down next to Kelsee and began to eat.

'He recognises me,' Kelsee whispered.

'Does that matter? Luca asked between mouthfuls.

Kelsee bit on her lip. 'I suppose not,' she eventually replied laying down. 'Your father had the right to know.'

Luca did not know what to say and felt the awkward silence. He had never been alone with Kelsee. He sniffed as he realised that thinking about just himself was a rare occurrence in recent days. There had been no time where he had not been influenced by Mercy or Eban. Being back in this shack made him behave like nothing had really happened. It had been too easy to slip back into the angry young man he had been before the Prize; the one that demanded his place and his peace, yet never obtained it.

He glanced at Kelsee who had curled up on the bed. What must she be thinking? Luca took his thin blanket that had been lovingly folded at the end, and laid it over her still form. She must have been exhausted to fall asleep so quickly in such a strange and disgusting place, if she was sleeping at all. It would be much easier to assume that she slept because then he would not need to talk about the stuff that was flowing out of him and hurting him most of all. He would not have to confront and then retract the Luca who belonged in Outside.

Luca's thoughts became clearer in the peace and stillness of the shack. Who did he really want to be? Mercy and Eban were not here but he could still hear them. His closest of friends would have encouraged him, even if it were with something sharp, like a word or laughing at his irrational behaviour, to step into who he was now. They would be right. Luca had left the person who belonged in Outside far behind, so he should not try to resurrect him now. He was new and different. He had to start thinking that way.

Luca looked at Kelsee and knew what he must say to her when she woke. Of course, *sorry* would feature widely. He was sorry that she had been dragged into this, sorry that she had to put up with his unfeeling and rude outbursts, sorry that she had to sleep in squalor. He had hurt her and he had done it thoughtlessly.

Luca shook his head as he attempted to work out what he had been trying to prove in his meanness. Kelsee was not to blame for the suffering of Amil, or the other Outsiders. She had been oblivious to the Outsiders' plight. Perhaps her naivety to the

Compassion Prize had wounded him deeper than he had thought. It was difficult to come to terms with the fact that she considered it all entertainment and not a real contest to be given the compassion of Tropolis. Perhaps he had wanted to punish her in some way and to show her the real world.

Kelsee's breathing deepened.

Luca couldn't help but feel the tug in his spirit though. He had grown to know her over the past few days. She had been so brave in getting them free when she realised it had all been true. She had taken the truth and allowed it to change all that she had ever known. She had trusted them, trusted him, to change her perspective. She really was extraordinary.

He would not wake her now. She deserved the rest.

Luca gently stood up from the bed not wanting to jostle Kelsee, and went over to the battery. He removed the wire and the shack became suddenly dark.

Luca unzipped his jacket, lay down on the floor and covered himself. He hoped that his father, with the little bit of nourishment, would be strong enough to move in the morning. If not, he would have to protect him somehow. Luca knew that he needed to rest and tried not to imagine what would happen if it came to a fight. Weary from all that had gone before it was not long before Luca sank into dream filled sleep.

A cold draft blew across Luca's cheek. He opened his eyes. Bright morning light, made indistinct by the stained plastic roof, reached into the shack.

Luca's side was numb from sleeping on the hard floor so he was grateful for the room to stretch.

He looked over to his father who was still sleeping and sat up pushing the blanket to one side. He peered at the bed expecting to see Kelsee still fast asleep but she was not there. On the empty bed was a folded piece of paper. The size was oddly familiar and then Luca noticed the perforated edge as if it had been torn from a notebook.

He quickly reached for it.
On the outside was simply written his name. He unfolded it.

Dear Luca,
I'm so sorry for everything.
I can't stay here.
I am going to my grandfather.
Please forgive me.
Kelsee x

How long had this note sat here? Luca read it through again. He had driven her away and hadn't had a chance to explain himself. She was apologising for his mistakes and now she was on her way back to her grandfather because he had been so cruel. Luca frowned at the note. He had to sort out this mess that he had created.

His father was still sleeping peacefully. Would there be enough time to stop Kelsee and rescue his father too? He had to make a choice between two people who meant more to him than he realised.

'Dad!' Luca cried as he rushed over to his father and began to shake him a little.

Amil looked blurrily up at his son.

'I've got to go again!' Luca saw the confusion cross his father's face. 'I've got to go after Kelsee.' Luca grabbed the pot from the stove. There was still a little of the pumpkin soup left. 'Breakfast. Eat it all.' He put it beside Amil. Luca pulled on his jacket and dashed to the door. 'A girl named Mercy should turn up,' he said with a frown, 'You can trust her, she's my friend. If she wants you to leave, you must go with her.' He rushed to slide the door open, bashing it against the rock outside. 'Do you understand? You can't stay here!'

Chapter 16
00h 33m

Luca had no idea how long Kelsee had been gone and could only guess where she would go. His only thought was the docks since Mercy and himself had mentioned them. He hoped that she would lose her way and that he would get there before she did.

The night rain had left the paths slippery and stodgy. The settlement smelt damp but the heat from the morning sun on the dark roofs caused streamers of mist to rise. The bright light teased Luca with false promises of warmth but the breeze bit into his body. Luca had taken the shortest route he could remember but that was still some distance.

It was not early, yet the roads were eerily quiet.

Luca spotted an Outsider ahead and raced to catch up with him.

'We're late!' the man said almost laughing at Luca's sweaty face. 'I thought I was the only one but you are much later than me.'

'Late for what? Luca asked puffing to keep up.

'The docks protest!' the man frowned. 'A young lad like yourself should have been there at dawn.'

'Protest?'

'I don't have time for this!' The man said picking up his speed. 'I'll miss the action!'

Luca was left to run along the empty pathways. Soon his sides stung and his lungs felt like they would burst.

As he drew closer to the heaps, the stench was more disgusting than he remembered. It was also different. The tang of rotting rubbish was just that, just rotting rubbish. Luca peered at the sky. There was no hint of smoke, no acrid chemicals in the air and no rumble of the furnaces. The power plants were silent.

Luca had never known a day that the fires had not burned. Tropolis would not allow for such a breakdown in the system as it had always worked them hard. The heaps were continuously busy with gleaners scavenging an existence before the rubbish that supplied them with life was burned for the sake of the rich city.

He remembered the intercepted message at the Campion sea fort. *URGENT INTERVENTION REQUIRED Power must be restored, able bodies to be deployed to Outside within 48 hours.*

Tropolis had already been in need of power and it had been about two days since the message. Soon, Outside would be flooded with able bodied Tropolite workers while the Outsiders protested at the docks. Luca's heart pounded hard. He had to find Kelsee before they did and before she was taken back to Tropolis. He needed to put things right.

He knew that the fastest and by far the most efficient way of bringing in a workforce would be by Maglev and that meant that the Compassion Gate would be in service.

Luca gasped. The map he had drawn for Mercy had shown the Compassion Gate. The Compassion Gate would be familiar to Kelsee as it was the starting place for the Prize and the exit from Outside. Would she think to go there? What if she was did?

Without further thought, Luca changed direction and took a side path, the gate was not far. If Kelsee was with the crowd of

Outsiders at the docks, maybe she would be safe, but if she wanted to be found she would make herself known. If she was discovered by the Tropolite workers, they would need to get her out and the gate would be their only exit. Luca's best hope for interception would be at the gate. Perhaps he could stop them from taking her.

Luca was grateful that his father was hidden in the shack. Suddenly there was a spark of hope; perhaps there were no records of him since he had no chip and he would be safe, perhaps he really was hidden without trace. Luca clung to the idea and pressed himself faster to the gate. But he wasn't free from worry. Mercy had promised that she would find them but she hadn't. She could be anywhere. The situation was too familiar. He felt like a little boy once again about to lose his mother. His breathing became shallow. Dark shadows flowed over his vision. His body was telling him to stop and give up but he battled on, trying to steady his breaths. With each intake he whispered to himself, 'This won't be like last time.' But all the time the whisper was becoming quieter under the harsh scream, 'You are alone! There is nothing you can do! It's all your fault!' Luca saw the open space, just at the end of the passage. He stumbled forward desperately.

The looming metal doors of the Compassion Gate that declared to the Outsiders that there was no hope were firmly shut. There was no view through the railings, only a second wall, as stark as the one that hemmed them in.

Luca breathed deeply once again. The scream went silent as he considered that he might not be too late for Kelsee, at least. He balled his fists as thoughts of both Eban and Mercy came flooding in trying to drown his optimism and he grunted in frustration.

He wanted to breach the empty space that stood in front of the gates. He took a step forward then movement to the side caught his attention. In the shadows of the neighbouring structures, Outsiders crouched. Luca peered at the shipping containers which housed the influential; even in those windows he could make out faces.

Maybe he wasn't the only one to remember the message at Campion. Luca half laughed, maybe Mercy had a hand in what was going to happen here.

A call of a non-existent seagull sent the Outsiders deeper into the shadows. Luca instinctively copied, ducking into a shack.

He peeked through a crack in the haphazard façade.

00h 00m

The gates eased open in silence. Row after row of green clad people with rifles over their shoulders, filed in. They had the appearance of an army but there was disorder in the way they moved and waited. The square was filling and the Tropolite workers were forced ever closer to the buildings.

The small number of Outsiders that had been left to keep watch would not be able to take on such a force. Luca could not see them anymore as they had vanished from windows and hiding places.

Luca stilled all his fidgeting. Just the thickness of the shack's wall and a couple of paces away was Thickset. His enemy's nostrils flared and he grimaced at the smell of rotting rubbish. He did not appear to be delighted to be back where he had begun, but he stood tall with his chest pushed forward and his shoulders back. The large muscles were tight under the green uniform. Luca felt his stomach churn. Next to Thickset, as ever, were some of the other Compassion Prize contestants, Maxim and Taja. Danita, who had won the Endurance test had tied her wild hair back revealing a nasty dark bruise across her cheek. Luca wondered if the Prize was still taking place and this was a new twisted task, or maybe the lack of power had forced Tropolis' hand in finishing the competition early. He smiled at the latter.

The army was full of unknown faces save for a few. He wondered at the contestants. Danita, who had been consistently confident, now stood wide eyed and trembling. Could he have re-entered Outside with a rifle strapped to his back? Luca could not imagine standing in his own city and attacking his own people.

Perhaps Tropolis had gone even further in administering poison to the contestants and given them sights of a Prize worth the anguish.

No one talked but there was a bustle of noise. The Tropolite army coughed and panted. Many appeared pale and sweaty from their journey.

'Tropolis reinforcements!' A booming and authoritative male voice came from the left hand side of the square as if he had walked in from the settlement. He was approaching the group with eagerness. Luca went cold. The voice was familiar. 'You know the drill,' he commanded, 'Containment and force.' The stocky Sargent strolled to the front of the rabble. Atticus, dressed head to toe in full combat uniform, smiled menacingly; a familiar pose from Luca's days in training. Atticus was no longer just bossing about a group of teenagers after the Prize, he had an army of Tropolites and contestants to command. 'The strike action will not be tolerated. Identify the ring leaders and take them down by whatever means necessary.'

Luca stared at the bloodthirsty commander. Suddenly he felt strong enough to take on the whole army in order to remove the smug smile from Atticus' face. He planted his feet apart ready to rush out. It was only his grip on the edge of the plastic wall that held him back; the grip that had to keep him in the here and now. His resolve to stay hidden was faltering. He wanted to roar and rage.

In a moment, everything changed.

'What do you think you are doing?'

Luca's breath was gone.

Kelsee had stepped from the street. Her curly hair bounced as she strutted forwards. The softness in her speech and face was gone. She carried a presence. She carried her grandfather's name. She was a Barret.

'Take them down? Is that what you said?' she questioned.

Atticus turned and suddenly the smile was gone. 'Miss Barret!' He stood to attention.

'Is that what you said?' she asked again.

Atticus frowned then smiled more dangerously than before. 'How good to see you so safe and well!' He relaxed to stand at ease.

'I asked you a question.'

'Yes Miss,' he replied, almost lazily. 'I said take them down. Strict orders from a higher authority you see.'

Luca could feel the tension and was about to leap out, but Kelsee spoke up.

'If you *take them down*, as you put it, there will be no workforce.' She paused, but only briefly. 'I do not think my grandfather would be very pleased if you, in your simple minded eagerness and misunderstanding of our society, killed off the source of electricity.' She paced to the front of the army. 'What does taking down mean to you?' she asked a green clad Tropolite. 'You may speak.'

'I don't know Ma'am.'

'Well then,' Kelsee said turning to Atticus, 'It appears that your army are in some confusion too. Would you like to clarify how to take down the workers?'

'Yes Miss, of course.' Atticus addressed the army. 'The workforce are to be preserved.'

'Indeed they are!' Kelsee said enthusiastically.

'But any leaders of the rebellion,' Atticus said turning to face Kelsee, 'Are to be arrested or shot on the spot,'

Luca watched, disbelieving as Kelsee confirmed that leaders should be exterminated. His breath came in a gasp. He did not recognise this girl.

'Excellent!' Kelsee replied. 'I'm glad that we have cleared that up.' She turned away. 'You there! Take me back to Tropolis.'

A tall man stepped forward, but he was not wearing the crisp white suit Luca was so accustomed to, instead, he wore a similar combat uniform to Atticus. Luca covered his mouth.

'I have hand-picked the reinforcements but since I will be elsewhere, I am handing them over for your command. Continue with orders Sargent,' Luca's uncle Alec instructed. 'This way Miss,' he said.

Complete silence fell over the gathering. Kelsee followed Alec out of sight.

Luca shook his head. Everything was back to front. Kelsee was agreeing with the capture and possible deaths of his people, leaders like Mercy were in danger, and now this. His own uncle, the one that had set them free from Tropolis was commanding Atticus to follow through with orders. Who could he trust? His uncle had set him free from Tropolis but had sent him to Campion who themselves were unwilling to take action. Perhaps it had been a guilt reflex; save his sister's child in order to ease the burden of not finding and rescuing her. Luca bit down on his lip and shifted his stance a little as his world seemed to tip on its axis.

A tune sounded out over the hush, one that Eban had hummed the first time Luca had met him. The gate slid silently open and Luca knew that Kelsee and Alec were gone.

'Enough time has been wasted!' Atticus bellowed, startling Luca. 'Get moving!'

The rows of the green Tropolites jogged after Atticus along the main road towards the docks. The sound of their heavy feet filled the space like an impending storm.

Luca began to shake. He knew that the army would reach the dockside and if Atticus had his way, the Outsiders would be punished into submission. Mercy was likely to be there. Would he be able to help her? He remembered the sound of the many voices in the shack that Mercy had entered the night before. Could he trust these unknown Outsiders to take care of her?

Outside was a large city with an unknown number of prisoners, but surely they would outnumber the army sent to bring them down.

His decision was made. One extra person in a mob would not tip the balance, but one friend could make all the difference if that was all you had. Kelsee had lost everything and was going home. Luca rubbed his forehead. He ought to be her friend even though he didn't understand her. He needed to remind her of who she was, just like she had done for him.

Outside had made its way back into him, since being here he had resorted to his old way of thinking but she had reminded him that was not the Luca that she knew, and that was not the Luca that he was anymore. She deserved an apology from him and he was determined that he would deliver it. He hoped that it was not too late.

As the last row left the square, Luca sprinted out of his hiding place and to the Compassion Gate. The scanner was still lit up. Luca hummed the tune as he tapped the series of buttons. It took four attempts for the tune to match the code, but the gate slid silently open. Luca squeezed through as soon as it was wide enough and ran down the passage. It was even colder than the streets of Outside. The tall walls stretched skyward but allowed very little sunlight to permeate the shadows. His footfalls echoed and Luca tried to tread lightly.

He could hear voices ahead. The curve of the wall hid Kelsee and Alec from sight. Luca proceeded carefully. Alec had carried a weapon just like the others and he didn't want to put either Kelsee or himself in danger.

'I don't want to discuss it,' said Kelsee in a more natural voice once again. 'Take me to my grandfather.'

'The power is only auxiliary. The lift isn't working. We'll need to take the stairs.'

'I don't care how we get there. Just stop arguing about it.'

A second set of beeps and a slow squeal of metal resonated towards Luca.

'This way,' Alec said.

Luca approached tentatively.

Kelsee and Alec were nowhere to be seen. But next to the doors of the elevator that were firmly shut was a squeaking sliding door that was closing. Luca slid through the gap quickly.

Luca had entered a plain and dimly lit concrete hallway. There was a small landing before steps led downwards and then turned a corner. He stood still and listened. He could hear the tapping of feet against the stairs. He peered over the banister and saw two hands on the handrail a few levels down descending into the darkness. Luca was grateful for the near silence of the soft soled trainers but still trod carefully as he followed them downwards.

The light to the lower landing flickered off just as he turned the corner to the next flight of stairs. Luca sped up, aware that he may be left in darkness. Quickly, the bulb lit again.

There was a hesitation in the tapping of feet below, Luca peered over the banister but quickly pulled back to the wall as someone below leaned out and was about to look up. Alec had seen the light come on. Luca inspected the lamp. Below it, were two angled sensors tracking movement. He had caused the light to come back on but could not risk being discovered, he must move closer to Alec and Kelsee.

'We don't have time for this. I want to see my grandfather,' Kelsee said urgently.

Luca crept down the stairs, using Kelsee's voice to cover his steps. At the next landing the lamp stayed on. Luca swept his hand over the sensor to ensure that it had caught his movement. He had found the right gap between them but was eager for them to move on so that he would not be discovered.

Luca remembered the sickly and cramped elevator trip to the Maglev station. He was not aware, until now though, just how far below the surface they had travelled. It must have been necessary to build a tunnel under the sea to provide for the Maglev. The road that linked Outside to the shore was obviously not enough or serviceable for the trains. Perhaps it was just to keep the Outsiders even more unconnected to the wealth of the world that was around them and for Tropolis to stay in control.

Luca was able to keep a safe distance but was relieved when the stairs came to an end in a small lobby. The exit door had been pushed so wide that it had caught on ground and was jammed open.

Luca approached the doorway cautiously. A stationary Maglev train waited at the platform with all the doors raised open. He could not see either Kelsee or Alec but he heard his uncle's voice.

'I am aware that this is an unauthorised request.' There was a pause. 'You do not seem to understand the urgency, put me through to Mr Barret's office.' Alec's voice was coming from one of the far carriages. 'Mr Barret may be busy, but I assure you that he will not mind being disturbed, put me through.'

'Is there a problem?' Kelsee asked.

'No Miss, we will get the Maglev on its way in no time.' Alec then changed his tone once again. 'I want to speak with Mr Barret please.' Luca crept out from the doorway. He crouched low and sped towards the open carriages. 'My authority? Excuse me, but to whom am I speaking?' Luca ducked into the closest doorway and ducked low so that he would not be seen through the windows. 'Mara Hutchings' office? I would prefer to speak with Mr Barret himself... Very well. I am requesting that the Maglev be moved from the recycling plant back to the city entrance building... Yes, I know, but a second Maglev can be sent in its place... Of course I wasn't going to disturb Mr Barret with this!...'

Kelsee's voice then interrupted. 'Tell them you have me with you.'

Alec paused. 'I have his granddaughter here... Yes I have the control panel unlocked... 600 yes... 508. Great! Thank you!... Yes, we will be coming to the entrance building directly.'

'Are we going now?' Kelsee asked.

'One moment Miss. Just setting the destination.'

'That's not the code for my grandfather's house.'

'No miss, we are going to the office.'

The door slid down the carriage roof and sealed Luca inside. His heart fluttered and he took a deep breath. He peered towards the front of the Maglev, but there were too many carriages to catch a glimpse of Kelsee. Suddenly, the Maglev was on its way back to Tropolis.

The train moved almost silently. Luca slouched to the floor. He had been desperately fleeing the place he was heading back to. Everything had flipped over. He was alone, chasing after a girl that had convinced him she was sympathetic but was proving his judgement wrong by running back to the man who had caused all the problems in the first place. He thumped his fist against the floor. How could he have been so stupid? His only hope would be that she would listen to his request, to think of Mercy's kindness and plead her case with the man of power. To ask her not to tell of his mother, Eban and the others in Campion. If only they had been able to avoid taking her with them when they had escaped Tropolis in the first place. If only he had listened to Alec.

Luca hung his head. It was his fault. He had been the one who had driven her back to the comfort and familiarity of home. He only had himself to blame. His unkindness, his selfish words, his running back to an Outsider's heart had hurt her so badly that she would return to a system that she had not agreed with.

He forced himself to focus on the facts.

The things he was certain of was that Kelsee had hated the Tropolite system and had wanted to escape too. She had also cared for Mercy and Eban and had at one time cared for him.

Luca closed his eyes, just sitting in the carriage seemed to stir up lies and he did not want to focus on them. He had dealt with his anger and pain by accusing her. He couldn't do that again. Kelsee did care for him. Her note had asked for forgiveness, that wasn't the language of a person who didn't care. He focused again. If he could talk to her, she would listen, he was sure of it.

Luca opened his eyes once more. The last time he had been on this journey he had been a very different person. His goal had been the self-centred ambition of an Outsider, desperate for wealth, but he had been changed. He had the choice to step out from this dark tunnel a different person. He was shocked by his lack of fear, he was prepared to risk his freedom for her. He would speak to her as soon as he could. As soon as the Maglev stopped, he would appeal to her and face his uncle. Maybe Alec would let him leave again.

It was only when warm light flowed into the carriage that Luca was shaken from his thoughts. The gentle vibrations of the moving train ceased and the doors slid upwards.

Again, the stark contrast of the extravagance of Tropolis to Outside, and to Campion, was frightening. The high vaulted ceiling was embellished with hundreds of mirrors. He was grateful for his decision to approach them, there would, after all be nowhere to hide in this space.

Alec had already stepped from the Maglev with Kelsee following closely behind. As they approached the sweeping archway that led to the stairwell, Luca jumped from the carriage.

'Wait!'

Kelsee and Alec turned.

'Luca!' Kelsee said first smiling them frowning at him.

'It was you!' Alec whispered. 'What are you doing here?'

'You can't go back to Barrett! Please Kelsee!'

'I need to speak with my grandfather. Get out of here!'

'I'm sorry! I'm so sorry!' Luca called as he rushed forward. 'Please, don't let him hurt Mercy or Eban. Don't tell him about Campion.'

Kelsee shook her head. 'What?' She seemed lost for words.

'I know you want to be back in Tropolis, I'm sorry I let you down.'

'Luca!' Kelsee began her eyes wide.

Alec grabbed Luca and pushed him to the side and held him up against the wall. 'Be quiet! Wait there!' He commanded. Turning Kelsee away from Luca, he directed her through the arch so that they could not be seen.

A few moments passed. Luca frowned. He could feel the heat rising in his face as he realised that Alec had left him alone. He gingerly stepped away from the wall and was about to peer around the arch to see where they had gone when he heard another voice.

'Excellent work Alec!' Her tone was almost sickly sweet. 'And you, my dear Miss Barret, are so well and so alive despite our worst fears.'

'Mara Hutchings!' Alec exclaimed. 'I wasn't expecting anyone to meet us, let alone you personally. I would like to see Mr Barrett,' Alec said quietly.

'There is no need for that. I will take her from here.'

'You must be busy,' Alec began. Luca thought that his uncle was trying to convince Mara Hutchings to leave Kelsee with him. Had they formed a different plan inside the train? Alec continued, 'I would prefer ...'

'I think you are forgetting your rank, Alec, I said I will take her. Just jump back on the Maglev and get back to your place.'

'I don't mind if Alec takes me,' Kelsee said, her voice shaking a little. 'Really, I don't want to bother you.'

'No bother at all, the same code should work the Maglev. Take her.'

'Ma'am!' a couple of gruff voices obeyed.

'Ow!' Kelsee said quietly. 'Let go of me.'

'Your grandfather will see you now. Come with me and stop making a fuss.'

'I don't want to see him when you are there!' Kelsee protested, or possibly pleaded.

'Now, now Miss Barret,' Hutchings cooed. 'The more you struggle the harder they will have to restrain you. We can't have you running off again now can we.' Her tone changed, 'Get back to your post Alec, immediately,' she commanded.

'Of course.' Alec obeyed.

Alec stepped back through the arch. He put out his hand and restrained Luca, urging him, silently to stay where he was. Alec was frowning and his shoulders were hunched. He boarded the front carriage of the Maglev. After a few moments the train moved away.

Luca heard the fading voice of Hutchings. 'Get in contact with Atticus,' she said, 'Tell him to deal with Alec so that I never have to see him again.' She paused. 'Really man! Tell Atticus to kill him!'

Luca was stunned. The platform was empty and the sounds of Kelsee protesting were fading fast. Luca had no way to warn his uncle of the fate this woman had just sealed and felt powerless to help Kelsee.

He stepped away from the wall and approached the archway. Glancing up he saw the words lining the arch and struggled, more than ever, to believe them.

WELCOME TO TROPOLIS

Chapter 17
Eban's Story
16h 08m

Eban threw the lock handle into the swelling water and it disappeared into the depths. He felt the firm grip on his shoulder. The Campion Brigadier was breathing heavily. Before Eban turned to face him, he knew that he was in trouble.

'What have you done?' Alard said.

'The right thing.' Eban replied confidently.

'How?'

Eban turned. 'Outsiders need you!' Alard looked at him through narrowed eyes. 'And if you won't go to them, they will,' he said pointing to his friends that were disappearing along the beach on the other side of the river.

'All you have done is put them and us at risk,' Alard said angrily.

'If that is the case, why do they go so freely?'

The Campion officer grunted. 'We have all you need here. Why expose Campion to Tropolis?'

Eban nodded. 'True, you have plenty here,' he agreed, 'And enough for many others. In fact, probably enough for all the Outsiders too.'

'How do you know that?' Alard began. 'Never mind!'

'You're not denying it then.'

'There is no point, since you already have all the information you need,' Alard said sarcastically.

'Yet you still choose to sit back and let them suffer?'

Alard continued to march Eban back along the beach away from the river. 'Outside isn't all that bad. Tropolis are supplying the care that the people need.'

Eban stopped suddenly and dug in his heels. 'Tropolis supplying care? Where did you hear that?' Eban asked thinking that Luca's assumptions of Campion's indifference was closer than he liked.

Alard let go of Eban. 'I've seen the supplies invoices and delivery dates. Tropolis have been backing your lot up for years. It is us they hate and want terminated,' Alard said regurgitating the Network propaganda.

'Outsiders aren't supplied with anything except the barges loaded with rubbish to sort through. Do you not understand that the Outsiders are trapped on that island?'

'I'm not talking about it with you. We have to deal with what you have done before Tropolis come after us.'

'Really? You want to be blind to what Outside go through just to survive another day? Where are you getting your information?'

'Come on Eban,' Alard said slowly. 'We have no choice but to go to Headquarters.'

'If you are gleaning your facts from the Network, you have got to take the blinkers off. The Network is corrupt and manipulates everything.'

'You know, I hate going to Headquarters. You had better not have ruined my life on land,' Alard said turning away from Eban and doing his best to ignore him.

Eban would not be deterred. He followed closely behind and persisted. 'You must have spoken to others in the past, other Outsiders that make their way to Campion.'

Alard crossed the small bridge over the gully that had flowed so full of water but was now emptying rapidly. But instead of heading inland, he continued along the beach.

'What about Willow?' Eban pressed. 'What has she said about Outside?'

'She is our story teller.'

Eban opened his hands. 'Meaning what exactly?'

'Meaning; she has no idea what is real and what is not.' Alard pulled the grey jacket tighter around him and dropped his gaze to the pebbles.

'I don't think you believe that,' Eban stated. 'She may have been with Campion a long time, but I doubt that the stories that she bought with her from Outside have ever changed.'

'Stories are not bought from Outside. When we have new members to Campion, they are told to start afresh.'

Eban nodded, remembering the instructions from Major Thomas, the woman officer with the severe haircut, who had interrogated the friends at Campion Headquarters. 'But I expect people still talk. I mean, you can't just walk away from one life and it not affect you?'

'Enough!' Alard said raising his voice. He quickened his pace.

'If you want to know anything about Outside,' Eban said much more gently, 'I'd be happy to tell you, but I guess you may not want to know.'

He followed Alard along the beach without saying another word. He wondered how long it would take to walk to the sea forts from the mouth of the river.

After a while, Alard took a path slightly higher than the beach where the pebbles had been overcome with grass and weeds. It was much easier to walk on and Eban began to hum a little.

The wind was picking up and the light was beginning to fade a little when Alard eventually stepped off to the side where some large rocks stood and a gnarled tree grew. He began to push aside the undergrowth. Eban approached.

A dark green tarp was tied neatly over a large object. Eban thought that it had been left there for a considerable amount of time by the stains and patches of deterioration to the surface. As Alard swiftly tugged at the ropes the cover lifted off and revealed a small boat. It was nothing like the camouflaged version that he had sat in before. This was much simpler. It didn't have any fancy rooftop or on board computer. A small, square motor was fitted to the rear and there were planks that spanned the width to sit on.

Alard began to drag it out from the hiding place. 'So, does Outside have guards on the walls?' he asked casually.

'I've never seen them,' Eban replied seriously. 'The walls are so high I can't imagine why they would need to put guards there.'

'Good.'

'So what's the plan?' Eban asked. 'I'm guessing we aren't going to headquarters.'

'We get them back before there is any more trouble.' Alard looked up at the darkening sky. 'I don't think I have any other choice if I want to stay on land.' He began to shove at the boat.

Eban did not want to collect his friends at all. He wanted them to reach Outside. Maybe there was something in Alard's plan that could work for them. If he could see Outside, the real Outside, maybe Campion would listen.

Eban grabbed the other side of the boat and lifted it with great effort. They struggled up to the grassy path and then down the shingle beach to the water's edge.

'You talk about living on land as if it could be taken from you,' Eban puffed out as the lowered the boat.

'I don't do well living at sea.'

'Well, I hope you cope with waves. I think there may be some bad weather coming.'

'It isn't the sea that is the problem,' Alard said half smiling. 'The waves don't bother me, but here,' Alard leaned into the hull of the boat, 'You will need one of these.' He tossed Eban a life jacket that had been carefully blacked out with dark paint. Eban shook the creepy crawlies off and quickly put it on.

They pushed the boat out onto the water and leapt inside. Eban wriggled his toes in his now sodden trainers. Alard pulled on the string attached to the motor several times before the engine started with a roar and a small puff of smoke.

'Not the most economical, but glad I kept it,' Alard commented.

The small boat skittered over the surface of the sea. The little engine pushed them fast along the route that they had taken. Within a few minutes they had passed the river mouth and had rounded the edge of the cliff.

'You sure there is no guard?' Alard called out.

'Can't be certain. But Tropolis can't spare anyone.'

'They'll see us from here,' Alard said.

Eban turned and glanced at Alard. He briefly saw Alard's furrowed brow and narrowed eyes. The Campion Brigadier would not turn back. Eban hoped that Mercy, Luca and Kelsee were far enough ahead so that Alard would get a good look at the prison that he believed Tropolis cared for.

Rain began to fall hard and fast. The wind rushed against them and increased the chill of the weather against their skin. The small skiff was working hard to move forward through the head wind.

Eban could just make out the glowing walls of Outside in the dusk light.

The tiny boat crept ever closer. The wind was kind in that it took the rainclouds away but still fought against the boat.

'Look!' Alard exclaimed. Eban had seen it too. A sudden but fairly brief light had shone against the wall. 'You said that there were no guards.'

'I don't think it is a guard, Eban replied. 'Surely they would use light all the time.'

'It might be them,' Alard said pushing the boat towards the patch of brief light.

Moonlight poured through the clouds as the skiff came closer to the wall. The cool beams highlighted the foam of the crashing waves against the rocks at the base of Outside island.

Eban clung to the sides. The boat felt especially insignificant dwarfed against the towering wall and dangerously close to the swell. He watched closely for any other movement above, although being this far below the base of the wall was a disadvantage for Alard but bought a smile to Eban. Even if they did find them, there would be no way to bring them aboard.

Eban caught sight of the thing that had drawn them in so close to danger. Alard gasped.

An old message was smeared on the wall. There were no words but the dark paint stood out against the pale render. A five petalled-flower had been painted there; large and bold. It was so different to the cold image that had graced the sea fort and not as careful as Mercy's tattoo, but the Campion flower stood firm. The surface had cracked and fallen off in places, taking some of the design with it. This painting had been here for some time.

Alard turned the vessel and continued to skirt the wall. Eban watched him closely. Alard pursed his lips then reached up to touch his mouth. He was muttering to himself.

'What did you say?' Eban asked.

'How did they know about us?' Alard asked.

Eban shrugged and did not answer. How did anyone know anything when they were trapped inside the wall? But they did. Somehow, someone had found out about Campion and were asking for help. He peered up at the wall again, wondering at the state of the people inside. He hoped that Luca had found his father.

The longer they searched the more Alard muttered as he directed the skiff around the wall. The pounding waves covered the sound of the engine and the moonlight ensued that the small boat would not be caught on the rocks.

'There!' Alard pointed.

Eban wanted to stand but didn't want to make it any more unstable. A dark figure was disappearing into the wall. He squinted into the pale light. He was certain that Luca was gone. Perhaps the line that ran up the wall was a crack or gap, perhaps they had found a way to enter Outside unnoticed.

'Luca!' Alard called loudly but his voice seemed to be drowned out by the waves.

Two smaller figures followed Luca closely into the concealed entrance. Eban thought that perhaps one of them had hesitated and turned, but they did not stop for the skiff.

'It's too late, they've gone!' Eban called to Alard who looked even paler in the moonlight.

'I have no choice then,' Alard said sadly, 'We have to go to Headquarters.'

There had been very little conversation as the tiny boat jumped over the dark waves. Eban had tried to talk, but Alard had given no reply. He had no idea how Alard knew where to go but soon the boat was slowing and the dark forms of the sea forts loomed over head.

Eban shivered. The rain had soaked him and the wind had chilled him, but it was what the Campion headquarters stood for that made him uneasy. He knew that Mercy had spoken the truth, as she always did about Campion. He understood that they weren't holding back from Outside because of their lack but only for their fear of lack.

He wondered if others had the chance to came back to the sea fort once they had been settled on land or if they were unceremoniously forgotten as they could take care of themselves.

Brigadier Alard fidgeted at the helm. He had cleared his throat several times and straightened his jacket. Alard removed his hat, folded it and tucked it into his pocket. Moments later he had pulled the hat back on again. Maybe the fort held a power over many people.

Eban purposefully relaxed his shoulders and took a slow breath. Within a moment, he was calm again. This was only a building that housed fellow humans. He could sense the adrenalin, that had obviously unnerved Alard. Eban's heart raced a little. He would not let Campion Headquarters produce fear, his being here should inspire him to hope.

A spot light dazzled Eban before he felt the boat rising into the air. The crane jangled but lifted them smoothly.

Eban followed Alard up into the holding bay where a young Campion soldier, a little older than Eban helped them in.

The flood light dimmed as the doors slid shut hiding the boat below them. Two caged lamps emitted a dull, warm glow throughout the room and the indicator on the camera in the corner showed it was recording their moves.

'Please inform Major Thomas that Brigadier Alard is here to speak with her.'

'Yes Sir!' the lad saluted and dashed off through the door to the right which shut firmly behind him. The circular handle twisted locking them in.

Alard removed his hat for good this time and smoothed his hair. He rubbed at his chin. Eban saw the grimace as Alard was frustrated that he was not as clean shaven as he would like to be. There was very little movement from Alard for quite some time. He stood very straight and tall, a posture that Eban had not seen in him before. Eban yawned then smiled at the stern glance that he received. Approaching the Campion flower he ran his fingers over the cold metal. Eban considered the design. The hammered patination was fine and precise, this symbol had once been an emblem not just of rebellion but also of courage. He would need to remind them.

A series of metallic bangs accompanied the turning wheel on the door just before it opened giving Eban warning. He moved away from the wall and stood a little behind Alard.

The door creaked. The young soldier had returned.

'If you will follow me. She is ready to see you Sir.'

'Yet she wouldn't come to me herself,' Alard said. Eban couldn't help but notice the irritation.

They were led along the narrow corridor. Eban peered up the stairwell at the end and was grateful that they were not being taken to the secure room upstairs. Instead, the officer opened the communications room. Eban could not help but bounce a little as he walked in. He looked intently at as many screens as possible, searching for news of Mercy, Luca and Kelsee. There was nothing. No images or news from Outside seemed to be evident except a highlighted Maglev schedule change on the screen nearest to him. One train with ten carriages was due to be arriving at the Outside underground station early the next day.

The room was strangely quiet compared to Eban's last visit. There was only the buzz of radio communications through headphones. The troupe appeared very busy though. Several were working away at their screens, twisting and shifting through images and diagrams, while others sorted through code, highlighting sections and manipulating sequences. It all appeared very neat and rule abiding as if they were trying to impress.

A hasty tapping and curt reply refocussed Eban's attention.

The soldier held the door open. 'Please go through, Sir,' he said politely.

'Thomas.' Alard bobbed his head once.

Major Thomas stood quickly to attention and saluted. Her short cropped hair remained unruffled but her wide eyes at the sight of Eban spoke differently. 'Sir!'

'At ease Thomas. Take a seat.'

'Thank you, Sir.'

A sturdy and slightly battered, wooden desk sat between Alard and Thomas. A small box with several flashing lights rested at one end of the surface alongside a thin tablet with a blank face. Behind the Major was a large roll down screen. Eban peered behind him and saw the projector mounted on the ceiling. Nothing was playing and the cord that would unroll the screen swung as if it had just been used. Eban could just about make out some scraps of coloured paper poking out from behind.

Major Thomas perched, stiff backed, on her chair, she did not appear at ease.

'Eban, you sit here,' Alard said placing Eban almost in the centre of the room whilst he pulled up a second chair and joined him.

'To what do I owe this honour Sir?' Thomas said after a few seconds of painful silence.

'Yes, I suppose it has been a while,' Alard replied not answering her question. Alard tightened his fists on his lap.

'At least five years.'

'No, closer to seven actually Thomas.'

'Sir, is the communication system down?' she asked hopefully. 'You could have sent word through someone else.'

'Communication is all,' Alard raised his wrist, pressed a series of buttons then spoke into it, 'Loud and clear!' The sound repeated from Thomas's wrist.

'So I see Sir.'

'I believe you have met Eban.'

'I have,' she replied shortly, glaring at Eban. 'I had commissioned the ex-contestants to your land group just as you explicitly ordered. Have they been causing trouble?'

'You have a lot of questions, Thomas. Am I making you nervous?'

'A little Sir,' Thomas admitted. 'We haven't had such direct orders from you for quite some time and now we have a visit too.' She smiled but it had no effect on the rage in her eyes.

'I should put you out of your misery then,' Alard said. 'What do you know of Outside?' Alard began, 'And specifically what the state of the people are there and how exactly they are being cared for.'

Major Thomas' gaze flickered towards Eban and then back to the Brigadier. 'The people of Outside are refusing, at present, to produce electricity for Tropolis. Tropolis are, however, working to re-establish power by moving extra workers into the community to motivate them. Tropolis continue to work with the people there in much the same way as we have seen over the past decade. They are, of course, unfortunately lacking in educating the community.'

'Hmm, interesting.' Alard got up from the chair and walked over to the window. He looked briefly out. 'And is there any need for us to seek out methods to help the community?'

'We only help those who seek us out, that is the policy that was set out by yourself, Sir,' the major replied, 'The ex-contestants are the most recent candidates.'

'Yes, Thomas, I know who wrote it.' Alard sighed. 'It is one of our covenant promises. To help those that seek it.' Alard nodded in agreement to his own statement. 'And what is our success rate for those that ask?'

'Success rate, Sir?

Alard came back to his chair, sat again and leaned into the desk. 'Yes! When asked do we help?'

Eban could feel the heat in Alard's question and he smiled to himself.

'Of course, Sir!'

'Then why haven't we gone to Outside?'

Major Thomas sat back in her chair confidently. 'They have no need for our help. They are a fairly contented people, who have found favour with Tropolis.'

Alard turned. 'Eban, is that correct?'

Thomas stood suddenly. 'Those that come into the care of Campion are not permitted to speak of their past.'

Eban was shocked by Major Thomas' strict employment of the rules. She had been adamant about their story being left in the past before. Eban rubbed his chin. Surely, what he had been through with Luca and Mercy had been what made them who they were. He looked over at Alard and frowned.

Alard was nodding. 'I know the rules, Thomas. But why was that rule introduced? It wasn't so that that we would never know what has happened, it was protect those that had stories that were full of shame and remorse. I know of those that had to do abominable things to survive, things that no one should ever have to recall. Isn't that right?'

Thomas sank to her chair. 'Yes, Sir.'

'So, if there are no further objections,' Alard said raising his eyebrows to Thomas, 'Eban, would you mind answering the question; have Outside found favour with Tropolis and are they contented?'

Eban made the most of the opportunity. 'I have no idea what she means by favour. The people there are kept under strict poverty. They have no way of escaping their misery. Day and night they work the heaps gleaning for food and anything that can be sold for credits. The children suffer and the community has been dying for years. The people starve.'

'It seems, then, that there are two very different stories, Thomas.'

'Be that as it may, Sir, they do not seek help.'

Alard cleared his throat. 'When was the last time that Outside was scouted by the sea patrol?'

'Er,' Thomas began frowning at the sudden change of subject, 'Do you want the exact date?'

He crossed his arms and sat back in his chair. 'Give me a rough idea.'

'It has been several years since we have sent out a sea patrol due to the heavily guarded wall and strong Tropolis presence.'

Eban sighed and stared at his hands on his lap. Several years? Eban bit down on his tongue to hold back the tears. Outsiders had struggled as if they were invisible.

'Interesting!' Alard said. 'How do you know about the security situation?'

'That information is confidential, Sir.' Eban looked up to see Major Thomas nodding at him.

'I will stop you if you start to say something that I am not happy for Eban to hear. Please continue.'

She looked at Eban through narrowed eyes. 'We have secured an intercepted channel on the Network. It relays the information on Outside. Everything from security to provision, competition candidates to barge numbers.'

Alard stood. 'And who controls the Network?'

'Tropolis, Sir. But this is a coded channel.' Eban knew that she was trying to convince Alard of the credentials.

'Does this source of information agree with Eban in regards to the state of poverty that he recounts?' Thomas shook her head. 'Does it verify the health status of the community?'

'No, Sir, but ...'

'Stop!' Alard slammed his hand on the desk. 'Did you think to confirm any of the information with scouts?'

'No, Sir.'

'Therefore, have you relied on a twisted form of communication to determine how we should act?'

'Yes, Sir.'

'Finally we agree!' Alard walked over to the tiny sea stained window. 'Eban and I have recently come back from the wall that surrounds Outside. It has no guards, and why would it when the wall is so high and the people are so down trodden that they sort through rubbish to find food?' Alard turned back to Thomas. 'We must learn to sift through the information and discard the lies.' His voice was softer now, and Eban saw Alard nod in agreement to his own statement. 'Eban and I saw a call for help painted on the wall. We must do something.' Alard placed his hand on Thomas' shoulder. 'You have been cut off from the land community and I have hidden away from the responsibility that was entrusted to me for far too long. I have let you and your team down. I'm sorry.'

Eban watched as Major Thomas swallowed hard.

'Thank you, Sir,' she replied. She looked at Alard full in the face. 'I am sorry that we have trusted in the wrong information, Sir. What would you have us do?'

'We work together,' Alard said, smiling.

Suddenly Eban wanted to thrust his fists into the air. Campion were about to act. 'Yes!' he said containing his excitement. 'Now that is fire and courage.'

Alard laughed. 'We noticed a small entry on the seaward side of the wall. I suggest that we get as many boats as we can to the that point and begin to ferry the Outsiders to land.'

'There'll be too many!' Thomas stated.

'Yes, for the boats, but we can go back time and time again. Tropolis already have issues with their electricity supply so they will not know that their workforce is gone until it is too late.'

'We may have a problem. Like I said before, Tropolis are sending in a new workforce early tomorrow morning.'

'How?' asked Eban. 'The people in Tropolis are sick, very sick. The streets are deserted and the people are restricted to their homes. Compassion fatigue is spread widely through Tropolis with only the very wealthy able to pay for treatment.'

'Really? Barrett's granddaughter said the same but I thought she was just trying to avoid questioning.'

'The average Tropolite will not be able to travel to Outside, so who are they sending?' Eban emphasised.

'I guess that may be propaganda too then,' Thomas suggested, 'But they need to restore the power supply somehow.'

'How many do you have in a fleet and how long before they can be ready? How many passengers can we take at a time?'

'We have a fleet of 26 boats, not all are designed to carry passengers though.'

'But can they?' Alard asked.

'They could. We could manage a skeleton crew on each – maybe up to 24 hours before they are assembled. The smaller, class A, vessels would take eight or possibly ten if the sea is calm. We have twenty of those. The larger class 2 boat will carry more people but wouldn't be able to get close to the wall. We have five of those. They may be bigger but they are for fishing. At a guess, maybe up to thirty people. We have one larger, but that is out on a distance trip and couldn't be back here until perhaps, four days' time.'

'So that is 350 people per trip. I need this fleet and crew ready to leave within six hours.'

'That would be difficult sir.'

'Difficult, but not impossible.'

'No sir. That would however, leave headquarters vulnerable.'

'I understand that, but we have left Outside vulnerable for far too long.'

Chapter 18
Mercy's story
12h 21m

'I think I should stay, just for a while and find out what is going on.' Mercy could not help but smile a little. To hear Gunter talking of other people as friends was far beyond what she was used to with him. She must see what had caused such a change in him and why he was eager for her to go with him. She reached out for Luca and squeezed his hand. 'You must go to your father.' She was confident that Kelsee would be able to help him and comfort him if needed. Kelsee had, of course, already shown that she was incredibly capable in the unknown and she obviously cared for Luca more than he realised. 'Where will you be?' Mercy asked, she would join them there.

Kelsee pulled Luca's notebook from her pocket and carefully passed it to him. 'Draw a map,' she suggested to Luca.

Luca took the book roughly and began to smear mud over the paper. Mercy glanced at Kelsee and watched her hopeful smile fade as she sighed.

The diagram Luca drew was simple but clear. 'My place is this side of the settlement, nestled into the rocks about three rows back.'

Luca carefully tore out the page. Mercy thought that the notebook may not be the item of little value that he had tossed away after all. 'Thank you!'

'I've got that. Go and find your father,' Mercy encouraged. 'I'll be there as soon as I can.'

Mercy had no time to watch them leave, she was already being led back to the shack.

The shacks seemed closer together and smaller than she remembered. Having been with Campion and out in the wide open spaces where the sky stretched out over the vast expanse, Outside felt cramped and closed in. Even the darkness was bleak, with very few spots of light and the starry sky was restricted to the edge of the wall.

Gunter opened the door and suddenly the talking stopped and then began again louder and more excited than ever.

'Mercy!' One lady stood and pulled Mercy forward.

'My girl, it is so good to see you.' Another patted her on the back.

'We thought you were gone for good.'

'Now we will not fail!' A man said confidently.

The room was full of people Mercy knew, yet they all seemed so different. There was still the evidence of life on the heaps but there was a joy and comradery between them.

Gunter pushed his way through the throng. He ushered those perched on the bench to move over and set Mercy on the seat.

'Can I just stay a bit longer?' Gunter asked.

An older man laughed. Mercy was so unaccustomed to the Outsiders laughing that it shocked her. She fixed her gaze on Griffin. He had lived in one of the shipping containers with his family for several years. She remembered his mother, who had been fairly old, by Outsider standards, when she had died. Griffin had taken on the role as foreman of the blue heap from her in his twenties. He must have had this responsibility for over half of Mercy's life. The problem with working in such harsh conditions had intensified already difficult problems with his health. Griffin had a deep curve in his spine and his hands were knotted with joint pain and movement issues. Mercy had often visited him when the days were cold and wet. He had struggled with his workload, and since his home was part of his work station, he had battled through the pain in order to care for his family. He did not want to burden his son with the task so had pushed through.

She smiled at the sound of his contagious laugh. 'Not at all,' he said. 'The younger folk need to be informed of the plan before it is too late. They must be stationed at dawn.'

Gunter nodded and shrugged. 'Don't say anything without me.' He squeezed back through the people and out into the night.

'You have a plan Griffin?' asked Mercy.

'Yes!' several voiced.

'Before we get to that, Mercy, how are you? We thought you would never come back.'

'I wasn't sure of what would happen either. So many contestants are sent to Tropolis and so few are successful in bringing their families out of this place.' She smiled sadly. 'I have missed you all so much, and yet here you all are. Together! Talking! What has happened to you?'

'I don't think any of us knew just how much you meant to us,' one woman said reaching over and squeezing Mercy's shoulder.

'Thank you, Gwenda,' Mercy replied reaching up and touching Gwenda's steady hand.

Griffin slapped his hands onto his legs. 'You made us all see each other again. We found a common loss that brought us together, when you left.'

Mercy nodded. She had hoped that one day the Outsiders would realise just what richness they had in their lives everyday with the people around them.

Griffin clenched his fists and flexed his muscles. 'It only took a few of us to start talking, and suddenly we were working together to bring down the monster that is Tropolis.'

Mercy shuddered Griffin's words. 'The world beyond the wall is so different,' she began. The unfamiliarity of the eager faces of those around her unsettled her a little. She was careful in how she continued. 'Outside has been kept under strict control of Tropolis, but Tropolis is not what you think it is.'

Griffin laughed. 'Is it free?' he asked sarcastically. The crowd were roused by his words.

'Yes … and no!' Mercy answered. 'It would be unwise to go about this without thinking about the consequences.'

Griffin stood. 'Are you saying we should let them continue to stamp on us? To scavenge a life from the heaps and feed their dominance. We have refused to work the furnaces, and that had felt like the only thing we could do, but it isn't. We can be free from them. They need to know that they should not underestimate us.'

Mercy raised her palms to him. 'Griffin, please sit down and let us talk this through.' She waited until he was seated once again. 'Tropolis are suffering, and not only because you have stopped the furnaces. They are desperate for electricity. Thousands of them are ill, so ill that they cannot leave their homes. They need your help. You have shown them that there is a need for communication.' Mercy saw that they doubted her. 'In fact, they are sending in extra workers to work on the furnaces in the morning.'

Griffin's eyes narrowed. 'How do you know that?' he asked.

'I saw an urgent message when I was with Campion.'

'Campion are real?' Gwenda asked.

Mercy thought of Eban. She knew his spirit and was certain that he would not let Alard and Campion ignore Outside. He would be working hard on their stubborn hearts. 'Absolutely!' Mercy replied. 'They found us after we escaped from Tropolis.'

'Then why haven't they done anything for us?' Griffin asked, but continued quickly. 'Because they are just as evil as Tropolis or as weak as we were. Are you with us Mercy, or are you with them?'

Mercy looked about the room and saw the faces of the people she had invested her time in. 'I am for you.' She paused, and pulled on the zip of her jacket, looking for the words to continue. She did not wish to take sides, there were so many hurting people inside this room but also in Tropolis and Campion.

'Glad to hear it!' Griffin announced enthusiastically and unaware of her thoughts. 'We are planning a rebellion,' he said nodding, 'And you are back just in time.'

'Rebellion?' Mercy exclaimed. 'Against what?'

He laughed harder than before. 'Tropolis of course!'

'Of course,' Mercy repeated frowning at him.

'The youngsters will be positioned at the docks at dawn. The power is down, and has been for days. We have discovered a chink in the enemy's armour! We can shut down the emergency supply if we can get the Tropolites that are here to be distracted. We will lead them over by the docks. Then we are going to send someone over the register gate and into the hut. It is just a matter to flicking the switch and taking out the fuse. Of course that will cause the cameras to shut down. After that the fence at the docks can be cut through and come down. The barges haven't had radio signal since the power cut so they will still arrive. We will take control of the ships, head back to Tropolis and take back what they have stolen from us for years.'

There was applause and cheers from all in the room.

'That is a lot!' Mercy commented.

Griffin indicated to Mercy. 'It all started with you!' he exclaimed, 'You got us talking and working together.' He did not wait for Mercy's response. 'If what you say about the extra workers is true, we will have to deal with them too. Ideas?'

'I expect they will use the Compassion Gate entry,' a man said standing at the back of the room. 'I suggest we station a gleaning group using the containers as cover. Whatever is gleaned can be quickly passed on and action taken. I doubt they would send more than a dozen workers, they would only need enough for the shifting machinery, they don't care about what might be burned.'

Griffin grunted. 'We'll need to re-direct maybe twice the number of Tropolis workers they'll send in so that we can ensure that they can be stopped. Volunteers?'

'I think I can spare about twenty from the docks group. They can be in place before dawn so that there will be no surprises.'

Mercy was shocked at the similarity between these Outsiders and the ones that they professed to be hating so much. 'What about helping Tropolis?' she asked.

'Why?' Griffin asked turning the corners of his mouth down. 'Why should we help them? It will be easier to take what is owed to us if they are as weak as you say. They can be confined to their luxurious and wasteful lives. It is time we took back what has been stolen from us and our families.'

Mercy could feel a weight sink in her soul. Outsiders had been mistreated for so long that it was understandable that they would seek revenge, but what else would they get in return? Would they be able to stop at just taking what was owed to them, whatever that might be. How do you evaluate the payment of the wrong doing of Tropolis? She knew the stories of each and every person crammed into this room. They each had a claim against their tyrant masters, but none of them were willing to love instead of hate. Mercy felt a shudder go down her spine.

'Griffin,' Mercy began, 'There must be another way.'

'You've seen the way they live and you know how we live. We demand that we be treated equally.'

'But what you are planning to do, is to force them into it,' Mercy said, 'Is that any better than they have treated you?'

Griffin shrugged. 'It is the only way they will listen,' he said and turning to the group, 'We must be heard.'

The volume of agreement drowned out any hope Mercy had of changing their minds. Tropolis had been too long in neglecting the poor and now they would pay their wages for doing so.

'Voices can be heard when you don't scream too. Please Griffin, promise me that you will think about it.'

'Sure,' he replied. 'Will you be with us?'

Mercy thought for a moment. 'I want Outsiders to be free, but I cannot promise to do this the way you have envisioned.' She stood. 'I will be with you, but if you or your rebellion get out of hand I will not be part of it. You need to remember that you have not been trained for combat, instead your lives have prepared you in other ways. Outsiders know how to be resourceful, they are able to give purpose to things that others may consider as worthless. We know how to give what little we have to the ones that we care about. Please, don't forget what a lifetime has taught you.' She moved towards the door.

'Where are you going?'

'My friend's father is likely to be very ill. I need to go and help.'

Griffin got to his feet and pulled Mercy into a hug. 'Thank you Mercy,' Griffin said quietly into her ear. 'I know that you have always spoken truth to me, even when I haven't wanted to hear it. Believe me, I will think about what you have said.'

She pushed away and saw the sincerity in his eyes. 'Thank you. I just don't want more lives to be wasted when they could be redeemed.'

'I know.' Griffin raised his voice a little. 'The docks will be occupied before dawn. I hope we will see you at the register gate.'

Mercy nodded. 'I'll be there.' She left the warm light of the shack and stepped out onto the dark street.

Despite the all the distressing, wild visions of what a rebellion might look like, Mercy was certain that it was time for Outside to act. She tucked her hair behind her ear and rubbed her neck. She knew with her whole heart that she would be there to support her people. It was the chosen method that caused her to feel anxious. If she were to inspire a different route, she would need to do so with the help of others and she wasn't confident that Griffin would be able to follow after her.

The street was empty. She glanced in the direction of the docks and although she could not see them, she knew that she would have to go there before dawn. She turned away. Her first concern was to ensure that Luca and his family were safe.

Mercy moved through the tightly packed and carefully constructed homes. There were no lights or voices from the friends that lived here. She supposed that they were sleeping and preserving as much energy as possible for the attack tomorrow. Each familiar shack she passed contained a friend and a story of desperation or suffering. She understood, fully, why the Outsiders had decided to take rebellious action. The battle of pride and anguish moved her to tears. Her friends had finally decided that they were family but they had fed on each other's bitterness. They had found their common ground, their hate for the tyrant of Tropolis.

The tiny houses that had once revealed the strength and resourcefulness of the people, now appeared littered with rubbish and held together with makeshift supports. Mercy forced herself to look deeper into the darkness. The maze of streets spoke to her of order, even in the haphazard buildings. She could not abandon the hope that she had for her people now. Perhaps order could still come.

The Lower-end Quarter was on the outskirts of the settlement. Mercy nodded to herself, knowing why Luca would have chosen such a place to live. When she had met him, she had found that he had been hiding from the world. She had not spoken to him before and even though she had actively sought him out, he always seemed to disappear as soon as she got close. He had shut out anyone and everyone. The Compassion Prize had, in fact, been the event that had changed his life and she was grateful for it. What it had offered was freedom from Outside, and Luca had experienced this to degrees that not even he understood yet. He had grown so much since Eban and herself had been with him. She could not shake the thought that the Lower-end Quarter would not be able to hold him back anymore.

She pulled out the scrap of paper with the muddy map and checked that she was heading in the right direction.

The dark wall felt more oppressive as she moved out from the centre of the settlement and closer to the outskirts. She knew how it was constructed but the façade spoke a different language to the hollow centre it hid. The rocks that stacked up either side of the slippery path were tall and strong. Luca had said that his place was in the third row, yet Mercy could not make out any resemblance to rows. Shacks were dotted here and there, nestled in the gaps between the rocks and sometimes, precariously under them.

'Luca! Kelsee!' Mercy spoke quietly. She leaned close to the homes and tried to peer into the dark rooms through gaps or distorted plastic. 'Luca? Kelsee?'

A small light filtered through a section of roof. Next to her a door slid to one side.

'Mercy!' Kelsee rushed forward and hugged her. 'You got here!' she said with a hushed voice.

'Luca?' Mercy asked as she pulled away. Kelsee's torch lit her face slightly. Mercy thought that Kelsee was stooped and had puffy eyes.

'He's asleep,' Kelsee said, 'He's exhausted. His dad is alive, but barely. Luca has done all he can, I hope it is enough.' Mercy thought that maybe that was why she appeared so sad. 'He hadn't eaten in days, possibly since Luca has been in Tropolis. He is so frail. Luca made him some food, fed him and now they are both asleep. Luca needs to rest, he is exhausted.'

'And you?'

'I've slept a little bit.'

'Is there anything I can do?'

'I don't think so,' Kelsee smiled a little. 'Luca has it all under control, but he isn't coping very well.'

Mercy peered over Kelsee's shoulder. The door was still open a little, but it was very dark inside. 'And you? Are you alright?'

Kelsee stepped away from the shack and sat on a rock nearby. Mercy followed her closely. 'What is it?'

'I had no idea!'

'Outside?'

'Yes!' She let her head droop and she covered her face with her hands. 'I don't understand how my grandfather could have let this happen.'

Mercy sat down next to her. She placed her arm around Kelsee's shoulder. Kelsee rested her head against Mercy.

Kelsee took a deep breath. 'I don't know what to think anymore. I do love my grandfather, yet all this,' she gestured to the street, 'all this, I don't know what this is, makes me think I don't know him at all.' Mercy rubbed Kelsee's shoulder. 'Luca has done all he can for his father but I can't help but wonder about what's next. What will happen to these people?'

Mercy sighed. 'We will find out tomorrow,' Mercy looked to the sky, '... or later today.' Kelsee turned suddenly towards her, pulling away from the hug. 'They are planning a rebellion against Tropolis if the workforce coming into Outside don't stop them.'

'How?'

'They will go over the fences and pirate the barges. It seems they will invade Tropolis and take what they think are due.'

'They are due a lot,' Kelsee said with fierce conviction.

'Yes, but I'm worried people will get hurt.'

'Tropolis won't be able to fight back,' Kelsee said carefully. 'It is a ghost city full of sickness. They aren't able to fight back.'

'Revenge is dangerous, Kelsee.'

'Then you need to make sure that they don't get revenge,' Kelsee said, then added quietly, 'But get justice instead.'

'I'm not sure that the leaders see the difference. I've been with them all this time and they are unable to change.'

Kelsee shook her head. 'Then talk to the people.'

'The younger Outsiders will be at the docks at dawn. I think that they might listen.'

'Good idea!' Kelsee replied. 'What about this workforce that Tropolis are sending?'

'I presume they will come via the Maglev and the Compassion Gate, but Griffin, the rebels' leader doesn't think it will be a large number due to the sickness with the Tropolites. He has planned a welcome party so that they won't get far. They were only coming to restore the furnaces and get the power back on in Tropolis.'

'I want to help. Can I come with you to the docks?'

Mercy saw that her friend was eager. 'I don't think that would be a good idea.' Kelsee lowered her head. 'If they know who you are, they may not listen to me at all.' Mercy squeezed her friend's hand. 'I don't want you to get hurt.'

Kelsee shrugged. 'I guess I'll stay here then.' She peered up at Mercy. 'Do you want Luca to help?'

Mercy shook her head. 'His father is very frail you said?' Kelsee nodded. 'Luca should stay here then.' Kelsee's shoulders were hunched. 'Perhaps you could come along a bit later, after I have spoken with them.'

'Alright,' Kelsee said cheerily. 'How do I get to the docks?'

'Follow this path until you get to the wider street, bear right. Hang on!' Mercy opened the map and pointed to the diagram Luca had drawn. 'The road will run parallel to the wall, take you past the Compassion Gate, past the shipping containers and eventually onto the docks. It isn't the fastest route, but at least you won't get lost in the back streets.' She handed the map to Kelsee who took a long look at it before she carefully folded it and placed it in her pocket.

'Great,' Kelsee said confidently. 'I'll see if Luca's father is well enough to leave alone for a while so that Luca can come too.'

'But if there is any sound of trouble, I want you to stay away.' Mercy wondered at her plan. 'Better yet, I will come and get you when I know you will be safe.'

'Will there be trouble?' Kelsee asked. 'You shouldn't go if you will be in danger.'

'I don't think I will be in danger,' Mercy replied shaking her head. She considered what the Outsiders might do if they knew who Kelsee was. She shivered at the thought. 'I can't reassure you, Kelsee, although I really wish I could. These are my people and my friends. I know their lives and I know what they want and I hope that they will listen to me. It's best you stay here.'

Kelsee sighed. 'I understand,' she said. 'You look tired. You had better get some rest.'

'I don't think there is time,' Mercy said once again looking up at the sky. 'Dawn will be here before long and I need to go to the docks.' She hugged Kelsee tightly. 'Wait for me.' Mercy let go and got up to leave. 'Take care of Luca. He will need a friend.'

'I'm not sure how to take care of anyone in this place,' Kelsee replied her eyes bright and wide, 'But I'll try.'

Mercy didn't look back. She felt tears welling and her breath came in short gasps. The weight that she had been carrying in her heart for such a long time seemed to lift a little, and Kelsee had taken some of that burden. Kelsee's pity for the Outsiders was changed; her outlook had been transformed. Being with Luca, in his tiny shack, had left her different. Mercy knew that she could do very little to guide Kelsee now that she had experienced true compassion.

Wiping the tears from her cheeks, and energised by what she had witnessed, Mercy sped through the maze of pathways and streets. She played through what she might say and found that she didn't have the words. She covered the distance much faster than she expected as she was so preoccupied with her thoughts.

The circle of sky was brightening. There was no horizon for the sun to rise above when you lived inside the wall.

The sign above the large concrete gateway, that separated the Outsiders from the heaps, was flashing red. The output for the incinerator and reusable waste were all at zero. The only indicator that suggested that the Outsiders were still functioning was that the gleanings were lit in the amber zone. The incinerator had to be accessed through this gateway, so Mercy assumed that the

Outsiders were still gleaning from the heaps in order to survive, but not completing the work that Tropolis demanded of them. Tropolis could not close the gate or stop supplying waste because they had to hope that electricity would be restored even if it meant sending in their own people.

A group of lads, maybe in their late teens, approached the gate. They offered their wrists, one at a time, at the scanning hole and entered.

Mercy approached. She looked at her own wrist. She balled her fist in frustration. Campion had disabled the chip that she had implanted at birth. She would not be able to follow them.

'Mercy!' a young man called from behind her. She turned. A tall, young man with dark tied back hair, was strolling towards her. He had more stubble than she remembered and she wondered if he was attempting to look older.

'Fielder! Is that you?' Mercy asked rushing towards him and laughing.

'My father said you would be stationed with those at the fence.'

'I know where he wants me to be. But I wanted to talk with you first.'

'We all thought that you were dead!' Fielder said. 'Did you know that they started to stream some of the footage of the Compassion Prize to try and get us to work?'

'No!'

'They thought that they would get the furnaces going by showing us that they were punishing you.' Fielder laughed. 'As if!' He began to walk towards the gate. 'It just made us angrier! Then you turn up alive anyway. I mean, we can't believe anything they say can we?'

'They aren't telling you the half of it,' Mercy began. 'Griffin, I mean, your dad has bought everyone together, but I am not convinced his plan will work. It needs to change.'

'There is no time for that. The plan is set.'

'But he hasn't been to Tropolis,' Mercy said. 'I have.'

'Then you should be on the barge when it takes us in. You can show us where to go.'

Mercy considered what he had said. Could she change their minds about revenge as they travelled to the place that would temporarily relieve them? Their passion would be too great.

She spoke slowly. 'Tropolis need our help not our hate.'

'I don't understand! They just want to use us.'

'It is all they have known, just like this is all we have known. The people are sick, they are dying and we have the ability to make them well again.'

Fielder snorted. 'Why should we do that exactly?'

'Because we are not Tropolites, we are Outsiders. We don't have to pay them back for what they have done. If we free them, they may well free us.'

'I can't see that happening!'

'You have suffered, I know that, but they are suffering now. If someone could free you, what would you pay them for doing that?'

Fielder scratched his head. 'You are messing with me.'

'I'm not,' Mercy answered. 'Why would they be different?'

'They are Tropolites.'

'They are humans.'

'But if we help them, won't they just put us back here when they are well again?'

'Maybe, but if we have really helped them, they won't want to.'

Fielder thought for a while. 'How do you propose we help?'

'You are the first Outsider to ask that. Thank you.' Mercy took a deep breath. 'They can only be made well again by us giving them blood.' Fielder shook his head and frowned. 'Wait! We have something that is worth so much more to them than electricity and wealth. We are able to free them of the sickness.'

'I have to give my blood to them? Haven't I already given them so much already!'

'Yes.'

Fielder waited. 'Yes! Is that it?'

'Well we have given them so much already. And no, they don't deserve our help. But will that stop us from doing so?'

Fielder pulled on his pony tail to tighten it. 'I don't know Mercy. You are asking so much of us.'

'I know.'

He straightened up. 'The plan is set though. We will still take the barges.'

'I understand that. But will you talk with your father, with your friends?'

'I'm not sure they will be convinced. We all want Tropolis to pay. I don't know that we can trust them.'

'Please.'

'I guess. I've got to go.' Fielder pushed his wrist into the hole and leaned on the turnstile gate. He turned briefly. 'I would like to believe you Mercy, but I don't think Tropolis are like us at all.' He did not wait for her reply but rushed away.

Mercy put her back to the gate and covered her mouth with her hand. Her message seemed hopeless.

She heard someone call her name. But she did not respond.

Time and time again she was recognised by the young Outsiders. Many of them were shocked to see her alive and were content to be with her until she challenged them to think differently. Soon there were large groups entering the gate but Mercy kept her voice loud enough for the individuals to hear her, even though they could not see her. She would watch as pockets of them would gather and chatter on the other side of the gate, often glaring back at her and shaking their heads.

The sun looked set to brink the wall. Her voice was hoarse and her legs ached. Mercy rested against the queuing barrier. The Outsiders had stopped coming.

Mercy lifted her face to the light and breathed deeply. The rain would not return today as the sky was virtually cloud free. At that moment there was a gentle chink of sound and the lights went out above the gate. The first part of the Outsiders plan was complete and the power had been cut.

She rubbed her neck. The sleepless night had crept up on her and the adrenalin that had sustained her was seeping away. Mercy was weary and alone. Her vision blurred with tears. She blinked and let them run down her cheeks and drip to the dusty ground. These Outsiders had been her friends and yet they had looked on her with distrust and anger. They did not want to hear her message and would not change their thinking. They were set for revenge.

Any thoughts about leaving were quickly banished, she could not give up on her people now. Mercy approached the turnstile which now shifted freely at her pushing and she followed the route towards the docks where everyone would be, more determined than before to get them to listen. She would not allow this to silence her. She wiped the tears from her cheeks with the tips of her fingers.

00h 00m

The seagulls' calls were gradually being drowned out with loud cheers and laughter as Mercy approached the dockside fence. The heavy wire mesh that had separated the Outsiders from the water's edge had been cut through. It had sprung back on itself, curling and twisting away from the tension that had once held it in place. Nearly all the Outsiders that had gathered had pushed their way past the barrier and were now standing on forbidden land. Mercy saw that the younger Outsiders had already been joined by the second group that had shut off the emergency power.

The huge jetty that extended out from the opening in the wall was teeming with Outsiders. They were evidently enjoying the freedom of walking on ground that had been prohibited to them for so long.

Mercy scanned the group. Over on the far side, right near the concrete mooring posts were a line of green clad Tropolite workers. They were tied and bound. The stooped form of Griffin stood nearby and he was holding a long piece of piping. Mercy pushed her way through the crowd towards them.

'Stop this, Griffin!' she cried out.

Griffin paid no attention. He was brandishing the pipe, pointing the end of it closely at his captors faces.

One Tropolite spoke up. 'You won't get away with this!'

'It appears that we have!' said Griffin laughing a little.

'They'll turn back the moment they see all this trouble,' the Tropolite continued.

'You're right!' Griffin turned. 'Get this place clear. The people have to move back. They need to move away from the dock, they can't be seen.'

There was a flurry of activity. Many of the people that Mercy had seen late the previous night began to usher the Outsiders away and out of sight. She was caught in the moving crowd until Gunter leaned in and grabbed her, pulling her through the mass of bodies.

Griffin turned to the worker. 'Thanks for the advice!' He laughed. 'Now. One more thing we will need.' He nodded to the last couple of Outsiders that stood by his side. 'Get their uniforms!'

'Gently!' Mercy said as she approached.

It was a bright morning but there was a chill in the air and the breeze that came across the water was cold. The Tropolite workers were stripped to short sleeved shirts and underwear.

'Is there anything else that they could wear to keep them warm?'

'They didn't care when we were cold!' the Outsider who was stripping them replied harshly.

'There are waterproofs on the pegs in the staff quarters,' the Tropolite worker called out.

Mercy rushed over to the shipping container that served the staff. The Outsiders hadn't ventured in. Mercy opened the door carefully. Inside, it was warm but a little dark. There were several soft chairs in a semi-circle facing the large screen attached to the wall. A long desk stretched the length of the far wall with four smaller screens, all dark and void of information. Mercy noticed that even here a Network camera was strapped to the corner of the room where it would record all the movements of the Tropolite workers. The space was clean and luxurious. Mercy sighed as she unhooked the fluorescent waterproofs that hung by the door, carrying as many as she could.

She dropped them at Griffin's feet. 'Okay,' he said to the shivering Tropolites, 'Grab some and get dressed.' He turned to the rebels with him. 'When they are done, tie them up again and put them in their quarters.' He lifted the green uniform and measured it against himself and threw it over his arm. He tossed the remaining uniforms to the Outsiders nearby. 'We've seen it a thousand times. Guide the barge in and tie it off. Mercy?' Griffin passed a uniform to her.

She stared at it for a moment. 'No thanks,' she finally said. 'Griffin?'

'The plan stands, Mercy, I just want Outside to be free.' He looked out to sea. 'Right on time! Clear the dockside!'

Mercy squinted out over the waves. Just coming into view was the dark shape of a barge moving steadily towards the dock.

Griffin was quickly fastening the front of the uniform. Had it not been for his unkempt hair, he would have passed for a Tropolite, and at the distance of the barges, that was all that mattered.

'Mercy, get out of view!' Griffin ordered.

The dockside was clear of all but the few Outsiders in uniform, a few trucks and crane. Mercy rushed from the substantial jetty, through the cut wire fence and inland to the sheltered opening of the wall at the edge of the dock. It was already crowded with chattering and excited Outsiders. When she peered over at the far side, where the wall began again she could see that the bustling community had primarily gathered there.

The shadow of the wall was no longer a threat to the people, but because they stood on the edge, they appeared to be enthused with hope and promise.

Several Outsiders began to hush the waiting people and as silence fell, Mercy remembered what had characterised them before she had left. They had been fearful and oppressed, unable to see beyond the moment in which they lived. She sighed. She was grateful for the courage that was rising up in them but could not quash the unease of their lack of seeing beyond the actions of revenge. How could she put an end to this and contain what had been started?

The clanging and shouts from the dockside indicated that the barge was ready for mooring. Several painful moments passed. The group of Outsiders were pushing forward but the leaders were straining to hold them back with silent actions and panicked faces. A final shout and then a cheer rose from the jetty. A few Outsiders ran for the fence and towards the noise.

Everyone waited.

The roar of an engine was approaching. The crowd pulled back, not knowing what was happening out of sight.

Suddenly, a large refuse truck burst through the fence, forcing the posts to bend and split from the ground. Further along the fence there were others doing the same thing, pounding the thin fence into the ground and opening the docks for all to venture onto.

There was a surge and the Outsiders poured out of their hiding place. Mercy was pushed and shoved, she had no option but to move with the swell. In the confusion she was able to catch a glimpse of the dockside and the three new Tropolites that were being escorted to the worker's hut.

Everything that Griffin had set out to do he had accomplished. Mercy could see the group of rebels circling him, slapping him on the back and cheering. She wasn't sure how to behave. She was elated that the Outsiders had found their voice and were now free, but at the same time the voice she heard was threatening and violent. It reminded her too much of Tropolis for her to celebrate.

A gun shot rang out over the people. A piercing scream and a sense of panic rose from the distant crowd nearest the gate entry. Fear spread quickly and soon the Outsiders were running to the dockside to escape. People fell under the onslaught and were trampled by others. The sounds of jubilation had twisted into shrieks and yells. People hurried to the truck sides and cowered beside the barge. They were trapped.

A dark swathe of people were advancing towards them. They were organised in lines which pushed back the crowd. The front row were following a lone muscular man and were aiming guns at the Outsiders.

Mercy took a few steps backwards.

Griffin had forced his way through the fleeing people and had stopped close by.

'Only a dozen! Whoever thought that was wrong!'

'I don't understand!' Mercy said quietly. 'Tropolis is deathly ill. Where did they get such an army?'

Griffin turned to her. 'Who do I believe?' he said raising his eyebrows and scowling at her. 'And you want me to be merciful to them!' He shook his head. 'I don't see any mercy from them.'

The Outsiders had filled all the running spaces and were unable to go farther. They now turned to face their enemy.

Mercy recognised the eagerness of Sargent Atticus at the head of the army. He was grinning so broadly that his teeth glistened. From the moment Mercy had met him in the Prize, she knew he had always been desperate for a fight.

Chapter 19
Eban's story
00h 54m

Eban grinned as the sight of the white walls of Outside grew ever nearer. He had known that this was the right thing to do, but had not been certain that Alard would go along with the plan. Dozens of boats followed in the foamy wake of his own craft. Alard had sent out a call to the Campion land settlements and many had rushed to volunteer, it was as if they had been eagerly waiting for such an opportunity. The boats that rushed forward were not timid but were boldly approaching the walls. Campion had gathered a fleet and they were advancing on Outside.

The early morning sun glanced off the tall walls but the campion flower stood out in contrast. It may have been old red paint but it gleamed a new message against the white. And the message was provoking a response.

Eban watched out for the place where he had seen his friends disappear just the night before. He examined the wall carefully. A thin crack was exposed in the wall next to one of the strengthening struts. He signalled to the fleet to drop anchor as they had agreed before setting out.

Thomas was at the helm of the small boat with Alard and two further crew.

'You ready Eban?' Alard began. Eban nodded. 'Thomas, keep the comms open. We will send out the Outsiders in manageable sized groups. Take the vessel in nearer.'

Major Thomas pulled the small boat as close to the rocks as possible but it was still a fair distance away. Eban tightened the life jacket and lowered himself into the cold water, which smothered his breath for a moment. Quickly, he was surrounded by about a dozen Campion volunteers. Some were swimming directly to the rocks, while Captain Scout stayed back and dragged him onward. She may have been a slight woman but she was a very strong swimmer.

'I'm grateful... you have come back... Eban,' Scout said in short bursts as she delivered him to Outsides foundations.

The concrete rocks were huge and relatively smooth, but because they were not all interlinked, there were places to clamber up. As a team of twelve they pulled, lifted and pushed each other over the obstacles.

Eban shivered as he reached the flatter rim that formed the base of the wall. 'I'm not sure how the Outsiders will manage to get back to the boats from here,' he said to Alard with a hushed voice.

'The currents are strong,' Alard said quietly and nodded, 'It might be best to take the fleet to the dockside after all. But we should secure that space first. Although I am not sure how.' He tapped his shoulder and spoke into the communicator on his wrist. 'Entry not viable. Await new orders. Keep radio silence. Over.'

There would be no way to hide once inside the confines of the wall so the plan was to become Outsiders.

Alard gathered the team in the shadow of the vast wall under the Campion emblem. He unfolded the top of his rucksack and handed out dry clothes and as they quickly changed, he spoke softly but urgently.

'We will need to secure the dock as that is the best and probably safest option in order to move the Outsider refugees. If we can overcome the Tropolite authority without Outsider help that would be preferable.' Alard checked the time on his communicator. 'We don't have any time to waste. We are cutting this fine as it is. A new workforce is being sent as I speak.'

He twisted the outer rim of his communicator and drew a pattern on the small screen. Suddenly, everybody's communicators lit up with a bright crimson light. Eban leaned in close, with his dry sweatshirt half on, to Alard and saw a detailed map three-dimensional map of Outside displayed at his wrist. The detail was astonishing.

'How?' Eban asked pointing at the map and causing the image to tip towards him.

'We have technology Eban.'

'No! How do you know so much about Outside?' He asked forcing the jumper over his damp skin.

'We gather information from every Outsider who has manged to leave.'

Eban frowned. He had never been asked for details.

'As I was saying,' Alard continued to the watching team, 'You have been selected as the elite for this mission.' He reached into his bag once again. He produced several small hand guns. He handed them out but missed out Eban. 'Sorry, but since you don't have the training you will have to go without. You will be with Debs who is an excellent shot. You are safe with her.' He addressed the team once again. 'At all times you must work as pairs although no verbal communication is recommended as this will single you out. We will be entering approximately here.' Alard pointed to a position on the map where the community was quieter and where there were container homes just a short distance from the main roads that lead to the heaps. 'The perimeter of the wall will be the most closely watched by Tropolis so I suggest that blending with the crowd would be best. You will not be noticed among the people there even as strangers.'

Eban could feel his chest tighten. There had been many times when he had felt like a stranger in Outside despite having grown up there but that was not how it was meant to be. Mercy had bought a whole new atmosphere with her wherever she went and she had changed that. When she was around, people couldn't help themselves. It was as if they had been woken up from some long sleep to see that they were no longer alone. And she was in there and behind the wall. She could change that description of Outsiders. The information that Campion had gathered may not be as accurate as they expected.

Eban looked more closely at the map. All the main pathways and landmarks were there. A few of the newer areas in the community were not registered but the team would not need to know those details.

'The main issue will be to get through the gates here and here,' Alard said pointing at the entrances onto the heaps. 'The Outsiders haven't been producing enough energy for Tropolis for a while so we may find that the crowds will not be available for cover. However, we must reach the docks so this is the obvious route.' Alard highlighted the link between the heaps and the dock where the rubbish was received for sorting.

'If the power is down maybe we can scale the fences,' suggested Captain Scout.

As Eban looked up the painted Campion symbol seemed to merge with the wall in the maps light.

'Yes Debs,' Alard replied to Scout, 'I believe that may be an option but we'll have to think on our feet. The power to the fences will be one of the last things that Tropolis decommission. The dock area will have to be fully secured before the evacuation. Intel tells us that the cameras monitoring the site as a whole have been intermittent but the dock remains online at all times. This means that this is the place that they are both the weakest and strongest. A new consignment of Tropolites are due in under an hour, it will be tight for time, but if we move fast we will have the upper hand. If we can stop them from entering the site by taking the docks we will be done. The fleet can take the force of a few Tropolites without too many problems whilst we evacuate the Outsiders. Understood.'

'Sir!' members of the team agreed and nodded.

Alard twisted the dial on the communicator and every wrist went dark. He ascended first and one by one the team climbed easily to the rift in the wall using convenient hand and foot grips. They disappeared into the hole.

The sun had risen steadily. Eban closed his eyes and let the gentle warmth eradicate the sea's chill. In the shelter of the wall, the wind was weak and felt like a sweet summer breeze. Eban hummed a joyful tune to himself. He could not help but be excited by the prospect of this being Outside's break from winter.

Eban was last to enter and he laughed a little as he saw that this substantial wall was little more than a concrete rendered cage. The wall was a metaphor for so many things about Tropolis. Its appearance not nearly as appealing as it actually was, the thin layer of strength, massive and domineering but now being exposed. The echoing sound of feet scuffing filled the dark space. A smaller hole marked the exit and the daylight flashed into the space occasionally as the Campion team crawled out to the other side.

As Eban approached the hole a waft from the heaps swept in. He peered out and saw Outside stretched before him in its tumble down shacks, dirt paths and multi-coloured hues of plastic, metal and other discarded materials. The morning sun hadn't reached into the community yet but the sight warmed him. This was home, and soon this people would be free.

He slid down the rubble bank and followed the other Campion team through the narrow gap between two shacks that had their backs to each other.

'The sooner we get up onto the main roadways the quicker we blend in. Let's go!' Alard waved the team on.

Eban was used to the near silence of Outside but he frowned at the empty paths. He paused at several huts but could not hear any movement inside. He jogged to the front of the team and tapped Alard on his back.

'Brigadier, there's something wrong,' he warned.

'What is it?'

'Haven't you noticed? There's no one here. Where are all the Outsiders?'

Eban and the rest of the team wove through the streets. Each time they came to a new junction they quickly scanned for Outsiders but not a soul was found. Alard appeared to be getting more anxious as he barked instructions and to keep searching even venturing into some of the shanty homes himself. Eban, however, smiled. His confidence was growing stronger. Outside was not the same and he thought he knew why: Mercy was back.

They had reached the wider road that led to the heaps.

Eban leaned towards Alard. 'We don't have time for this distraction,' he whispered. 'We need to secure the dock.'

'You're right!' Alard turned to the team that were checking in the shacks and down narrow paths. 'This way, hurry!' He pointed and began to run. He leaped over the water filled potholes, focused again on reaching the dock. The team followed closely.

The concrete gateway could be seen from a fair distance over the low buildings. The dull angular grey was a contrast to the colour of the shacks that were thinning at the approach. The indicator lights that had shone every day were lifeless. Eban raced forward.

At the turnstiles was a lone figure.

'What's going on?' Eban asked slightly out of breath.

Alard stopped nearby, and listened for an answer.

'Have you seen my boy?' The man was pale and incredibly thin. He was holding himself up against the gate. 'I sent him here, every day. I am evil.'

'We all came here every day, that doesn't make you evil. What boy are you looking for?' Eban asked. 'We haven't seen anyone but you.'

'Took care of me for years. I hate myself.' Tears trickled over the sallow cheeks of the man.

The team had just caught up and were struggling to catch their breath.

'We all had to come here to survive,' Eban replied.

'I never came.'

Alard leaned over the man. 'Then you should be ashamed of yourself.'

Eban frowned at Alard. 'Because we all do exactly what we should, is that right Alard?'

'Sending children to this place so that you don't have to is not the same.'

'In your eyes,' Eban answered. 'You don't look well, what happened to your boy?'

'Left me. Said he would come back. I waited.'

'Not surprised, I did that too. It is the only way to escape a prison.' Alard said under his breath. 'Where are all the Outsiders?' Alard pressed.

'All at the docks. Rebellion!' The man's breath rattled. 'My boy might be there. He'll save us.'

'Hang on,' Eban began. 'Your boy left you, but not because of anything you had done, was it? He was chosen for the Prize. Luca? Are you talking about Luca?' Eban asked.

The man stumbled towards him and grasped Eban's jumper. 'You know him?'

Eban laughed. 'I certainly do! He is my friend. I'm Eban.' He supported the man by the arms and smiled at him. 'He came back to you. Did he find you?'

'We don't have time for this!' Alard said. 'Rebellion at the docks he said, let's go!'

Eban raised his hand. 'Did he find you?'

'Yes. I'm Amil, his, want for a better word, father.' He patted Eban's chest. 'Him and a girl. She was like me, she didn't fit here.'

'Kelsee!' Eban laughed a little. 'Very insightful. She isn't an Outsider, but a Tropolite, just like you.'

Luca's father stared wide eyed. 'You know?'

Eban nodded. 'So does Luca.'

'Overheard her talking in the night,' Amil said with effort. 'Another girl there. Said there was rebellion at docks at dawn. They were gone long before dawn. Didn't see Luca again. He must be here.'

'Dawn!' Alard said. 'Then the Outsiders are all there. Let's get moving.'

'Something else ...' Amil said breathlessly. 'Tropolite workforce at Compassion Gate.'

'Yes we know about them,' Alard said nodding and trying to push past.

Amil shrugged his frail shoulders. 'Tropolis will send a large number. More than Outsiders think. It will be dangerous.'

Alard took in the frail man's appearance. His shoulders drooped a little as it seemed that even this weak warning was to be heeded. He turned to his team. 'We'll need to split up. I don't want to do it but I don't think I have a choice. If Amil is right, the rebellion at the dock will need to be protected. Eban, can you take Mason, George and Debs with you to the docks. Debs is prepped for the securing of the area. I'll head back to the Compassion Gate and see if we can head them off.' Alard held out his hand to Amil. 'Sorry I judged you. I know that Tropolites can't glean, you had no other option but to send your boy here. Your boy and his friends have made a huge difference to Campion and we will find him for you.'

'Campion? Campion does exist and has come at last!'

Eban took a sharp breath. 'You know about Campion?'

'I left a message a long time ago.' Amil sighed. 'Before ...' He stopped and closed his eyes whilst he shook his head. 'On the wall.'

'We saw it,' Alard said standing to attention. 'Sorry for the delay in our response, sir. We are here to do what we should have done years ago.'

'So much suffering and waiting. Then the suddenly! Seems like a dream!'

With a swift salute Alard gathered the seven other members of his team and ran back down the track.

'We should be on our way too,' Mason urged.

'I'll wait here,' Amil said sadly and rubbing his hand up his arm, 'No chip'

Eban pointed at the dead lights. 'You aren't going to be left behind.'

Amil was weak and exhausted but Eban would not abandon him.

Tropolis had kept the road from the dock to the heaps well maintained. Their power relied upon the incinerator being fed and the rubbish being sorted for re-usable materials on the heaps. A large concrete hanger was the only building on this side of the gate and resided on the far side of the heaps and parallel to the dock. It made up the entrance to the furnace where the rubbish would be incinerated. Outsiders were not permitted to enter that area but there were no fences to hold them back. The potential danger would be from the rubbish shifting vehicles and the heat. Trucks would force the rubbish over the tipping point and the conveyors carry the tons of waste to the processors to be compacted and then burned. The drivers paid no attention to what was in the way and there had been many deaths and fatal injuries. The zones had been set up by the Outsiders to protect themselves from this danger.

Amil panted trying to keep up. His legs were shaking and he used a wooden stake to stabilise himself.

Captain Scout puffed. 'We need to move faster!' she said.

'You go!' Eban suggested.

'Brigadier Alard's orders were to stay together.'

Eban shrugged. 'Then you are going to have to go as fast as the slowest of us then.' Eban turned to see just how much difficulty Amil was having. They didn't seem to be any further away from the stinking heaps or from the bunker. 'Unless,' Eban called out to Scout, 'We can make us all move faster!'

00h 00m

Chapter 20
Mercy's Story

00h 00m

The army drew close. They were trapping the Outsiders on the dockside where they would have nowhere to run to. Even the seagulls' cries were silent. The only sounds were the rhythmic marching of feet, but even that appeared off.

Mercy was exhausted. She had so little to focus on since her perspective was so different to the ones around her. The Outsiders had pinned their hopes on resisting Tropolis and rebelling; they had wanted revenge and now Tropolis was interfering with their plans. The people were terrified that at their first attempt in decades to be free, they would be imprisoned just as they tasted sweet freedom. The fear was seeping through the community. Several began to sob and a few fell to the ground covering their heads with their hands.

It was so difficult to understand. They had been strong all the time that adversity had been absent, but now they cowered.

The fear that rippled through the crowd stirred something else in Mercy.

She straightened her shoulders and took a step forward.

'What are you doing?' Griffin, the bent over rebel leader, asked, reaching for her.

'Mercy!' Fielder called out running towards his father. He began to pull him back into the crowd. 'They'll kill you!'

Mercy turned to Griffin and touched his hand. 'Let me speak to them.' She looked at the fear in Fielder's face but refused to respond in the same way. 'Perhaps I can be a mediator.' She did not wait for permission.

She took several steps towards the army.

Atticus raised his hand and halted the approach.

'Sargent, welcome to Outside!' Mercy greeted.

'It appears that I arrived at just the right time. Since when do Tropolis workers defend Outsiders?'

Mercy turned and at once understood. From where Atticus viewed the scene, it appeared that Griffin and his rebels in uniforms were Tropolites. They were the ones sitting in the large trucks holding the fence down, they were the ones at the forefront of the community.

'Do you remember me?' she asked.

'Should I?' Atticus squinted at her. 'You are of little consequence to me girl. Get out of my way!'

Mercy stood firm. 'Do you think that your troops can overcome us? Just look at the numbers, my people will not allow you to hold us down anymore.'

'You have no weapons and even I can see how terrified they are. Each of my soldiers are worth more than fifty of *your* people.'

A loud and strong voice called out from behind him. 'Yes, but you are surrounded!'

Suddenly there were several, armed people moving from the rear of the Tropolite army and down its flanks.

'Hardly!' Atticus laughed.

Three more strangers stepped out from the shadows.

'Alard! It is good to see you.' Mercy quickly counted ten Campion soldiers with their leader.

'Miss!' Alard nodded but did not stop glaring at Atticus. His weapon was held steady. 'We are everywhere!' Alard announced. 'I suggest you lay down your arms.'

Atticus didn't move but his gaze darted about as if he were checking if that were the truth. No one dared to move.

A gasp caught Mercy's attention. In the second row of the army a girl with a deep purple bruise across her cheek and thick hair tied back stared wide eyed at Mercy.

'Danita?'

Atticus turned briefly then stepped in front to block Mercy's view.

Although Danita belonged in Outside, she had been part of the Prize alongside Mercy, Eban and Luca. It seemed strange that she would be here in this capacity now.

'My orders are to restore power to Tropolis by any means that I wish. I suggest that you step aside or I will have you and this meagre guard shot.'

Mercy began to scan the army. Familiar faces peppered the troops as far as she could see. She could not help but laugh a little.

'Death is funny to you is it? Are you crazy?'

'I've faced death before,' Mercy said, 'Haven't I Seth?' she nodded to the larger contestant that Luca had named Thickset, 'Maxim, Taja, Cayden ... Kit?' catching the attention of her old competition companions. 'I'm not afraid.'

Seth, Luca's enemy from the Prize leaned forward and raised his rifle pointing it directly at Mercy. The barrel shook a little in his unsteady hands.

Suddenly, a faint cry came from the ranks. 'Ma!'

The army began to shift and stir. One by one they were focusing on the Outsiders a short distance away. The Campion soldiers stood firm.

A tall, fair haired man ran from the army towards the Outsiders. He threw his rifle to the ground as he sprinted at a woman who had covered her mouth in shock.

Atticus turned, aimed and fired.

Alard sprung forward to knock the rifle but he was too late to divert the bullet.

The running man crumpled and fell to the ground, dust rising from the fall. The woman screamed through her fingers and dashed for the injured man. She dropped to her knees and cradled him on her lap, stroking his face tenderly. Mercy was certain that she had done that countless times when he was a child and had comforted him.

Mercy faced Seth. His rifle dropped a little and his eyes flickered, searching the crowd of Outsiders. Then they locked on someone. His gaze stammered between Mercy and the familiar face in the crowd.

'I came forward to speak to you,' Mercy said breaking the silence. 'To mediate some sort of peace or understanding, but it seems that someone has already begun that process when they chose your army.'

Atticus snarled. 'Alec!' he spat, 'No wonder they wanted him dead!'

One by one the rifles were dropped to the floor and members stepped from the ranks.

Mercy opened her hands. 'It seems that your army will not restore power by any means you wish.'

'Get back in formation!' Atticus commanded. He turned and he pointed his gun at his own army. In return several rifles were turned on him.

'I was told that my family were dead!'

'So was I!'

The tension was broken. Suddenly Outsiders and Tropolite army were rushing towards each other. There were hugs and shouts, names being called and clasped hands.

Mercy's heart felt like it was going to explode. So many families were being reunited, so many griefs were thrown away only to be replaced with ecstatic tears. There were however, a few who had their grief doubled. Some of the older recruits had no hope of finding lost family members; their Outsider relatives had lived the lifespan expected of this place. But many of them still wandered about in the throng soaking in the joy of others.

Atticus' face had turned from red to white. He stared at the Campion weapons aimed at him.

'You came from Outside too,' Mercy stated. 'Did Tropolis tell you anything about your family?'

'That is none of your business!' Atticus replied curtly, but his gun had fallen to his side. Seth however still pointed his weapon at Mercy.

'Can you see them?'

'Shut up!' Atticus snapped. 'You and your people have nothing to do with me anymore.'

Griffin laughed as he stepped up next to Mercy with two other uniform clad leaders. 'Isn't this wonderful!' He beamed.

Mercy nodded and patted his shoulder.

Griffin turned to Atticus and his smile disappeared. 'You will have to come with me,' he said sternly. Griffin took the gun from Atticus' hand and grabbed him by the forearm. Seth raised his rifle.

'Don't be stupid!' Atticus said and pushed the barrel down to face the ground. 'You can't kill them all!'

'Take him too,' Alard instructed nodding towards Seth.

He tapped his shoulder. 'Area secure. Advance to alternative secure area. Over.'

Atticus and Seth were led away, through the joyous Outsider reunions, to the staff quarters. A thickset man, sure to be Seth's father followed closely. Seth shouted abusively at him, then he stopped in his pursuit of his son and began to sob.

Griffin stepped towards Alard. 'Don't get me wrong, I'm glad you showed up, but who are you?'

'Brigadier Alard. I am part of an extensive group named Campion,' Alard answered. 'We live away from the rule of Tropolis.'

'No Tropolis? How?' Griffin asked.

'On the mainland we have settlements that are not controlled or maintained by Tropolis unlike Outside.'

'Maintained? You think Outside is maintained by Tropolis.'

'We believed so.'

'You knew about us?' Griffin asked angrily. 'And you did nothing?'

'We did nothing because we believed your community was being maintained.' Alard raised his hand sharply. 'In order for you to understand why we are here now, you need to listen.'

Griffin closed his lips tightly.

'We *believed* ... that is something you need to understand. We *believed* that Tropolis were maintaining this community with care. The network, the communications, everything appeared to say that you and your people were content. It is only with the arrival of the three escaped prize contestants and their friend that we have been able to see things differently.'

Griffin glanced at Mercy. 'She does have a habit of being able to do that.'

'Indeed!' Alard smiled a little which surprised Mercy.

'Alard,' she said smiling widely at him. 'I am sorry that we left you at the bridge, but I presume that Eban had something to do with your being here and it was not just my influence.' Mercy began to scan the Campion crew, but Eban was nowhere to be seen.

'He did, miss.' Alard gave a little salute before turning back to Griffin. 'I think that you have every right to be angry at Campion. If we had looked at the trickle of evidence that had come our way over the years we should have seen that not all was as it appeared.' Alard bowed his head slightly. 'We have done you wrong. We should have come sooner but we cannot re-live that time. We have come today.'

'And not at a bad time too!' joked Griffin. Mercy knew that the present victory was playing heavily with Griffin's judgements and she was glad of it for Campion's sake.

'Quite!' Alard laughed. 'It seems that the timing was about right.'

'You say you have land communities; how big are they and could they house my people?' Griffin asked.

'I had not accounted for so many of you.' Alard scanned the swelling crowd. Griffin looked away and brushed his hands together. Alard was not deterred. 'But our resources will, I think, be enough.'

'My people know how to work,' Griffin said desperate to prove their worth.

Alard nodded. 'Adjusting to living as a free people will require a change.'

'Free people,' Griffin repeated. 'Sounds like a dream.'

Alard offered his hand. Griffin took it and they shook in agreement. 'A reality,' Alard assured him. 'We can take your people with us today. A fleet of boats are on their way as we speak.'

Mercy patted Alard on the back. 'Thank you so much for your generosity.'

Griffin raised his other hand and placed it on Alard's shoulder. 'But first we will take your boats to the mainland and to Tropolis. We have some unfinished business.'

'Tropolis?' Alard questioned. 'It is best to leave them as they are.'

Griffin released Alard's hand sharply. 'I don't think so! I know my people will have other plans.'

Mercy realised that the danger had not passed, her people needed to hear some truth. She looked around a little franticly.

A loud horn sounded from the truck that had wrecked the wire fence.

The people stopped what they were doing and Mercy squinted through the windscreen. There were two people in the cab. One of them she knew very well.

'Eban!' She ran towards the truck.

Eban opened the door and offered his hand.

'I knew you would be in the middle of it all!'

'I am so glad to see you!' She leaned in and hugged him tightly. A pale man sat in the other seat of the truck.

Eban gestured to the man sitting next to him. 'This is Amil, Luca's father.'

'Is he here? Is Luca here?' Amil asked looking out over the crowd.

'I thought he was with you,' Mercy said frowning. 'He will be with Kelsee.

'They're not with you?' Eban asked.

'The last I saw of Kelsee was very early this morning. I told her to stay back at your place,' Mercy said to Amil.

Amil's shoulders drooped and he shook his head.

'Amil,' Mercy said gently as she leaned over and touched his arm. He looked up, startled. 'Luca is very strong. Please try not to worry. He will be wherever Kelsee is, and looking after her.' She was certain that Luca would be the very best of friends to Kelsee but that did not mean that she could forget that they were missing. He was strong, much stronger than the last time he was in Outside. He had grown and she knew that he would be there to protect Kelsee at all cost. It was how he understood friendship as it was how friendship had been modelled from both Eban and herself.

'We don't have time to look for them now.' Mercy focussed on Eban. 'I am so glad that you brought Campion but Griffin wants to take their boats and the people to attack Tropolis.'

Eban nodded. 'You can't have thought that Outsider's would do anything differently without guidance. Mercy, you're not done with this situation yet.'

Mercy conceded. 'The Outsiders want retribution. I have to stop them.'

'Campion are coming and they have been moved into action but you are able to set the plan in place. Climb up here. Let the Outsiders see you.' Eban smiled. 'I believe in you.'

He sounded the horn once again. The crowd turned and went silent.

Mercy breathed deeply then clambered up.

She turned her back to Eban and looked out over the expectant people. She felt stronger knowing that Eban was there. 'People of Outside!' she called, 'I know so many of you have had precious loved ones returned to you today.' There was a cheer and many clapped. 'We must change the plan.'

'We have the Tropolis army!' A middle aged man called out hugging a strong lad to his side. 'Let's take the city!'

'They've lied about our families!'

Many in the crowd shouted out their agreement.

'Nothing has changed! Tropolis must fall!'

Eban sounded the horn, Mercy raised her hands and silence fell. 'Tropolis has said and done a lot of things to protect themselves.'

'They had no right!' An Outsider voiced

Mercy shouted over the angry voices. 'They thought they had no choice. Tropolis needed Outsiders to make them well again. The people there are sick.'

Outsiders began to group together, trying to drag and include the Tropolite army with them.

'We have no need for them anymore,' Griffin shouted as he approached Mercy. 'Let them die! I won't help them!'

Mercy balled her fists.

A dark haired woman rushed forward. She wore the Tropolite army uniform but had untucked the neat shirt and had swung the rifle to her back. 'I am 60109. I lived here for fifteen years.' The crowd gave her full attention. 'I am also Josetta and have lived in Tropolis for fifteen years. I have family here, family that I haven't seen or known about, but I also have a family in Tropolis. Please, I appeal to you to help them!'

Griffin stepped in front of the woman. 'Why? I mean, really, why should we help them?' He frowned at the crowd silently asking for an answer. 'They are not worth saving! We should take the city. Now is the time!'

Fielder pushed forward and stood face to face with his father. His pony tail trembled as he shook his head. Reaching for Josetta, he pulled her out into the open again. 'I think we should listen to the other side before we make such a quick decision.' Fielder ushered Josetta up onto the hood of the truck. Mercy offered her hand helping her to get higher.

Mercy spoke quietly. 'Be bold! You may be the only voice that they hear for Tropolis.'

'I hope that I do them justice,' Josetta said then took a deep breath and turned to the crowd. 'Outside is different. You have grown as a community despite the dire circumstances in which you live. If we had known that you were alive we would have come back, we would have, perhaps, done something. But we didn't know and we didn't see what has happened here. Tropolis don't tell anyone what is happening here. But that does not mean that they would not want to know. The people of Tropolis, the real ones, are more like you than you know.' The crowd began to get restless.

'Let her finish!' shouted Fielder.

Josetta smiled. 'I remember when I lived here that Tropolis was the place of luxury and waste, it felt like it had turned its back on us.' The murmur spread through the crowd. 'I guess it had. I vowed that I would not turn my back on Outside when I got selected for the Prize. But here I am, a lifetime later, having done just that. It wasn't intentional. I wanted to bring my family out but I was told that they had died.'

'Me too!' called another in the army uniform.

Others agreed with shouts and nodding.

Emboldened by the crowd Josetta raised her voice and continued with passion. 'Tropolis was a comfortable place to settle. We made new families and new friends. Real Tropolites are held back by the law, but they are real people. It is the law that needs to be punished. The law that needs to be changed. There are those in authority who have kept the truth from you. Kept the truth from us! They have kept the truth of Outside from the Tropolite people. This wall has become your prison, and sickness is the prison of Tropolis. My friends and family in Tropolis are dying while I am somehow immune. I cannot abandon them. I beg you, please be strong. Together we can be full of courage and be different.'

The Outsiders stood in silence. Griffin leaned against the truck. 'That may be the case, but we need to think about ourselves because you can be sure that they won't. What about us? Who will give us what we need when Tropolis are spared?'

'Griffin wait!' Mercy bent down and placed her hand on his shoulder. 'I understand what Griffin is saying. It appears, from what we have experienced before that as Outsiders, we need to grab at this chance to take back what we deserve. I know that he wants what is best for his community, for his family. I hope that since you have begun to talk to each other that you have discovered just what each person here has had to carry and live with. Griffin has taken the burden for his family in more ways than one. He has suffered ill health as well as all the other ailments that come with being an Outsider. He wants what is best for us. He wants justice to be served because of his compassion for you.' The crowd shuffled at the use of Mercy's term. 'We need to reclaim the term "compassion". Compassion isn't a prize that has to be fought over and won. It is something that can only be felt deep inside and then given freely as a gift. Griffin has it for you. He sees your plight and wants to give you dignity. He is soft,' Mercy smiled widely, 'He really is you know! He feels it when you hurt and he hates that you have had to endure more when he can't do anything about it. Griffin is a great leader. He leads following his heart. He wants you to be free.'

Griffin had sunk lower as Mercy had spoken. Fielder stood closer to his father and gently fist punched his upper arm. 'Dad, you know it is true!'

'Griffin would be right. You should receive justice, you have been treated unfairly and cruelly. But he hasn't got it all right. If we follow through with taking Tropolis we will not be free. We would still be acting as prisoners, grabbing at what we feel is ours. Josetta is right. Tropolis know nothing of what has become of Outside and are innocent of creating it. Yet all are guilty of upholding it whether they like it or not. Justice must be served to the ones that have caused this atrocity. The ones that have continued to hide the truth must be held accountable. But in order for us to be free, it is up to us to give them a chance to change their minds and turn their backs on this way of life. It is essential that we do not walk from one prison straight into another one where we have blood on our hands that will never wash off.'

Griffin turned. His anger was all but gone. 'How can you be sure that we will be treated fairly this time?' he said quietly.

'I can't,' Mercy replied. 'But I do know that the Tropolites who have been family to the prize contestants will probably feel the same way as Josetta. Griffin, for the sake of all the people, we have to try.'

Griffin cleared his throat and breathed out a heavy breath. 'We have an opportunity to change the way we live,' he called out. Mercy clenched her fists and held back tears of frustration. 'We have the means to change the way Tropolis treats us. But Mercy is right,' he said looking up into her face, 'I say we go into the city and we behave like Outsiders. We give what we have gleaned in these years; our generosity, our lack of waste and our,' he paused and tapped Mercy's foot. 'Our compassion.' She wiped the warm tear that had run down her cheek away. Griffin smiled a little as he stood straighter than he had done in years. 'Let us show the Tropolites that we will not measure back to them the cruelty that we have suffered. Let's be a people that pours out the richness that cannot be counted out in credits. We promise we will have justice, but it will be contained and considered. Now is the time to act, now is the time go to them with a compassion gift.' Griffin took several steps towards Alard and offered his hand. 'Brigadier, are you and Campion with us?'

Alard looked up at Mercy and stood to attention then saluted her. He then stepped forward, and shook Griffin's hand. 'You will have Campion with you as you deliver your compassion gift.'

Chapter 21

00h 00m

Luca was stunned. The platform was empty and the sounds of Kelsee protesting were fading fast.

He stepped away from the wall and approached the archway. Glancing up he saw the words lining the arch and struggled, more than ever, to believe them.

WELCOME TO TROPOLIS

Terrified and confused, Luca felt immobile. He had to do something about Kelsee but did Alec deserve to die? He turned toward the Maglev track. There was no sign of a train but a dark smudge of movement was growing as someone approached. Alec was running along the dim tunnel towards him.

He climbed the metal rungs at the trackside and pulled Luca into the shadows away from the arch.

'What are you doing here?' he asked urgently. 'What does it matter? I need to get you out!'

'I'm not going anywhere. We need to stop her! She's going to see her grandfather. None of us are safe.'

'We're not safe, you are correct on that count,' Alec replied unwrapping the roll of torn fabric from his hand. Alec looked intently at Luca.

'I'll go after her myself if I have to.'

Alec shook his head as he made a decision against his better judgement. He looked down at his hands. There were small cuts on his knuckles. 'I won't have a place in Tropolis for much longer when they discover the army I just sent. Do you think Campion would take me?' he said sarcastically.

'That Mara Hutchings woman gave orders for Atticus to kill you.'

Alec snorted. 'That I don't doubt!' He peered through the archway. 'And a task he would willingly complete.' Alec looked intently at Luca. 'This is your last chance. Are you certain that you don't want to go back? If so, now is the time.'

'I can't leave Kelsee to tell them about everyone.'

'Tell them? She just wants to get back to her grandfather.'

Luca pulled away. 'Then we can't wait. We have to stop her before she tells him about Campion, Mercy and Eban.' Luca had to convince Alec. 'And you.'

Alec grabbed Luca's arm. 'Who do you think Kelsee is exactly?'

Luca struggled to be free from Alec's grip. 'She was my friend.' He shrugged his shoulders. 'I don't know anymore.'

'She isn't going to tell her grandfather about you, at least not in the way that you think. On the train she told me about the state of Outside, as if I wasn't aware of it. She was heartbroken for you and your father.' Luca looked at his uncle and frowned. 'She wanted to appeal to her grandfather to change how Outside are treated.'

Luca smiled. 'Then it will all be fine,' he snorted angrily, 'If he listens.' Luca ran his hand through his hair. 'But he won't listen will he. He never has.' Luca peered towards the archway. 'So I don't know if she needs me anymore.'

Alec shook his head. 'I not sure about Barrett, he's never done anything for Outside in the past.' Alec paused and sighed. 'But it is that woman, Mara Hutchings, the one who took Kelsee, that we need to worry about.' Alec opened his hands. 'I've been watching since you've been gone. She is dangerous.'

'Then why did you let her take her? Do we need to get Kelsee out of there?' Luca glared at his uncle. 'You will not do this without me.'

'They wouldn't let us back into Tropolis until they knew that Kelsee was with me. It was her choice, not mine,' Alec explained. Luca shook his head. 'It's too late to change that decision now,' he justified as he moved towards the arch. 'I don't know what will happen to Kelsee, but I can't shake the feeling that Hutchings is not what she seems.' Alec straightened up. 'I can get us in but you will have to trust me.' Luca nodded.

Alec stepped through the arch and began to climb the stairs. Luca followed. There was no sound of anything other than their footfalls on the polished steps as they climbed ever higher. Luca recalled the struggle and effort when he had first encountered the entrance to Tropolis, how Thickset had wanted to rest but Crisp had pushed them on without a hint of care. Luca jogged, barely out of breath and had no need for the handrail to support the accent. Now he followed after Alec, a man no longer hiding in the Tropolite shell of indifference.

Warm morning light trickled down the stairwell on the final flight. As they stepped into the glass and steel atrium Luca could not help but be impressed. He wanted to hate the space, but in reality, it was beautiful. The white marble floor reflecting the slightly yellow light threw the darker struts into contrast. It was a powerful space. The bank of frosted glass doors lined one wall, but Alec was not leading Luca to the cleansing rooms. He was walking with confidence towards the empty gable ended wall on the left.

It was only as they drew close that Luca noticed the faint and fine outline of a doorway. This must have been a separate building to the contestant's quarters.

Alec pressed his palm against a very slightly raised plaque of marble. A red strip of light ran the length of his hand and the door hissed as it pulled in and then slid to one side.

Luca hadn't been in this building but the stark memories of a similar space came flooding to the surface. The bright corridor reminded him of the introduction to the banqueting room and of being questioned. It was only the sight of a desk at the far end that differentiated the floors. No one sat there and there was little sound from any of the rooms either side of the corridor.

Suddenly Alec grabbed Luca's wrists and held them tightly.

'Trust me!' he whispered and tilted his head to a camera in the ceiling.

Luca saw that there was the familiar red light and knew that somewhere there would be an image of them being broadcast. He lowered his head to hide his face a little.

Alec walked fast towards the end where the desk stood opposite two lifts. Alec peered at the panel that indicated the floors where they had stopped then punched the button to call for a lift.

Luca's stomach was churning a little but he was relieved that when the lift door opened and the walls were not made of glass. Alec led Luca inside and pressed the button, the doors shut and the lift rose.

'They've stopped on the media floor but her grandfather won't be there,' Alec said releasing Luca and pacing the lift. 'What is she doing?'

Luca looked about. There were no cameras here. 'Where are we going?'

'A couple of floors below. We'll take the stairs from there.'

Luca nodded. Wherever Kelsee was being taken was where he wanted to be. He couldn't speak, he thought that maybe movement of the lift was making him feel a bit sick but wasn't certain. Scenarios of what could be said to Kelsee were playing over in his mind and he could not find one that made what he had thought she was doing any better.

The lift slowed and Alec took hold of his prisoner once again. The doors opened onto another deserted corridor. The doors to all the rooms were shut and the glass was dim and void of light. The cameras on this floor were not as sophisticated as in the contestant rooms. They were angled with the lenses fixed in one direction.

Alec kept Luca close to the wall, pushed open the first door on the left and stepped through. The stairwell was simple and lit by the tall windows at the top of each flight. Alec let go of Luca once again.

'No cameras?' Luca asked.

'Perk of the job!' Alec answered starting to climb. 'The stairs don't get used by the Tropolites, they chose the lift every time. I made sure that there would always be a way of unseen escape.'

As they reached the first landing Luca looked out of the tinted window over a section of Tropolis. It was a large city with hundreds of tall buildings but it was so still. He recognised an automatically driven vehicle trundle along the road below but there were no Tropolites out on the streets and no noise.

After the third floor and the third check for life Luca had to ask, 'Where is everyone?'

Alec stopped and looked out over the same scene. 'They are there,' Alec paused as if to think about the question, 'But inside. No one goes out onto the street because of the fatigue. They're just too ill.'

Luca wondered how anyone could survive being confined to the inside. He considered the luxury and riches of this city but that was not real wealth at all. They were not free to step outside. Suddenly, Luca realised that they were, perhaps, just as trapped at his own people. 'Are there many Tropolites?'

'A city full, or so I am led to believe from records that I think can be trusted. But I have never seen more than twenty in a room.' Alec raised his eyebrows. 'People don't act like people here. Tropolites cut out the world around them. They don't think that they need to interact with other real people. The fatigue has forced them survive in apartments where tiny and handpicked communities are always looking suspiciously inward. The fatigue has done more than make them ill, it has created deadly fear that the person nearest you could kill you. That's why I sent the army full of ex-contestants back to Outside. They needed to be reminded of humanity. They will have to remember where they came from and what happened to them when they are face to face with it. I just hope it works.' Alec turned away. 'This is the media floor. I don't know why they are here but you can be certain that there will be Tropolites. This floor is busy day and night but funnily enough, also has a lack of cameras.' Alec tilted his head and half smiled. Luca knew that there must be a reason to hide here too. 'Follow me closely.'

Bright spot lights were directed to the floor but the corridor was dark. It was not the same as the other floors, the walls were not stark white but had been decorated exclusively in images from the network. There were pictures of Harland Barret, Nolan Smythe (the Prize presenter) and other characters that had been shown on the screens over the years. Luca caught his breath as he saw scenes from past Compassion Prizes devoid of any sense of human life, but contestants portrayed as entertainment. There were other images of the perfect Tropolis, something that Luca had never witnessed on either of his visits to the city. Luca could hear the faint buzz of voices coming from behind closed doors.

Alec indicated Luca to follow and they crept up the dark corridor, drawing themselves out of the lights and hiding in the shadows. A strip of glass down one edge of the door let multi-coloured light filter through. The plaque on the door read 'Monitor suite 1' and as Luca peered through the glass he saw a large bank of screens each showing a different scene. There were three people sat at the desk surrounded by dials, sliders and buttons. One was rewinding footage while another spoke into the screen of a white room. Suddenly Harland Barret appeared on the screen.

Luca let out a gasp and motioned to Alec. After only a moment of viewing the screens Alec nodded and coaxed Luca away. Alec moved quickly as he briefly peered into the glass strip of a door several rooms further up the corridor. The moment later and he was inside. Luca ran to join him.

'It will be here somewhere.' Alec was standing at the only monitor that was switched on and showed the series of coloured lines of the test card running across it. Luca closed the door quietly and crossed the room. Although the monitor was furthest from the door, he was aware that it was emitting light.

Alec was twiddling a dial and with each click a new image appeared on the screen. He stopped when Harland Barret stood in the white room.

Luca began switching on all the monitors.

'Stop that!' Alec warned.

'One monitor is too obvious,' Luca said turning his back on Alec. 'If someone looks in they will see us. This is the best way to hide.'

Alec puffed. 'We are not intending to stay long. I just want to know what he is doing.'

The screens were all lit and many of them were showing the same footage that was in the other suite without having to re-tune them. One screen, on the far side, showed the live Network stream. The program being broadcast was not familiar to Luca.

A speaker hummed as Alec continued to flick a couple of switches on the desk. 'Ok, you're running in 5, 4, 3, 2, ...' The voice began.

'It is for your own good that you are being held,' Barret said. He was staring out of the monitor that Alec had tuned.

'Pull in for the close up shot.'

Barret continued as if no-one had spoken. 'You are home but before you can be welcomed back there are some things that I need to be certain of.'

'Cut.' The screen than cut to a closer image but it was still waist up.

'Kelsee, are you willing to answer my questions?'

'I don't have the answers you want,' Kelsee's voice replied shaking just a little.

Luca scanned the other screens. 'Where is she?'

Alec flicked another switch and twisted the dial. The image on the monitor next to the one showing Harland Barret began to change.

'You know that you have the answers that I want and you are refusing to give them to me. Do you know where you sit?'

Just then the monitor showed another white room and in the centre of it was a large chair where Kelsee was sat. She looked so small. Her arms were tied to the arms of the chair with wide straps. Luca could see her pulling and tugging at them. When she raised her head at the question, a deep red gash showed under her right eye. Luca clenched his fists.

'No,' Kelsee answered.

'You don't recognise it? Surely you would if I did this?'

Kelsee jumped in the chair and let out a squeal.

Luca gasped. He looked at Kelsee's ankles and there were the other fabric strips that were lined with wires. Harland was using the Intelligence test on his own granddaughter. 'What's he doing?' he asked in disbelief. Luca knew the pain of the electric current passing through him, only he had been able to avoid the ongoing torture by cheating in the test during the competition.

'That was just a little appetizer for you. I want answers and I will get them.' Barret smiled but there was no affection and only malice. 'How did you survive?' He paused for a minute but Kelsee did not reply. 'It is a simple question, don't make me shock you again.'

'I'm not telling you anything. I want to see my grandfather face to face.' Kelsee twitched and screamed. Luca knew the pain.

'Increase the voltage?' asked the voice over the speaker.

Harland nodded to the camera and then continued to address Kelsee. 'You won't get an audience with me until you are fully decontaminated.' He paused. 'You will, however, answer me,' he ordered.

'I will not!' Kelsee shouted. Luca was awe struck by her loyalty to him.

'You will!' Barret sent a shock and Kelsee arched her back. 'How did you survive?' She screwed up her face. 'How did you get to Outside?' She yelled in pain. 'Who is helping you?' another attack. 'Where are the others?'

'Heart rate is erratic,' the voice from the other suite announced.

'Why are you back here? What have you told them?' Barret shouted angrily. Kelsee shook violently and went deathly pale before she slumped in the chair.

'She's out!'

'Get her back!' Barret said approaching the camera and then leaving the shot.

'Take to the holding room!' Hutchings shouted down the corridor. 'I don't want to see again until she is ready to answer. You used the backdated software, idiots!'

Luca ran to the door and watched as Hutchings marched angrily past pulling a sticker with a training cable from her face. A moment later and Kelsee was being dragged in the other direction by two of the people from the other suite. Her head hung with her hair falling limp over her face. She didn't struggle at all. She was unconscious.

'She's being taken that way, back to the lift,' Luca whispered urgently and pointed. He pulled the door open a little.

Alec joined him. Then suddenly there was a familiar voice coming from the speaker.

'Greetings from Outside!' Luca turned and saw the familiar and friendly smile of Eban.

'Shut it down now!' Hutchings screamed down the corridor.

The live screen cut back to the previous Network program.

Alec rushed back to the monitor and twisted the dial. The video link from Outside was running but the sound was not being played through the speaker.

'Who's seeing this?' Hutchings voice could be faintly heard.

'Just us,' replied the worker in the other suite.

'Did it broadcast?' she asked.

The worker was obviously flustered. 'For a few seconds … maybe.'

There was a thud. 'Arghh!'

Eban had set the camera to pan the area. Luca could see the mass of Outsiders gathered. Eban then appeared back on screen as if he were holding the camera directed at himself. He was talking and smiling. He shook his fist and nodded.

'Wait!' Hutchings said with a tone of excitement. 'We are recording this, yes?'

Alec was flicking off the monitors. 'We've got to go now, while she is distracted,' he whispered.

Luca took one last look at his friend and switched it off. He was encouraged. Eban and Mercy had been able to unite Outside and were reaching Tropolis, be it only for a few seconds.

Alec and Luca crept back along the corridor. Luca hoped that he would see Harland but had suspected that he was tucked away somewhere in luxury not caring about anyone but himself. As he passed Monitor Suite 1 the door was wide open. He carefully looked in and could see Hutchings leaning over the man at the desk. She was busy rewinding a section of Eban's broadcast.

'Trim it to there and then stitch that section on the end,' Hutchings said. 'Take that speech and cut it up. I want the phrases separated.'

Hutchings was so engrossed in what she was doing that she didn't turn. Luca hurried away to the open doorway that Alec held and to the relative safety of the stairs.

Luca waited until the door shut behind him. 'What is she doing with that?'

'It looked like she was editing it,' Alec replied as they climbed the stairs. 'Whatever it is, I don't think it will be in Eban's favour. Hutchings is control crazy and won't let others dictate to her.'

'Did you see the crowd though!' Luca said smiling widely. 'I knew Mercy would do it. There is just something about her that you can't escape. It isn't control like Hutchings, but it's like a magnetic force or something!'

'Whatever is happening in Outside will have an impact on Kelsee. I'm not sure that Hutchings will leave her alone for long.'

'We have to get her out of here.' Luca's joy was short lived. He dashed past Alec to reach the top of the stairs. 'Who knows what else her grandfather will do.'

'He is a strong man and his following is more committed than it has ever been. People look to him as someone who hasn't changed in years. He is the one thing that is solid in Tropolis, the one thing that hasn't been diminished because of the fatigue. Just last week he was promising power restoration and free sickness treatment to the masses. I guess the invasion on Outside didn't go as planned.' Alec put his hand on Luca's chest. 'I have learnt a great deal whilst I have been here, but one thing that can cause unexpected reactions is failure.' Alec removed his hand from Luca and rubbed his brow. 'Failure or protecting yourself from being seen as a failure can make a man turn to desperate measures.'

'Harland is going to be more dangerous now than he has ever been isn't he?' Luca asked, but he knew the answer. 'We've got to get her out of here before she gets punished.'

Alec shook his head sadly. 'I don't have access to this level. I can't get the lift to even stop on this floor, I just don't have the codes.' He lowered his gaze to the floor. 'I have only ever opened this door. I can't get you in further.'

Luca patted Alec's shoulder. 'I'm not meant to be here anyway but I'm not leaving without her. She needs a family and she's not got that in Tropolis.' Luca pulled on the stairwell door and opened it ajar. The corridor was dark except for the warm light streaming from the open lift.

The click of a lock from across the hallway made Luca start. He slunk back into the stairwell a little. One of the technicians who had carried Kelsee away had strolled out and had tapped his shoulder.

'Yes ma'am. We are on our way. Over.' He casually approached the lift and began tapping on the control panel. 'You better get a move on,' he shouted across the corridor and through the slowly closing lift. 'She won't want to be waiting for you! I'm going!'

'I'm coming! Don't lock me out!' came the reply and the other man came rushing out, flinging the door wide and running to the closing lift. 'You idiot!' he spat as the lift doors sealed and the corridor went dark.

Luca sprinted from his hiding place and managed to get his hand to the closing door just before it shut. He turned to see Alec laughing a little. 'It seems I have an access code!' he whispered.

Chapter 22

00h 00m

Luca was grateful for the arrogance of Tropolis just this once. The unit must have been considered so secure by the right people that there were no cameras or staff. Luca bit down on his lip; or it was very secret.

The darkness seemed characteristic of this level in the building. The lights were triggered by motion but as soon as you moved on they switched off. It was very disorientating.

Luca began searching; pushing at all available doors but nothing would open. There were no windows to the hidden worlds that were barred. Luca pressed his ear against the next door and listened. There was the gentle hum of a machine on the other side but no sound of movement. Some muffled beeps and clicks came from another room while others were completely silent.

'Kelsee?' he called a little nervously. 'Kelsee?' he repeated louder. No one came running, the floor was completely abandoned. With his confidence growing, Luca began to bang on the doors as he passed them. 'Are you in there?'

At the far end of the passage there was a large communal area with several huge sofas. There were tall lamps and other electrical appliances all devoid of life. The room, however, was dominated by the screen covering almost the entire wall.

'They bought her here,' Luca said, 'so where is she?'

A sudden tapping began. Luca spun around but couldn't determine where the noise came from. He crossed the room and the lights came on automatically.

'Kelsee?'

The tapping continued and he heard a muffled voice. The steady and wide spreading light revealed a single dark coloured door set apart from the rest, leading from the space.

He rushed forwards and banged on the door. 'Are you in there?' A fast tapping replied.

Luca turned to Alec but knew that there was little his uncle could do. There was no keypad, switch or button to unlock the door. He ran his hands over the close fitting indentation that marked the next room. There was nothing to help him. As he reached the upper section where the door met the wall Luca hesitated. The ceiling was tiled and he saw that the wall dividing the rooms did not reach beyond the suspended ceiling.

'Help me!' Luca called to Alec as he began to drag one of the sofas over to the doorway.

Luca climbed onto the back of the seat and reached up. He pushed at a tile and it lifted. He quickly peered into the hole he had made and saw that the wall dividing the rooms stopped just below the suspended ceiling.

'Luca!' Kelsee called.

He shifted two more tiles and then lifted himself into the ceiling void using the partition wall to support his weight. The air was dusty. Luca could see through the small slit into the next room and Kelsee was slumped against the door but her gaze was on him.

'You ok?' Luca asked. He was aware of her cut face and lack of movement 'We're going to get you out.' He felt for the next tile and lifted it out of place. Grit and dirt showered Kelsee and she quickly turned her face away.

'What can I do?' Alec asked.

'You are going to have to help lift her out from here,' Luca said. 'You alright doing that?'

'Won't be a problem,' Alec replied climbing up on the sofa. 'I don't think we should be here much longer.'

Luca knew that he needed to get into Kelsee's room. He searched for the best place to land. There were two chairs and a small table in the stark white room. The only other colour were the smears of blood on the floor. They hadn't held back on violence against her here. If the holding room was designed for such an interrogation, why had they taken her down to the media suite? He braced himself as he jumped into Kelsee's room. He rushed over to her and wrapped his arms around her. He took a deep breath knowing that now he might have the power to keep her safe. Luca pulled away but reached towards her and cupped her face in his hand. Kelsee leaned into his touch seemingly unaware of the cut across her cheek.

He was so close to her. He lifted her hand that was on her lap and brought it to his lips. She lifted her other hand, wanting to hold his face close to hers. He leaned into her and gently kissed her.

Kelsee shut her eyes and smiled.

'I'm so glad I found you.' Luca didn't want to move on but knew that he had to. 'We'll get you out,' he said quietly. 'Can you stand?'

'Yes, but I feel all shaky. It hurts.'

Luca grit his teeth and helped to lift her. 'I can't understand how he could do this to you.'

'It was Hutchings,' Kelsee corrected.

Luca shook his head but did not answer her. 'Wait here!'

He propped her up against the wall and pulled the table towards the door just as Alec appeared at the hole in the ceiling.

'Can you get ...' Luca began, but Kelsee was already shuffling herself up on the table. 'That's it, well done!' Alec leaned down with hands open. 'Let me help!' Luca said lifting Kelsee as carefully as possible. She winced but did not complain.

Luca pushed her up and Alec grabbed her upstretched hands, pulling her to the ledge. Alec helped her through the hole and she was gone. Luca clambered after them. When he got to the other side, Alec was just supporting Kelsee to one of the other sofas. He put the tiles back in place to hide Kelsee's escape for as long as possible.

'Are you alright?' Luca said as he pushed the sofa back to its place. 'Do you think you can come with us?' He smudged the track-lines out of the carpet as he went. Not paying attention, he nudged the coffee table. Suddenly, the room was bathed in blue light.

'Don't worry about me. You have to see this,' Kelsee said weakly. As the large holographic sprang into life. 'This was active when they bought me in before, I'm glad they've not shut it down.' She looked like she was in so much pain that Luca just wanted to get her to safety, to a place where he could help her. 'It is bad!' she said with a sigh.

The blue light from the cubic sensor was bright even against the lamps. The graphic showed a tight grid with undulating hills and wide sea. In scrolling letters, imposed over the map were the words 'Extinction commencement sequence – Code word: Emundabit. Stage One: complete. Stage Two: instigated'.

'Tropolis,' Alec pointed.

Luca looked down the coast. 'And Outside.'

'That's not all,' Kelsee said waving her hand in the blue light. The image tightened as she pulled the focus. Several sections of the map appeared either green, amber or red. 'Oh no!'

'They know about Campion.' Luca took a sharp breath.

'They do, but I think it is worse,' Kelsee manipulated the graphic again. In the top corner there were three clock countdowns in the same corresponding colours. The red countdown had reached zero, the green clock, although only showing a small number of minutes was stationary, whilst the amber was ticking away.

   00h 00m   01h 57m   00h 30m

   'When I was brought in here before,' Kelsee said urgently, 'Campion wasn't amber, it was still green.'

   'Outside is red now,' Alec said. 'And has already been invaded and attacked. If Campion has changed from green. This is a countdown.'

   'Campion sea forts are amber,' Kelsee whispered, 'So they'll attack them next. They have under an hour.'

   'Eban had got to Outside, he might have had some of Campion with him. But what about the land settlements?' Luca paused, tracing back the route they had made to Outside from his mother's settlement. Her home was amber. He felt lightheaded and had to sit down. 'They aren't safe either. None of them.'

Chapter 23

00h 00m **02h 57m** 00h 30m

Alec frowned. 'I didn't have to assemble an army for anywhere else?' He rubbed his hands as he thought. 'There just isn't enough of a healthy population. They know that, I told them that.'

'We need to warn them,' Kelsee said wincing a little. 'The countdown gives just a few hours.'

Luca reached over to Alec and gripped his wrist. 'Can you get a message to them?' Alec shrugged. 'Willow is still alive and that is where she is. You have got to help her.'

'Alive?' Alec said wide eyed. 'Are you sure?'

'I've seen her.' Luca released Alec and swallowed hard. He had not left her with the friendliest of goodbyes and was now feeling ashamed. What if that was the last time he ever saw her? 'Can you get them to evacuate?' he asked desperately.

Alec shrugged but then got to his feet quickly, 'I can try.'

'Where can I take Kelsee for medical supplies?' Luca asked. 'The Death Room?'

'Too heavily watched,' Alec replied. 'Head for the basement. That is where all the supplies come into the city, there is bound to be something we can use to treat her wounds down there. I'll be there as soon as I have sent Campion a warning.'

Luca moved over to Kelsee and gently supported her as she stood. He could feel her body trembling and her quick but shallow breathing made him wonder how much pain she was in. He wouldn't force her to move faster but was worried that they would be found or Campion destroyed if they couldn't move faster.

The exit consisted of a simple release button. Luca realised that it had already taken far too long to get to the stairwell.

'Go on ahead,' Luca urged Alec.

He nodded. 'Take the stairs to the floor with the fixed cameras and then call a lift. Go to the lowest floor and wait there for me. But don't leave the lift there, send it back up just in case they start looking for her – we need to cover our tracks.'

Luca pushed his uncle away. 'Got it. Go!'

Alec didn't turn back but ran down the stairs, his feet tapping frantically as he sped downwards. Luca was left following after him, helping a struggling Kelsee.

'Try this.' He lifted her so that she sat on the banister and had her lean on his shoulder. It seemed that this gave her some relief. Movement still caused her too much pain to speak so they descended quietly. Upon reaching the correct floor, Luca followed Alec's instructions and took the lift to the lowest floor he could. The level number flashed on the panel and they descended. There seemed to be a longer pause between the ground floor and the basement. When they eventually arrived, they exited hurriedly. Luca quickly sent the lift back up to a random floor number.

Luca had thought that the basement would appear to be much the same as the Maglev station since that was also underground, but he was wrong. Strong round pillars supported the upper floors but they were difficult to make out with the volume of goods that filled the space. Stacked from floor to ceiling were plastic wrapped pallets loaded with boxes and crates. Each package was labelled clearly with a zone number and row designation, although they were not organised into groups where they were piled here.

The only access that was left was a long passage formed by the towering parcels and since Luca did not want to be left exposed he thought it best to hide. He wrapped his arm around Kelsee's waist and they tottered deeper. Luca searched for a safe place for Kelsee to rest but the further that he travelled into this extensive holding area the more distracted he became with Tropolite extravagance.

An opening, almost the height of the space but with walls thicker than he was tall was cast out of concrete. Curious, Luca stepped in.

There was a sudden succession of pings as hundreds of long ceiling lights came on as they entered.

They stood at the top of a ramp overlooking a huge open space laid out in a grid formation. The lights shone between the neatly stacked boxes that had been placed on vast shelves.

'Wait here!' Luca said helping Kelsee to the edge of the ramp. 'Nothing will fall on you here.' He jogged down the slope and up to one of the rows. The sign on the end read: Zone 6, Row 46b. Below that there was a small gridded map and a green First Aid box. He unhooked it and looked at the map of the space with the area marked where he stood. Below that there was a list of zones.

Luca read down the list: Food, clothing, household, sanitary, chemicals, energy, communication, hardware and in Zone 9, medical. He pulled the map from the side and quickly located the medical zone. It covered several rows. He rubbed his forehead and blew out his breath. This place was vast and incredibly organised. He ran down the nearest row to investigate and the further Luca ventured the more uneasy he felt. Who would need all these supplies? Towering over him and packed tightly were row upon row of brown crates and shrink wrapped boxes. The supplies outside the entrance were destined for this store house but there were no spaces left on these shelves.

He had seen enough and Kelsee's pain was too urgent to investigate further. Dashing back to her, he dropped to his knees and flipped open the first aid kit. Everything was wrapped and sterile, something that Luca was not used to. Having had to treat injuries in Outside with whatever could be found or reused, Luca had a moment of confusion. He shifted some of the contents into the lid, putting the tight bandage and packets of dressings to one side.

'Let me see,' Luca said holding out his hand to Kelsee.

She showed him her wrists. There were long red and slightly swollen patches almost encircling them. Kelsee reached into the box and pulled out a tube of antiseptic cream.

'Will that help?' he asked. Then he opened it and gently smeared the cool lotion on her burns. Kelsee gasped. 'Sorry!' He applied a clean pad of gauze. 'I can't believe he did this to you.' Then wrapped them in bandages.

'Thank you!' she said quietly cradling her arms close to her body. 'Why did you come after me?' she asked.

'Just as well I did.'

'Yes, but that wasn't what I asked.'

Luca stayed silent for a moment then changed the subject. 'We need to deal with that too.' He tilted her face into the light. The cut across her cheek was quite deep but had stopped bleeding. He swabbed off the dried blood and tentatively cleaned the wound. It started to bleed once again. Searching through the kit he found some small paper-like strips and stuck them over the gash to hold the skin tightly together. This seemed to stop the flow. Not wanting to aggravate it further, he left it alone. 'Anything else?'

'I don't think so,' Kelsee replied. 'My ribs hurt a bit but there's no cuts there. I think my legs feel a bit more steady now too. I haven't felt this human in a long time!' She stretched her legs out in front of her. 'Luca?' Kelsee pulled his body to face her. 'You didn't answer me.'

He bit on his lip. 'You're my friend.'

'So are Mercy and Eban, but they aren't here?'

'Eban was with Campion.'

Kelsee frowned. 'I know that. What aren't you telling me? Why did you come?'

He sighed and swallowed hard. 'You said on the note that you were going to your grandfather. I don't know what I was thinking. I guess I got worried or scared or something and thought that you were going to tell him about all that you had seen. I just wanted to stop you.'

'Why stop me? He is one who could make all this change.'

He looked away. 'I didn't think you wanted it to change, it sounded like you are going to tell him about everything, you know, Outside and Campion. I thought that you had seen enough and were going back to Tropolis for good.'

She gripped his arm tightly. 'Why would you think that?' she asked angrily.

'It's my fault. I was horrid to you and I thought that you would … well, would be like me and … well, you're so not like me. But your note made me think that you were.'

'But you wouldn't do that to your friends.'

'No, but I wouldn't want to live on the run either if there was a place here in Tropolis.'

'There isn't a place in Tropolis for me, I told you that before. I couldn't live here before and I certainly can't live here now, knowing how others live.'

Luca turned away and they were both silent for a while.

When Kelsee spoke again her voice was soft and kind. 'I don't know how you did it,' she finally said. Luca peered back at her. 'You survived in Outside, you and all those others. I couldn't just let it continue. I thought I might be the only one who could make a difference. I had no real choice.'

'You couldn't make a difference and there isn't a choice anymore. I think your grandfather made that perfectly clear.'

'That wasn't my grandfather!'

Luca sighed and turned to face her. 'Kelsee, you have to see him as we see him. He isn't who you think he is. He did that to Outsiders!'

'No!' Kelsee said wide eyed. 'That wasn't my grandfather. As in it wasn't him, it was fake, made up, not real!'

Luca frowned at her. 'What?' He looked at her cheek and thought that perhaps the blow had confused her.

'My grandfather hasn't looked that well and young for a long time. It wasn't him.' Kelsee said reaching out to Luca. 'I need to see him and talk to him.'

Luca waved his hand. 'I don't think so! Not after what has just happened.'

'I came back to Tropolis to speak with him.' Kelsee began to get to her feet. 'I can't go without at least trying.' She stood and wobbled a little. 'It wasn't him, Luca.'

Luca stood quickly. 'You can't go!'

Kelsee put her hands on her hips. 'You can't tell me what to do!'

'You are injured!' Luca pointed out.

'And you have sorted that out for me, thank you. But I can't stay here!'

'You've got to stay!'

'Why, Luca? Tell me why!'

He briefly covered his mouth. 'Because he will hurt you again. And we are waiting for Alec.'

'It wasn't him!' Kelsee turned away. 'I'm not just going to sit around while everyone is made extinct.' She turned to face him again. 'I know you saw that too. I know you read it. *Extinction commencement sequence – Code word: Emundabit*. That was what it said on the plans.'

Luca did not deny it. He took a deep breath. 'Let someone else sort it out. Alec is sending Campion a message. They can do it.'

'That is a good choice Luca,' Kelsee agreed nodding, 'But is it the right choice?'

Luca hung his head. He had protected her, found her and wanted to rescue her. But in reality, it was not something he could do at all while Emundabit loomed over his world. What would be the right thing to do? Luca looked up at her. He saw the girl from Tropolis had changed. Kelsee was not like him. She was much stronger. When she came back to her home, she had not slipped neatly back into her old ways. He saw the dressed cut on her face and sighed. 'I thought I'd lost you before, when I was supposed to be looking after you.' He shook his head. 'I can't do that again.'

'Don't you think I have thought about it?' Kelsee asked. 'When I left Outside I didn't know if I would see you again but I knew that I had to try and change things. Who has access to the one leader that can stop this?' Kelsee softened her tone. 'I care about you ... and about Mercy and Eban, and your father and Willow. I care what happens from this point on to Outside and to Campion. If there is something that I can do, I think I should do it. It may not be a good choice, but it is the right one.' She stepped closer to him. 'Please, Luca,' she said reaching for him. 'I need to do this.'

Luca couldn't find fault in her argument. He took hold of her outstretched hand. His rapidly beating heart revealed more than his fear. If he took her away from Tropolis where could they go that would be safe? But if he let her go to Harland Barret, what else would he do to her? She seemed convinced that Barret hadn't hurt her.

He ran his hand through his hair and stood straighter. 'Alright, where is he?'

She hugged him tightly. 'Thank you!' she whispered. She pulled away and seemed to stand straighter. 'He'll be in his house, out of town. I can get us there but I need a Maglev station. I think the one we came on will work.'

He sighed, wondering if this was at all wise. 'This way.'

A moment after they left the large warehouse of supplies the lights went out and the excessiveness of Tropolis should have been hidden once again had it not been for the towering piles of supplies right up to the lift doors.

Luca instinctively pushed at the door next to the elevator knowing that he would find a stairwell. Despite Kelsee's eagerness, progress was slow.

The distance between the basement and ground floor was three times as that of the floors above but Kelsee kept silent if she was in any pain. She pushed him on.

Warm light filtered through the glass pane on the door and Luca peered through it to see the unmanned desk. He put his finger to his lips briefly and crept out with Kelsee close behind.

Luca beckoned her to move faster in the bright corridor, but Kelsee was looking tired as she tried to keep up. He offered some support and she took him by the hand. There was no way of telling what would be in the lobby but Luca, having never encountered any trouble confidently hit the simple exit button. The door opened and they moved into the large, bright lobby. It was silent and empty.

'Come on!' Luca pulled Kelsee out into the open space and forced her to dash towards the Maglev exit.

They had crossed half of the floor when the light streaming into the space began to grow dim. Luca tried to run faster. He looked up and saw that the glass ceiling was becoming opaque and dark. He could feel the tears welling in his eyes as the fear of being caught overcame him. There was nowhere to hide. They were as exposed as they could be. He spun around to see who would be coming for them.

Suddenly Harland Barret shouted unnaturally into the place. 'I am sending you a warning!' Luca looked about frantically. How had they found them? But there was no movement and they were still alone. A slight movement above him caught his attention and he looked up. The glass roof had become massive screens. 'This was received a few moments ago from Outside. One of the rogue Compassion Prize contestants has taken it as his divine right to threaten our peace. Please give this your full attention.'

The image changed and Eban's face filled the ceiling. The images were coming from Outside.

'Tropolis have treated Outside wrongfully,' he began. 'The people here are united!' The screen fuzzed a little as if there was some sort of static interference. Luca only remembered the crisp and clear images that had come through to the media suite, and they were nothing like this. 'You would be right to think that we...' again static fuzzed across the screen for a moment. '...angry and want revenge.' Eban's image stuttered, broke up a little and then flickered back to life. 'Get ready! We are coming!' Then there were extensive shots of the people of Outside who could have been angry and organised. There were so many that as the camera panned the interference cut in once again before it cut back to the continuously panning shot of the huge numbers of revengeful Outsiders.

Harland Barret appeared once again. He stood in the same white room as before. He paused a moment, silent and wide eyed. When he spoke it was slow and measured. 'They have sent us warning that they are coming for us.' A faint scream could be heard. Luca wasn't sure where it had come from until Barret turned to the side as if he heard it too. 'Please, I ask you to stay calm and not to panic. It is true that these people have already starved us of our electricity and now they want to take our homes. I am endeavouring to do all I can to protect Tropolis but I will need your co-operation.' Barret was focused. 'You must protect your homes and your families. They have become the enemy and they will stop at nothing to destroy all that we have built here. It is your duty to not let that happen.' Barret stepped forward as if to climb out of the screen. Luca backed away. 'I am working hard to see that all is done to ensure our survival.' Harland Barret raised his hand and in it was a small gun. 'I suggest that you arm yourselves, don't listen to what they say to you, you cannot trust them. You have seen that they are coming to take away our freedom ... Don't let them!'

The daylight returned as if nothing had happened but everything had changed.

Luca's chest tightened and he could feel his muscles tensing. 'He wants them to kill Outsiders!'

Kelsee glared at him. 'It is not him Luca!'

Luca shook his head. 'Just like that was not Eban!' He began to run across the marble floor.

Muffled shouting and screaming filtered into the lobby. Both Luca and Kelsee were shocked as they peered through the tall glass wall. The street was beginning to appear almost normal. People were leaving their buildings and going onto the streets. A large man stumbled up to the glass wall and banged heavily on the barrier. He was shouting something about safety.

'We've got to go!' Kelsee said as she dragged Luca away from the spectacle.

Luca couldn't look away from these true Tropolites. They were dressed differently from Outsiders, but were they really that different? Some of them looked very ill and frail, but they were all scared and desperate. The Network screening and Barret had created such a fear and panic that they had been driven to gather on the streets, the one place they had avoided for all this time. Why would he do that? Surely, having heard that Eban and the Outsiders were on their way to Tropolis he should have just mobilised the defence. But Tropolis was without protection, all that they had was sent to Outside and the only way to save Tropolis was to summon the people to defend it themselves. Luca's breath caught as he considered if fear was the best motivation. These people may well defend their homes, but who would they defend against? Did they even know who their neighbour was? This would end in disaster. Tropolite could easily turn on Tropolite. Luca felt cold when he considered the endorsement of weapons that Harland Barret had made. Fear would tell these people to attack before they had time to think. Barret had made it clear that this situation was urgent and frightening. No one was safe. If this continued only the fittest and strongest would survive. The sudden thought made Luca gag. They would be loyal to Tropolis and all that it stood for having fought so hard for it. Perhaps this is what Barret wanted. Harland Barret would not be to blame, but would instead, be the heroic leader with more power and loyalty than ever before.

Chapter 24

02h 24m

The light dimmed once more and Harland Barret appeared once again on the sky light screens.

'People of Tropolis!' he called out. The people out on the street stopped, turned and looked towards the same façade. Luca knew what they saw because the ceiling showed the same message. 'Listen to me! You must return to your homes. Protect them.'

Luca had heard and seen enough. He gripped Kelsee's hand firmly and ran for the Maglev exit.

The stairs twisted down under the building, although it may not have been lower than the basement storage space. When, at last they came to the bright, but empty, platform Kelsee was out of breath but managing to keep up.

The mirrors that covered the vaulted ceiling and strong walls created fractured sparkles and distorted reflections. Luca approached the edge and was about to clamber over the side.

'Where are you going?' Kelsee asked. She looked up and down the platform and then walked a little way to the right. She stopped and pressed her hand against a square glass plate. 'My grandfather has his own Maglev train, and I have the code.' The glass lit up with a number keypad. Before Luca knew what Kelsee was doing she had punched in a set of numbers.

'They'll trace it!' Luca called out.

'A possibility ... but I don't think that the train is far away. We'll be gone before they will know it.' Then, as if she had said some magic word there was a rush of air and a moment later a smart, silver and blue Maglev sped up the track.

Luca frowned at her. Kelsee just sighed and stepped into the carriage. He followed her.

The train was spacious and unlike any he had been in before. The chairs were deep and soft, there was a large screen at one end and the windows were tinted. The carriage was fitted out like the communal lounge that the contestants had, only the furnishings were much more luxurious.

'You hungry?' Kelsee asked as the door slid shut behind them.

Luca let out a bark of laughter. 'How did you do that?' Kelsee tilted her head in response. 'How did you know the Maglev wasn't far away. Not any Maglev, but this one?'

'Oh,' Kelsee nodded as she punched in a code to the control panel to set the destination. She then made her way over to the chilling cabinets at the far end, 'Hutchings was in the building so I assumed she had used it to get there.' She pulled out two packets, placed them onto plates and put them into the oven. She tapped a few buttons. 'Here!' she said passing Luca a bottle of green liquid and then opened one for herself. 'She's reorganised the food a bit, and the drinks are more to her liking.' The oven beeped, Kelsee set down her drink and then fetched the steaming hot food. She offered one plate to Luca and then sat down on one of the chairs. 'It will take a little while to get there. My grandfather lives out of town. Sit down and eat up. You are hungry aren't you?'

Luca took the plate and sat opposite her. He split open the packet and the aroma of the deep filled pie, with its creamy sauce made his mouth water. He had not realised just how hungry he was.

They sat quietly. Luca was lost in his own thoughts. He stabbed at the pie aggressively when he thought of what he had just witnessed. He had been wrong about lots of things. He had once believed that Tropolis was the ideal place to live but now knew that it was full of sickness and isolation. The prize had offered to save himself and give him freedom from caring for his father, but it had only opened his eyes to his own neglected wealth. And now, despite all those years he had been envious of Tropolites and hated them for their waste and riches, he discovered that in reality they had very little more than himself. They had been held back by domineering and influential leadership. He could feel all the hatred that had once been for the Tropolite people being funnelled onto the one man who started it all and would not stop it. Once the connection was made, Luca could not shut it down. The years of hunger, mistreatment and grief only made his anger burn brighter. Then a dark but liberating thought came to him; he was about to have the opportunity to stop it all.

Luca couldn't look up at Kelsee but he knew that she was watching him. He could hear her gentle cutting of her meal and the quiet chink of cutlery to the plate. He tried hard to reduce his own sharp and loud sounds but they just seemed to grow louder. When he had finally finished, he put down his knife and fork, cleared his throat, composed himself then glanced up.

'Are you alright?' Kelsee asked, extending her hand.

Luca nodded. 'So,' he began, 'Why does your grandfather live so far away from everyone?'

Kelsee sat back a bit. 'I think that city life was too much for him. I know that Mara Hutchings found this house and knew that she could get the transport to work if he needed it. He prefers to be outside.' Kelsee put her plate on the side table. 'I guess that if they knew about Campion, they must have thought about where he could live and decided it was safe.'

Luca sucked on his lips and nodded again. He turned away and looked out the window. The cityscape was in the distance and there were wide fields that separated them. He was grateful that the view could be measured as a distraction. He could not shake the heavy pain he felt as he considered Kelsee's definition of safe. He recalled his mother sitting in her chair, tucked away with all those books, her people busy in the tumble down streets and the large warehouses hiding the crops ready for harvest. He stared, hard, at the disappearing buildings. Harland was safe from Campion, he was never under threat from them, he was safe from everyone. Nearly.

Luca had to stop that thought sharply.

He focussed on the plight of the Tropolites and their dependency on the Outsiders producing electricity for them. He knew that they had been rationing the power to Tropolis, yet here he was, sitting comfortably on a Maglev, travelling at high speed without a problem. He wondered at the possibility of separate power supplies. Harland, would, of course not allow himself to be without. The fiery heat of anger would not go but kept on feeding. Luca balled his fists. He wanted to shout and rage, desired to burst out in a string of accusations and demand justice, but he stayed silent. He held it all together for Kelsee's sake. Her grandfather was not who she thought he was and he was far worse than Luca had ever understood him to be.

The gentle rocking of the Maglev was soporific but everything in Luca felt pumped with adrenalin and he could not rest. When the carriage finally stopped, Luca was relieved that he would at least be able to move without excuse.

Kelsee stood first and waited by the door. As it rose she glanced at Luca and sighed. Turning back to the outside she briefly shut her eyes and bowed her head. She looked sad. Luca stood up and as she stepped out, he instinctively reached over to his plate, grabbed the knife and slipped it into his pocket.

The Maglev had halted at a short platform which was flanked by tall, dark hedge. The barrier stretched far both ways. Directly in front of them and up a few steps, a wide and ornate gate creaked slightly as it opened automatically. Kelsee entered without hesitation. Luca looked up at the gates but couldn't detect any cameras or obvious surveillance. He wanted to wait, to check that they would be safe but at the same time there was nothing that could get him inside and face to face with Harland quick enough. Luca searched again, hoping that some tough guard would come and grab them, anything to stop him from having to do what he knew he needed to do. But they were alone and unchallenged.

Beyond the gates, up a long straight path, the pale historical façade of a grand house remained untouched, it seemed, by time. But warm lights illuminated a few of the windows telling Luca that it was inhabited. He had never seen any building like it. It did not resemble the clean and crisp glass apartments in Tropolis. The shapes of the windows set into the walls and the slanting roof, the seemingly calculated and symmetrical view, even the way that the greenery climbed the walls all related to Campion better than Tropolis. He noticed the oddity and ornate pattern built into a curved section higher up that may have been some type of viewing tower. He scanned the spaces, searching for manned security, but found no one.

Suddenly, a started deer leapt from behind one of the hedges. Its pale body, sleek and strong, jumped out of the patch of garden where it had been nibbling the plants. It sent the stone chippings flying into the air as it fled deeper into the grounds and out of sight.

Everything seemed to glisten with the previous night's rainfall. The fallen leaves softly carpeted vast sections of the gravel path and had been piled up against the taller plants, arranged by the gusts of wind, where they had begun to rot. The shapely plants had not been attended to and had sprouted shoots that disturbed the geometric designs. Had it not been for the lights in the building beyond, Luca would have thought that this was place was abandoned.

The building towered over them as they approached. Kelsee's confidence did little to help Luca's nerves. She strolled right up to the door and pulled down on the handle. The large door swung open with an earie squeal.

Luca went to grab her, but she was already out of reach. 'We can't just go in!' he whispered urgently.

Kelsee looked over her shoulder. 'This is my grandfather's house. I can do what I want here.' She walked away.

Luca huffed. 'Kelsee!' he called.

Kelsee would not stop, so he followed her inside.

He quickly closed the door but regretted his decision as the space was very dimly lit. A huge and richly carved staircase curved lavishly in the centre of the space and followed the dark wood panelling that spanned the walls up to the next floor. There was some sort of roof window above as greenish hues of daylight filtered down to the treads of the stairs and glanced off the polished parquet. Massive paintings hung in ornate gold frames in between the wide wooden doorways. There were old master landscapes alongside bold abstracts and, among other portraits, a Barret family composition. He huffed and shook his head at the expense and extravagance since the likeness of Barret and his two sons was inadequately inaccurate.

Any resemblance of boldness in Luca had wilted. He was tiny in this domineering place and he did not fit. He shoved his hands in his pockets. His knuckle caught the handle of the knife and he knew that he had to go on.

Kelsee had already avoided the staircase and was about to enter one of the rooms on the left.

'Wait!' Luca called. His voice felt like a roar but since they had not been challenged he did not worry about it disturbing anyone.

Kelsee beckoned to Luca. 'Hurry!'

She paused for only a moment and then went in.

Dusty and ancient tapestries hung over the entirety of the wall. The colours were faded but it was clear that the scenes depicted men and women on horseback with dogs scurrying about their hooves. There were large, saggy sofas and chairs, dark wood side tables and cupboards. Marble busts and ornate vases sat precariously on plinths while shelves were stacked with books showing their faded spines.

The room was flooded with light from the ceiling height French doors that led out to a glass conservatory.

Still there were no people, no one to turn them away. Luca's arms prickled as the hairs began to stand up. Something wasn't right.

Kelsee continued towards the glass doors as if there was nothing wrong.

'Where is everyone?' Luca asked quietly.

'Grandfather doesn't like the house to be busy. He prefers his own company that's why he sent me to live in Tropolis.'

'You didn't live here?'

'It's been years since I have stayed here. The last time was to punish me for my bad behaviour and lack of commitment to studies. But I loved it. All this space and colour.' She paused. 'Perhaps I loved it too much and they heard how happy I was, that's why I was taken back to Tropolis.'

'He didn't want you to be happy?'

Kelsee shrugged. 'Hutchings collected me one morning and I haven't seen my grandfather since, not really seen him, face to face, anyway.'

Luca wanted to state that her grandfather was too busy taking happiness from everyone else to bother with her. 'When I found out who you were related to, you said that you weren't that impressed by him.'

'Harland Barret has done a lot of damage,' Kelsee looked Luca full in the face. 'But I don't think that was who I knew when I was last here.' She smiled. 'It is making sense, don't you see?'

Luca was tired of her defence for him. 'He's different now. You've seen and experienced what he has done.'

'He is not the man that was on the video or the man who was hurting me,' Kelsee said, counting off on her fingers. 'Luca,' she said frowning at him, 'If that wasn't him, why can't all this other stuff not be him too.'

Luca couldn't look into her eyes any more. He was here to do one thing, he knew that this man was to blame and had to pay.

'You'll see, Luca,' Kelsee said confidently.

A warm gust of air floated into the room as Kelsee opened the doors and entered the conservatory. The gentle tinkling of water from a fountain in the centre broke the silence of lack of life. Rich scents of earth and a heady flowery fragrance overpowered the dusty and neglected smell of the room where Luca stood with slumped shoulders.

He looked up and followed her. The pool was full of water lilies and bright coloured fish. But beyond the splashing pond was a jungle of green, lush leaves and tropical blooms. There, a lone figure dressed in what appeared to be pyjamas, sat in an oversized armchair. In one hand he held an open book and the other a delicate bone china cup with a steaming drink.

Luca stopped mid stride. A deep, animal growl rose to Luca's throat and he pulled out the knife.

Harland Barret looked up from what he was reading.

Chapter 25

00h 00m **01h 52m** 00h 30m

Harland coughed and then squinted at them across the pond.

'Is that my little Kelsee?' he asked punctuating every syllable. 'I must be dreaming!'

Luca held the knife tightly; it seemed like the only real thing at that moment. The man sat, overwhelmed by the expansive armchair, was grey haired and wrinkled, his skin was thin and papery. His eyes were not bright but drooped with age and weariness. He was not the familiar wild haired man that had been in the Tropolis video archives, the orderly and powerful leader or the one that had tortured Kelsee, she had been right. Luca tilted his head and squinted back at the old man. Yet he was Harland Barret.

Everything had led Luca to this moment but he hardly recognised this man. His muscles were tense but was he ready? They hadn't been stopped and it appeared that no-one was aware that they had even entered the house. He could do what he knew he should and be out before anyone could stop him. But what had he come to do? Suddenly the knife was cumbersome and awkward. Could he really finish it all?

'It's me!' Kelsee replied but she did not approach her grandfather. 'I'm not a dream.'

The cup began to shake and the hot liquid spilled over the side. 'But you died. They assured me that you had died and that I would never see you again.' He put down the book and cup. 'This is it. This must be it. My time has obviously come. It is much sweeter than I expected it would ever be. I will go with you Kelsee. Surely, if you are there, it is a wonderful place!'

'I'm not dead, and neither are you,' she said seriously.

Luca could not shake the phrase that Barret had used: they had assured him she had died. This was the man that was familiar to him and that he had hated his whole life. Luca needed little other excuse. This man would stop at nothing; even his own family. Luca raised the knife. 'But you should be!'

Barret hadn't even acknowledged he was there and that he could be a threat until now when he stared at him.

'Luca, no!' Kelsee stepped between them. 'It's not who you think. This is not the Harland Barret you know.'

Luca peered around her. 'You are Harland Barret, aren't you?' he asked.

'I am indeed.' Barret raised his chin proudly and puckered his lips. 'Kelsee, dear, I am Harland Barret, your grandfather.' He reached out to her. 'Are you not well? I haven't seen you for a while but it is me.'

'I know who you are!' Kelsee said gesturing at her grandfather.

Barret laughed a little then turned to Luca. 'But who are you?'

Luca jabbed the knife in the air. 'I'm an Outsider,' Luca said through a tight mouth. 'No one of importance to you.'

'Ah, Outside: a well-oiled machine!' Barret said staring up at the ceiling for a moment. 'Tell me,' he said almost with excitement, and looking back at Luca without any hint of fear, 'Have they installed the new power plant yet? The mechanics of it are sheer perfection. I was so impressed with the drawings that I said, I did, that it should be put into service as soon as possible. The power output alone gave my heart palpitations!'

'No!' Luca said with disgust, frowning at the absurdity of this arrogant man.

'Shame!' Barret shook his head, 'I will have to instigate that as soon as I can.' He pulled a pen from his pyjama pocket and searched about for something to write on.

'You don't care at all!' Luca shouted and tried to side step Kelsee. 'Let me through!' She grabbed his arm and he turned on her, fiercely. 'I'm sorry!' Luca lowered the knife a fraction. 'I don't want you to get hurt, but he has to pay!'

'Is he your friend? I don't much like him.' Barret had shuffled to the edge of his chair with the pen still in his hand. 'Outsiders are all the same. He has very little to endear him to yourself, Kelsee, darling.'

She spun around to face her grandfather. 'You are not helping!'

Luca could feel heat bubbling inside of him.

'Help? Why would I help?' he said laughing. 'My security will be in here in no time and remove this insignificant dissident.'

'You have no security!' Luca hissed.

'Of course I do! I am an extremely important person and I have the most imperative role ...' Barret frowned and shook his head. Some of his wild grey hair fell into his eyes. 'I do don't I Kelsee?' He shuffled back in his chair, pushed his hair back into place and picked up his drink to take a sip. 'Or I did.' Barret swallowed a mouthful and then sighed dreamily staring at the pen. 'Did we close the contract? Maybe ... I am universally loved after all.'

'What's he going on about?' Luca asked Kelsee.

Barret glared at Luca. He spoke loudly. 'Outside! Yes, I remember Outside. It was a great idea, probably one of my most splendid. I recall the board meeting. The enclosed labour force was a stroke of genius.' Barret coughed to clear his throat and began to tap the pen against the arm of the chair. 'Yes,' he said with a thoughtful tone putting the pen down, 'Outside.'

He reached for a small bottle with purple liquid that rested on the elaborately carved side table. He unscrewed the cap and tipped a couple of drops into his cup. He replaced the bottle and then took a large swig of his drink. He looked up at them over the rim. 'Mara stood by me and made sure that it all happened. She is an excellent woman. Give her a job and she gets it done.' Barret peered about. 'Where is she?'

'Mara Hutchings?'

'Yes! She should be here somewhere. She does love a good cup of tea and a chat.'

Luca whispered to Kelsee. 'Is he alright?'

Kelsee shrugged.

'I am quite well. Thank you! Did you want a cup of tea?' Barret chirped merrily.

'No!' Luca replied angrily. He may have been clutching at the knife but felt quite disarmed by the man sat in front of him. Luca took a deep breath and tried to focus on his task.

Kelsee glared at Luca. She placed her hand gently on his clenched fist holding his weapon. 'Please, Luca,' she whispered. 'There's something wrong here. You must feel it?'

He grimaced and lowered his arm, but did not let go of the knife.

'If you are not staying for tea, what did you want?' Barret asked with a blank expression. 'Only, I have just got to the really good bit in my book.' He picked it up again and began to leaf through the pages.

'Grandfather?' Kelsee began as she slowly edged around the pond and approached him. 'Can I talk to you about something incredibly important?'

'Kelsee?' he said frowning at her. 'How did you get here?'

'That's not important right now,' Kelsee replied. 'What we need to talk about is something that might be a little bit strange. Do you know what Emundabit is?'

Harland Barret grabbed his cup once again, but Kelsee was close enough to push it back to the table. 'I think that is enough tea for now.'

Barret looked longingly at the cup. 'I don't think so, I'm very thirsty.'

'Perhaps you can have some after we have talked.'

'I want it now!' Barret barred his teeth at Kelsee. Luca rushed forward.

Kelsee raised her hand to Luca. 'It's alright. My grandfather wouldn't hurt me.'

Luca shook his head. 'Really! That's not what I have seen.' But he respected her caution and stopped within snatching distance of her.

She turned back to her grandfather who had not taken his gaze from the cup. 'We need to talk about it. Do you know what Emundabit is?'

'Just a little sip.'

'No,' she said firmly. 'We talk first.'

'Emundabit means cleanse,' Barret said looking hopefully at his granddaughter, but she did not offer him the cup. 'Emundabit is the cleansing sequence for Tropolis.' He reached out.

'Not yet!' she commanded. 'Who had authority to initiate the sequence.'

Barret laughed and looked up at his granddaughter. 'No one!' He relaxed back into his chair. 'It was an idea that we had ... oh, years ago. An idea that is all.'

'It's not just an idea!' barked Luca.

'Who thought of it?' Kelsee asked ignoring Luca. 'Grandfather, what makes you say it was just a plan.'

'We talked about cleansing Tropolis as a solution. You know, getting rid of the riff raff and weak. Even using it to stop the fatigue from spreading. It was just an idea that Mara Hutchings and I formulated back when the fatigue started to become serious. The days when you were diagnosed and there was no halting its advance on higher society.'

Kelsee peered around at Luca. 'It was never more than just that; a plan?'

'Of course not,' Barret replied.

Luca avoided Kelsee's knowing look. 'What was the idea? What did it involve?'

'Seriously,' Barret sneered, 'What is it to you?'

'The details!' Luca said lifting the knife. 'What are the details?'

'Emundabit would have involved a few stages of operation.'

Luca pointed the knife towards Harland. 'Outside being the first target.'

'Yes, actually!' Harland Barret seemed surprised at Luca's intuition. 'But that would only be the first call if there was ever any trouble because the power that Outside produces is essential for Tropolis ... but don't tell anyone I told you that!' Barret winked. 'The stages would have been arranged depending on the emergency. The end result would be the creation of an ark,' he giggled unnervingly, 'You know what that is? A safe place to be when everything around you is, for need of a better word, cleansed.'

'Cleansed?' Luca spat out the word. 'How would the extinction take place?'

Barret reached for the cup once again.

'Answer Luca!' Kelsee instructed taking the cup away.

Barret swallowed and shook his head. 'We discussed implanting explosives throughout the city, chemicals in the water system, drones with the ability to set fires in the hills, just in case they came to Tropolis. There were plenty of notions being thrown about. We knew that it wasn't just Outside and Tropolis that would need to be dealt with in order for a superior group to immerge.'

Luca began to nod. 'And you would have a vast supply of provisions for the ones to be kept in your ark too.'

'Of course!'

Luca tugged on Kelsee's sleeve. 'We've seen the ark.' He side-stepped Kelsee and prodded Barret in the chest with the tip of the knife. 'You lie! This isn't some random idea. You've set this up and it is happening now.'

Barret pushed Luca's hand away from him. He was deceptively strong for his age. 'It is *not* happening now. I would know, I have the code to the countdown.' Barret's eyes widened. 'Must be time for some tea now. Do you want some?'

Luca swatted the cup that Kelsee held and she gasped as it slipped from her hand. The liquid spilled and the cup smashed with a musical tinkle on the conservatory floor. Luca saw Barret's gaze quickly fall on the small bottle of purple solution that sat on the table. He reached forward and grabbed at the bottle before Barret's slower aged reactions allowed him to do the same.

But Luca's smile was short lived. Barret swiftly rose from his chair and grasped Luca with both hands about his throat.

Luca gasped. The strong leader was lifting him from the floor. He dropped the bottle which rolled in a circle at his feet and tried desperately to help himself. Luca stabbed wildly with the knife. The blade made contact. Barret winced but would not let go. Luca pulled at the knife and thrust it again but the blade snagged on the baggy pyjama fabric. Luca reached up, instinctively to free his airway and grazed his cheek with the dull blade. He dug at the old man's fingers, desperately attempting to loosen the determined grip. The useless weapon fell from his clenched hand in the struggle.

'Stop it!' Kelsee screamed. She tried to prise the exceptionally firm grip from Luca's neck. 'Stop! You'll kill him!' Her fingers scratched at Luca and the old man's hands.

Just as quickly as he began, Barret let go. He slumped into his chair, placed his hand over his rib and stared off into the greenery.

Luca breathed in with a wheeze and wobbled as he regained his balance. He swallowed and winced, rubbing at his neck.

'What is the point?' Barret muttered. He lifted his hand and revealed a small blood stain. 'I've become one of those unworthy charity cases I always despised.'

Luca huffed. He kicked at the bottle. It cracked as it hit a raised floor tile, scuttled across the floor and dropped into the pond with an insignificant splash. A trail of purple stained the floor.

Barret watched it and sighed. 'I have!' he said staring at Luca. 'I have nothing.'

Luca clenched his fists and leaned closer to Barret, ready for any fight. 'You have everything, how dare you say have nothing!' Luca said gruffly as prodded Barret in the chest. Luca smiled when Barret grunted in pain. 'You want to see what nothing looks like?' Luca coughed. 'Live in Outside!'

'I wouldn't last a day there.'

Luca laughed cruelly. 'You'd be dead the moment they saw you.' Although Luca believed it, the unnerving appearance of Harland Barret brought doubt on his argument. He was different to the cold blooded dictator they knew.

'Instead, I will rot here.' Barret gazed at the pond. 'And I will pay for a while, at least until Mara brings me a new batch of medicine.'

Luca shook his head. 'You never pay for anything.'

'That, boy, is probably the truth,' Harland stated soberly.

Luca rubbed his forehead. Who was this strange man? He had been an actor all those years before, but this appeared genuine. Was this remorse?

Kelsee crouched down in front of her grandfather and rested her hands on his knees. 'They've started the Emundabit sequence. If you have the access codes, do you think you can stop it?'

'If I wanted to, I expect I could.'

'But you don't want to!' Luca sneered.

'It's not that,' Harland replied. 'I want to, but the price is too high.' He sighed again. 'If I shut the program, I live, if it goes ahead I die and so does everything that tortures me.'

Luca turned away and faced Kelsee. 'It is only ever about him, do you see that?' Kelsee did not take her gaze from her grandfather's face. 'Mass execution or cleansing, whatever you want to call it so that you no longer have to live with what you have done?'

'The medicine helps, but the reality is still there.' Harland said weakly, the strain of the burden finally showing. 'I thought living away from Tropolis and having no hand in it would give me freedom, but I feel more trapped than ever. Emundabit, if it really has begun, will end it all for me. I just have to make one more decision. It isn't even one that I will have to live with for long. But it is a good choice. It's nearly over!'

'It's only a good choice for you. What about me?' Kelsee asked.

'Wait! You don't run Tropolis and don't have a place in the ark?' Luca asked.

Harland nodded. 'I gave up rule when Kelsee first became ill...'

'Then who rules?'

'I do!'

Luca and Kelsee spun around. Mara Hutchings stood in the doorway of the conservatory in her neat tailored outfit and wide smile. She was pushing a wheelchair.

'Sweet Harland is wrong about his place in the ark though. He has a very significant reservation. If he didn't, how would I continue to hold power?'

·

Chapter 26

'But we agreed!' Harland protested.

'That was before Outside rebelled.' Hutchings pushed the chair past the pond and closer to Harland. 'What a wonderful reunion!' she said sneering before she glared at Kelsee. 'You just won't disappear will you?' Hutchings laughed. 'But I think I may have resolved that problem.'

'We'll do the broadcast now, please, just leave me.'

'That will not do. We must have witnesses,' she looked down her nose at Kelsee and Luca, 'that will live long enough to back us up. Especially, as we both know, the Network broadcasts can be manipulated to say whatever we please. Unfortunately, without your physical say so, I think my standing as president will not be recognised. They have after all, been following you, or so they believed, these past years. I hate to admit it, but I need you,' her upper lip curled, 'dearest Harland, for my continuous reign to run smoothly. I do not want the people to lack any confidence in me.' Hutchings laughed again. 'Well, the people that matter that is!'

'Do it now!' Harland kicked the knife towards Luca. 'I won't resist!'

Hutchings was closer than Luca. 'I'll have that!' she said stamping on the blade. She picked it up, saw that it was dirty and threw it over the nearby plants. 'That's enough Harland. Roll up your sleeve and give me your arm.'

Harland's lips began to tremble and he blinked rapidly. He clasped his hands together. 'Please!' he begged. 'Leave me here. They'll believe you, they always do.' He grabbed the pen from the table. 'I'll sign any document you want. Please leave me here. I can't live with this any longer.'

'They'll need something more convincing than a signature or a video, Harland. Get in the chair.' She produced a clear plastic box with a hypodermic inside, from her top pocket. 'This will numb it, and besides, I know how little you like the drone transport.'

Harland was unsteady on his feet as he transferred himself into Hutchings' chair. His hands shook as he began to fold back the loose sleeve of his pyjama top. All colour had gone from his wrinkled face.

Luca wondered why this wasn't as satisfying as he would have expected. Emundabit was under way and he was certain that he would die in the cleansing, but Harland would live with his memories of what he had done. Luca considered the way Harland had even described it as torture and pondered how long Hutchings would make him live to endure it, maybe she would even use it against him. It would, perhaps, be a fitting way for this coward to die. Luca would not be a witness to it, but the thought seemed, somehow, just.

'I'd like to say something,' Luca stuttered.

Hutchings glanced at him but ignored the Outsider.

'Barret,' Luca continued, 'you have been the one person I have wanted to see dead for my entire life. You may have gleefully thought up Outside but not once did you consider the lives of the real people you enslaved there. My mother tried to escape and I was told she was crushed by the rubbish barges. The barges loaded with fuel for your precious Tropolis, the curse of the whole of Outside. I grew up having to glean scraps from your table, from Tropolis waste, in order to survive and to keep my father alive.'

Harland had stopped rolling his sleeve and looked down at the ground. Hutchings laughed slightly as she placed the box down. 'Don't stop Luca, we all want to hear your pathetic sob story.' She continued to roll the sleeve up roughly. 'I'm sure Harland needs a little more fuel on his fire!'

Luca frowned. Hutchings really would make Harland suffer.

'I was selected to enter the Compassion Prize.' Luca paused as thoughts of Mercy and Eban flooded his mind. He took a sharp breath as he realised what he should do. 'The prize was not as it seemed. It was all a rouse to get fresh blood stock to heal the people, there was no compassion at all on your part. I was attacked and forced to compete. But I made friends who showed me what life really is. Mercy took my place in the death room, Eban gave me time to save my father and Kelsee, well she looks beyond what others see.' Harland sniffed and took a deep breath. He rubbed one eye.

Hutchings unclipped the box.

'Would you wait? I have just a few more words and I want him to hear them.'

Hutchings smiled and her eyes narrowed viciously. 'Go ahead!'

'You stole my life away. You owe me my mother, my freedom and a full stomach. You owe me respect and care. You owe me a life without poverty. You owe me the rights of being a human and not a slave. You owe me so very much. You owe Outside the neglected years where you have let someone else be in control when you should have been repairing what you had almost completely destroyed.' Harland was weeping. Luca compared the faces of Tropolis that were before him. Hutchings was gleeful at the tales of suffering, Harland crushed. Luca took a deep breath. His heart was beating so fast he thought it might burst out of his chest. 'I choose to not hold any of it as debt. I forgive you.'

'What?' Hutchings spat angrily.

'What? questioned Harland looking up, tears running down the furrows of his aged cheeks.

'You regret it,' Luca said knowing it was the truth. Harland nodded quickly. 'Even if you didn't, I can't live with this bitter hatred towards you anymore. You need to know I won't hold this against you.' Luca could feel a great weight lifting from his shoulders and he let out a small relieved puff of breath before tears then began to swell in his eyes. He breathed in long and deep. 'Hutchings may take you back and hide you away in the ark, but know this, what little power I have over you I choose not to increase your suffering.'

Kelsee jumped up and rushed to hug Luca tightly.

'Luca?' Harland said through gasps. 'Thank you so, so much.' He crossed his arms over his chest and he breathed slowly. 'It is a gift that I don't deserve but one I will treasure.' Harland leaned forward and grabbed hold of Kelsee's sleeve. 'The day my Kelsee was born was a very special date indeed!'

Harland had pulled Kelsee towards him and gripped her arm.

'Ouch!' Kelsee said pulling away but Harland did not let her go.

Harland continued to stare at her and nodded. 'If you had not been born, I would never have such a gift.'

'Oh!' Kelsee said softly.

'I want you to have it,' Luca said clearly. 'I don't want it to determine who I am anymore.'

Harland turned to Luca and smiled peacefully.

'My Kelsee has discovered real humanity.'

Hutchings took the needle and stabbed Harland with it. She forced the contents into his arm. 'Enough!'

'Luca!' Harland said slurring. 'Kelsee's...' his speech had slowed right down. His eyes shut. 'Remember,' he murmured.

'Fool!' Hutchings announced pushing Harland's slouched body back to a sitting position. 'Now, if you will excuse me,' Hutchings sniggered, 'as if you have anything better to do than die! I, however, have somewhere I need to be.' She laughed as she strutted out of the room pushing an unconscious Harland ahead of her. 'Enjoy your last moments of freedom Luca, now that you have it!' she called as she left.

Luca could not consolidate his feelings. He had found freedom, but Hutchings had soured the taste.

Kelsee was watching Hutchings leave eagerly. She bounced on the balls of her feet as if she had some renewed energy that had to be expelled. The loud bang of the door out in the hallway acted as a starting pistol.

Kelsee grabbed Luca's arm. 'This way,' she said dragging him out of the conservatory. 'Come on!' Luca had to jog to keep up. 'Hurry!' she urged as they sped through the lounge, skirting the chairs and ornaments in the next room. The tapestry flapped in the draft that they created as they rushed past.

She ran up the hallway.

'We can't escape, Kelsee,' Luca said slowing down. 'Even if we did get back to Tropolis in time.'

'I'm not going to Tropolis,' she replied without turning. 'I'm going to stop Emundabit.'

Luca rushed after her. 'How?'

Kelsee ran past the staircase and flung open the first door on the right.

The room was full of shelves with hundreds of books on each shelf. A long ladder rested against the distant wall obviously used for selecting tomes from the higher levels. The library spread from floor to ceiling on all the walls except for the deep window recesses and the chimney breast.

Kelsee ignored them all and rushed to the large painting in a gilt frame that hung over the fire.

The canvas had been painted in a similar style to the paintings in the hall. A young, curly haired girl sat on a window seat looking out into the garden beyond.

Luca frowned. 'You?' he asked.

'He made me sit for hours,' Kelsee said smiling. 'But I didn't mind that much. I loved the garden.' She glanced over to the window. 'It was my favourite place when I was little and prone to get really sick. I'd be sent out here because it seemed to be the best type of recuperation. He used to read to me from these books.' Kelsee laughed. 'Our favourite stories were espionage and mysteries. People don't read them anymore, I guess they are not fashionable, but we loved them. That's why,' Kelsee said, grinning and reaching up to the frame of the painting, 'I know where he keeps his safe!' She pressed the golden plaque at the centre of the frame, there was a click and the picture swung open on a hinge. 'He let me find it once, set up a whole adventure for me with a story about a thief and everything.' She pulled open the picture wider and a smaller metal door was hidden behind. 'But he never told me the code, until now.'

'He didn't tell you a code.'

'Special date!' Kelsee said, 'My birth date!' She twisted the dial to the right, she slowed as she reached 14. Then she twisted it to the left and stopped at 02, and finally back right again to 87. Luca realised she was just under three months younger than himself. A deep clunk came from the door. She pulled down the handle and it opened slowly.

The open door revealed a stack of files stuffed with papers with a small silver cube sit on top. Kelsee pulled out the entire contents and spread them out on the floor. The deep red folders were covered in scribbled handwriting with many words underlined and starred.

'The cube,' Luca said pointing to it. 'It's too similar to the one that held the plans in Tropolis.'

He reached over and picked it up. It was small enough to be held in between his thumb and forefinger. He turned it over and inspected all six sides.

'How do we switch it on?' he asked shaking it. There was no evidence of indentations or joins.

Kelsee held out her hand and Luca dropped it in.

'It was already switched on in Tropolis,' she said, nudging it just as Luca had done, hoping that it would spring into life. 'I never saw how they did it.' She put it down, defeated.

Luca stared at the tiny object. How could the fate of so many be enclosed in such a small space? He was certain that Hutchings had begun the extinction sequence. She had come to collect Harland so that must mean that everyone in Tropolis who hadn't been selected for the ark were also in danger.

'There are no buttons ...' Luca muttered to himself, puzzled by the cube. 'But there must be a code or something like it.' He tutted. 'Harland wanted us to open the safe, and I really think that would he want us to stop Emundabit too.'

Suddenly the edges of the silver cube began to glow bright blue.

Kelsee clapped her hands. 'How did you do that?'

Luca shrugged but smiled widely. 'Perhaps Emundabit...' The glowing stopped suddenly. '...is a code word! Emundabit!' The cube lit up once again.

A small hole opened up on the top of the cube and the blue light dimmed from the edges and streamed towards the spot. A focussed holographic of the same tight grid that they had seen before, with hills and sea filled the space between them. The scrolling letters had barely changed. 'Extinction commencement sequence – Code word: Emundabit. Stage One: complete. Stage Two: instigated' but there was an addition that made Luca catch his breath. 'Stage Three: instigated.'

'Can you get us to the countdowns again?' Luca asked desperately.

Kelsee waved her hand over the holograph and pulled the image into a tighter focus just like she had done in Tropolis.

There were no sections that were green. Outside remained red, Campion and Tropolis were amber. The two amber clocks were ticking away relentlessly and were now in unison.

'Campion have been docked time too! We've got to stop the countdown,' Luca held his head. 'Can you stop them?'

'I don't ...' Kelsee stuttered, 'I can't do that, I don't know how. I'm so sorry Luca!'

Chapter 27

00h00m   00h29m   00h29m

A huge explosion outside shook the building. Kelsee screamed.

It was followed by a second and louder blast. The windows rattled and swirls of dust misted the room.

'You ok?' Luca called. He glanced at the countdown and they were ticking away undeterred. This wasn't some work of Emundabit.

There was a sharp series of gunshot and then, a third bang was accompanied by a flash of light.

Luca ran to the window. A tall pillar of dark smoke was rising from behind the hedges of the once neat garden. The tip of a crumpled white aircraft wing was almost engulfed in flames. There was a crashed drone in the garden. A large rubbish truck with a hole torn aggressively through the hopper sat abandoned along the path. The doors to the cab were open.

All the noise had stopped, several shadows of people came rushing out of the smoke. Luca was mesmerised.

'It's Mercy and Eban!'

Luca flung open the window. The acrid smell of smoke was carried on the breeze. There was third person struggling as they carried a fourth. He leaned out and waved his arms trying to capture their attention, but they didn't see him. He rushed back to Kelsee.

He grabbed the cube still glowing with the holograph and ran for the front door without turning to see if Kelsee followed. He sprinted out of the mansion and sent the gravel on the path flying as he sharply skirted the corner of the building. The garden was laid out to hedge and grass but the dark smear of smoke led the way.

'Eban!' Luca shouted towards the cluster of people on the lawn. A figure turned, got to his feet and ran to Luca with arms wide.

Luca laughed as he ran to hug his dear friend.

'You alright mate?' Eban asked looking Luca up and down.

'I am now!' Luca gripped Eban's hand and pulled him into another hug. 'What are you doing here?'

'Alard!' Eban said pointing at the group on the grass. 'He checked Kelsee's tracker and we knew you'd be here too.'

'Tracker?' Luca asked.

'The chip they put in at the sea headquarters.' Eban replied. 'What's that?' He pointed to the blue light coming from Luca's hand.

'Maybe you could break it! It's the plans for the extinction of Tropolis, and all of us, only Kelsee and I can't work out how to stop the countdown.'

'Just as well I am here then!' Eban smiled and reached out to Kelsee who was running up to them. He put his arm around her then gently spoke. 'Your grandfather is hurt.'

'No, Hutchings gave him something that knocked him out.'

Eban shook his head. 'Kelsee, its more than that. There is a lot of blood. Alard and Mercy are doing all they can.'

She pulled away and dashed towards Mercy. Luca was relieved to see his two friends together again but as Mercy held Kelsee tightly he knew that it was a bitter sweet moment.

Luca nervously approached.

Harland had a large shard of metal embedded deeply in his leg and several gashes across his face and chest. His eyes were still shut and despite the horrendous injuries he appeared peaceful and almost dreaming in his pyjamas.

Alard had tied his long grey hair in a bunch but several stray sections had fallen and hung over his face. He leaned over Harland and was busy attending to the injured man. He had torn a section of the blood soaked sleeve and had tied it tightly above the metal shard but blood still flowed out. A small puddle had already formed in the short time that they had been there.

Luca bent low and squeezed Mercy's shoulders. She was holding Kelsee who was sobbing. 'It's so good to see you!' Luca looked around. The lawn was free from debris and the smoke rose from the other side of the hedge. Alard attended to Harland, Mercy consoled Kelsee and Eban had already set the cube on the grass and was working on the holograph, the bright blue dim even against the putrid smoke. 'Where's Hutchings?' asked Luca as he spun around.

'The woman?' asked Mercy. 'She left Barret and ran for the drone when she saw us coming. She attacked the truck. Alard shot back and caught the propeller which grounded it. Before we knew it, something exploded which caught Barret. Then there were flames everywhere.'

Luca ran his hand through his hair. Mara Hutchings should have been held responsible for what she had made all the people endure. But there was little he could do now to right that wrong. It seemed that there was, perhaps some justice in that she had not made it to the ark.

'She was running it all! Harland hadn't been in control for years.' Luca glanced at Eban. 'It's worse. She had arranged for everyone to die and the only way to stop it is in that computer program that Eban is working on.

Alard focussed harder. He began to pack his own jacket around Harland's wound. 'All the more reason to save him!' he said. 'If we can get him inside, I'm certain he will have supplies. He's losing too much blood, he needs a transfusion.'

'I can't give him any of mine,' Kelsee sobbed, 'We're not a match.'

'But he can have mine,' Alard said.

Eban turned. 'I could do with a little less light and a firm surface.'

Alard had already lifted Harland and was staggering towards the house. Luca quickly caught up with the older man and took half the weight by looping Harland's arm around his neck. He linked hands with Alard providing a type of seat for Harland's unresponsive body.

'This way!' Kelsee said as she walked ahead with Mercy.

Luca breathed in short bursts under the burden. 'How,' he whispered to Alard, 'Do you know he can have your blood?'

Alard frowned and looked away.

'If you give him the wrong blood it will kill him and it doesn't look like you want him dead since you are going to all this trouble.' Luca gripped Alard's hand tighter before it slipped free. 'You don't want him dead and you know your blood will work for him. How do you know?'

'Luca, don't push it!' Alard commanded. 'There will be plenty of Outsiders who will want to see him go to some sort of trial, I just want to ensure that they get justice.'

Luca grunted and slowed his pace. 'It wasn't him!' he said repeating the phrase that Kelsee had used.

Alard fixed his lips tightly, adjusted his grip and then marched quickly after Kelsee and Mercy. Luca had no choice but to keep up. The gravel crunched loudly under their feet and the extra weight that they carried. The thunderous sound only emphasised the silence of the Brigadier.

Luca glanced down the long path that led up the house. The ornate gates stood open wide, wider than appeared comfortable. The open landscape, unaware of what was happening to the world. He squinted at the scene thinking that there was something missing. His concerns were put aside as he realised that the rubbish truck had obviously taken the short cut across the garden as plants were bent over or squashed and there were dark scars across the green.

The hallway seemed full of ghosts as the portraits stared blankly past their injured owner being stretchered in. Alard hesitated as they passed the family portrait. Kelsee took them back to the library and led Alard to the window seat. They gently lowered Harland onto the bench and Alard carefully placed a cushion under his head.

'Kelsee, I need medical supplies. He has some, he must have.'

She ran out with Mercy.

Blue light quickly filled the room. Eban had placed the cube on the reading table and had already moved away from the gridded reference of Tropolis, Outside and Campion. He was scrolling through line after line of encrypted coding. He highlighted a single line, enlarged it then pulled open a second holographic screen so that they formed a corner, similar to the cube beneath. Eban then flipped the screen and a third layer was produced, but this time Network footage was being shown rather than streams of mindless letters and numbers.

Luca watched, almost hypnotised by Eban's skill. The footage was as if it were close circuit camera work showing a large unattractive building with rows of white objects. A person walked into shot and the scale of the building and winged drones was suddenly apparent.

Eban opened a fourth screen with a long list on the left and timers on the right that were set at lower increments to the main countdown. As one timer hit zero a whole row of drones lifted effortlessly from the floor of the building and floated out of shot.

Luca read the description next to the timer. 'Fire launchers to zone 7'.

'Where's zone seven?' Luca asked.

'Not good,' Eban replied, 'It's the land that surrounds your mother's community.'

A second timer reached zero. 'Chemical drop to zone 4', another six drones left.

'You've got to stop them!' Luca pushed as three more timers reached their limit and more drones were sent on missions.

Eban worked faster. He flicked through the screen with the code again. Luca couldn't focus on anything but it seemed Eban knew exactly what he was after. He highlighted a single coded phrase and opened it. A fifth screen came to life. It was almost blank except for a rectangular box with TERMINATION PASSWORD written above it.

'Any ideas?' Eban asked as he tapped the box and a keyboard appeared. He didn't wait for answers but began to type out words and hit enter. 'PASSWORD incorrect.'

Kelsee arrived with a box full of medical equipment.

'What password would your grandfather use?' Eban asked before she had even put it down.

'Your birthday Kelsee,' urged Luca.

'February 14th,' Kelsee said quickly undoing the box.

Eban typed it in using a combination of both numbers and words. 'No!'

'You can ask my grandfather,' she said not even looking at Eban, 'He'll be better soon.'

Luca looked back at the screens. Another five drones were sent out. 'It will be too late by then!' he muttered angrily.

Alard slumped to the floor. 'Too late now,' he said with almost a quiver to his words. 'He's gone.'

Kelsee knelt down next to him and cried against her grandfather's chest.

Mercy laid down the bandage that she had been holding and reached out a hand to both Kelsee and Alard. Luca bit down on his lip. It was strange that Mercy considered that Alard would need the same comfort as Kelsee.

Luca hadn't noticed how Mercy had carried the dirt of her work with her until now. The tears that rolled silently over her cheeks washed the grime from her efforts in Outside and with Campion away. She sat silently for a moment and unashamedly let them flow. Luca could not help but be moved by her love of people, no matter what they had done.

Selfishly, Luca thought, he was glad that he had been able to release forgiveness to Harland when he had the chance. He clasped his chest. He felt no guilt or hatred towards the man. It was an unexpected and unnerving experience.

Mercy looked up. 'Try *Valentine*, Eban. Kelsee was born on a very special date that used to celebrate love.'

Even before Eban had completed typing Luca knew that she was correct.

As Eban entered the final letter and hit the enter key a sixth and final screen appeared.

Large sections of the encrypted code transferred to the last screen, they changed from blue to red and then vanished. The list that showed on the fourth screen disappeared just as suddenly.

'You've done it!' Luca shouted.

Luca and Eban ran over to Mercy and Kelsee. Amid the tears of sorrow there were shouts and cheers of victory.

'Brigadier Alard! Come in Alard!' came a slightly desperate tone from Alard's communicator.

The sweet success was broken in a moment.

Alard tapped his shoulder and spoke into the communicator. 'Received Thomas.'

'Request your presence at the entrance to Tropolis, Sir,' Thomas began amid the muffled sounds of shouting and loud bangs. 'Resistance from the city is violent.'

To be continued in …

THE COMPASSION FIRE

Other books in the Compassion series ...

The Compassion Prize

WHAT IF COMPASSION WAS NOT AN EMOTION THAT EVOKED A RESPONSE,
BUT WAS A PRIZE TO BE WON?

Luca leaves the poverty of Outside and enters affluent Tropolis in the hope of winning the Compassion Prize. With the help of friends Mercy and Eban, he discovers that true compassion cannot be won.

The Times of Kerim

Bruja hunts her, hungry for power. Japh waits for her, trusting in a promise. The Remnant plans for her. And I guide, watching as the storm begins.

Kerim is tired of running. She has escaped. Her wounded hands ache and her weary body needs rest. She hides in the shadow of a strangely familiar rock crevice. Japh has been waiting years to find her, but is he prepared for the perilous events that will unfold at her discovery?

Is she ready to listen to me, her messenger? Is she ready to step into her destiny?

Kerim discovers that mankind is not all the same. That some are called to be saved.

The Days of Eliora

Si dominates her, eager for respect Caleb notices her, detecting someone unique The Remnant shuns her And I watch over, as turmoil encompasses the land Eliora lives between worlds. Disowned by one and mistrusted by the other; she has no identity. Finding solace in conflicting friendships will shape her future beyond recognition. Caleb brings relief to her testing days, but can he bring startling revelation about who she really belongs to. Will she still her confusion and listen to my message? Is her heart prepared for the battle?

Eliora does not fit. Neither the palace nor the settlement offers her a place to be who she is called to be. Join Eliora as she discovers her calling amid the slavery of her people and the tyrannical Pharaoh. Discover the unfolding story through both the human and supernatural realm.